GALAXY'S EDGE
CREATED BY MIKE RESNICK

ISSUE 55: March 2022

Lezli Robyn, Editor
Lauren Rudin, Assistant Editor
Z.T. Bright, Slush Reader
Taylor Morris, Copyeditor
Shahid Mahmud, Publisher

Published by Arc Manor/Phoenix Pick
P.O. Box 10339
Rockville, MD 20849-0339

Galaxy's Edge is published in January, March, May, July, September, and November.

Please check our website for submission guidelines.

ISBN: 978-1-64973-115-9

SUBSCRIPTION INFORMATION:
Paper and digital subscriptions are available (including via Amazon.com) . Please visit our home page: www.GalaxysEdge.com

ADVERTISING:
Advertising is available in all editions of the magazine. Please contact advert@GalaxysEdge.com.

FOREIGN LANGUAGE RIGHTS:
Please refer all inquiries pertaining to foreign language rights to Shahid Mahmud, Arc Manor, P.O. Box 10339, Rockville, MD 20849-0339. Tel: 1-240-645-2214. Fax 1-310-388-8440. Email admin@ArcManor.com.

CONTENTS

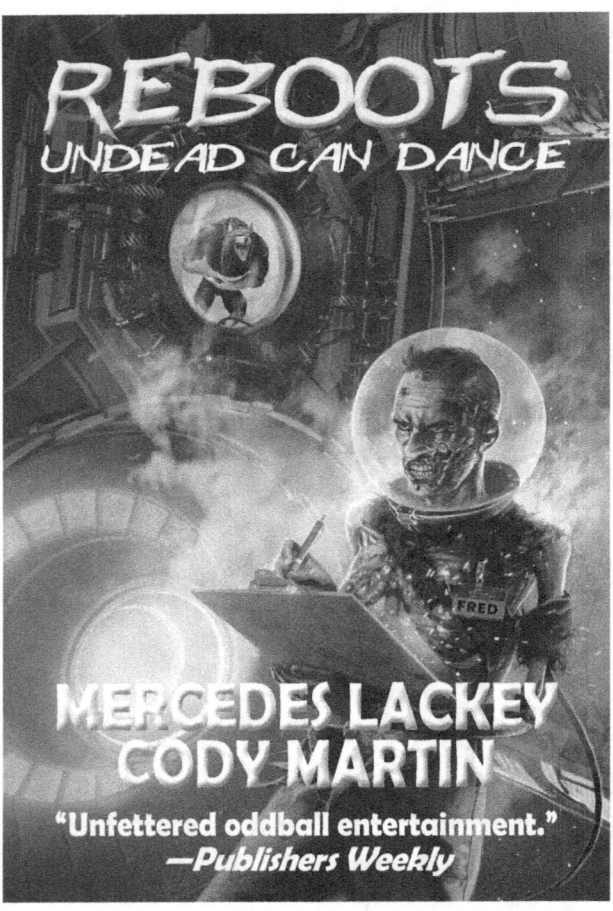

"We like this book, we like this book a LOT!"—Scribbles Worth Book Reviews

"Unfettered oddball entertainment."—Publisher's Weekly

Oklahoma author Mercedes Lackey, the popular and prolific author of 150 books, is joined by Florida author Cody Martin in this hilarious and immensely entertaining collection of four adventures from the world of Reboots – Bad Moon Rising, Just The Right Bullets, Diabolical Streak, and The Somnambulist Waltz.

A suggestion of the kicks ahead is present even in the opening lines of the first story – 'You know what they said in that ancient movie, about being in space? Well here's a news flash for you: in space no one give a s**t if you scream. Especially not your shipmates.

Oh, you'd think your shipmates would care, right? I mean, it's just all of you against all of the dark and vacuum and whatever crap the universe has dreamed up to kill you? Another news flash: no. Especially if your shipmates are a bunch of sociopathic dirtbags that think dead puppy jokes area laugh riot...So much for the glamour and excitement of interstellar ravel.'

Attempting to overview the contents of this book is best achieved by the authors' summary – 'Humans aren't alone anymore—in fact, they share a planet with undead and near-dead beings, living in...semi-harmony, depending on who you ask! This is the world of Reboots—where zombies, vampires, and werewolves live side-by-side with humans, taking whatever jobs they can in order to coexist peacefully. So, what better job to give almost-dead or dead beings, than one that consists of no air, cosmic radiation, and a lack of life-sustaining essentials? Follow Skinny Jim, a zombie who conceals his ability to speak to avoid being exterminated after an ill-fated war launched by a zombie emperor, leading to an alliance between Norms, the Fangs, and the Furs. And then there's Humph the Boggart, an ethereal parahuman private investigator who navigates interspecies relationships in claustrophobic extraterrestrial environments with his friends, including Fred the werewolf. And what happens when you put them all together in a confined space?'

Injecting fine parody and satire into this series of space operas intensifies the pleasure of reading. The writing uses a plethora expletives (you know, that language that permeates all movies and television these days!) and speeds through irresistible wild tales that consistently entertain. Relax, and spend some 'great escape' time with REBOOTS.

Grady Harp Reviews, December 21

ON SALE NOW

EDITOR'S NOTE

by Lezli Robyn

The 56th issue of *Galaxy's Edge* is a milestone issue for the magazine for several reasons. For one, we are officially entering our tenth year of publication! We also surpassed 600 purchased stories, all carefully curated for your reading pleasure from new and famous authors in the science fiction and fantasy field! If that weren't enough, our late editor, Mike Resnick, would have turned 80 just five days past the publication of this issue, had he still been here to share his natal day with us.

As a special treat, Alvaro Zinos-Amaro approached me with a really unexpected and beautiful idea. He had the thought to write a homage to Mike Resnick's "The Elephants on Neptune." Not only did I find the idea so well timed for the story to appear in this issue, but I was so curious how Mike's rather unique story could even inspire a sequel, written in the same voice as the original. To say that Alvaro knocked it out of the cosmos is an understatement. Not only did he match the voice and tone of the first story, making it feel as if Mike was writing again, but he added his own keen intelligence to the follow-up discussion about confronting your persecutors and prejudice. "The Rhinos on Jupiter" captures the delightful absurdity of the first story, but also the depth and impact of its predecessor. We recommend you read Mike's story first, to really appreciate the care and expertise Alvaro infused into his follow-up story. A fitting tribute.

This issue we have a brand new story by Katharine Kerr. Psychic Agent Nola O'Grady belongs to the Agency, an organization so secret even the CIA doesn't know it exists. Together with Israeli secret agent Ari Nathan, she must deal with the supernatural, paranormal, and apocalyptic while juggling family problems. Described as a "female James Bond with magic rather than violence," you are sure in for a treat when you read "A Leaf in the Wind."

ZZ Claybourne returns to our pages with the beautifully poignant "Giant Mechs in the Distance, Forever Fighting," about an older man who is heartily sick of war, and also just plain heartsick. This short story is the perfect example of how a writer can still make an emotive impact with very few words. It will stick with you long after you have read it.

We also have two new writers this issue. In "With our Songs of Scars and Starlight", by J.R. Troughton, we are introduced to a rather bewitching mother and her twin daughters, who are all able to manipulate the weather with song and magic. The author hauntingly tells a tale about the devastating consequences of choices. In "Feel," Torion Oey—finalist for The Mike Resnick Memorial Award—explores how advancing technology and the implementation of a robot can help a paralyzed woman walk again, in what makes for an engaging and moving read.

We are gifted with another striking recommendation by Yang Feng, which is written by Chinese writer, Tai Yi, who is known for adding a distinct Japanese flare to their fiction. We also get to enjoy the second half of "Killer Advice" by Kristine Kathryn Rusch, the second part of John Scalzi's interview, Recommended Books by Richard Chwedyk, and a regular writing advice column by L. Penelope. And our issue couldn't be complete without the continued serialization of Harry Turtledove's novel, *Over the Wine-Dark Se*a.

If anyone can think of a better way to start off our tenth year of publication as a magazine, I will be impressed. Mike was an atheist and thus didn't believe in heaven, but I would like to think that if his essence is out in the cosmos somewhere, he would be especially chuffed to see that one of his stories inspired another author to write fiction. Whether it is through the continuation of this magazine, his memorial award for new authors, or his fiction inspiring others, there is no doubt Mike's presence is still felt by many, and we are all the better for it.

Happy birthday, Storyman.

Mike Resnick, along with editing the first seven years of Galaxy's Edge magazine, was the winner of five Hugos from a record thirty-seven nominations and was, according to Locus, *the all-time leading award winner, living or dead, for short fiction. He was the author of over eighty novels, around 300 stories, three screenplays, and the editor of over forty anthologies. He was Guest of Honor at the 2012 Worldcon.*

THE ELEPHANTS ON NEPTUNE

by Mike Resnick

The elephants on Neptune led an idyllic life. None ever went hungry or were sick. They had no predators. They never fought a war. There was no prejudice. Their birth rate exactly equaled their death rate. Their skins and bowels were free of parasites.

The herd traveled at a speed that accommodated the youngest and weakest members. No sick or infirm elephant was ever left behind.

They were a remarkable race, the elephants on Neptune. They lived out their lives in peace and tranquility, they never argued among themselves, the old were always gentle with the young. When one was born, the entire herd gathered to celebrate. When one died, the entire herd mourned its passing. There were no animosities, no petty jealousies, no unresolved quarrels.

Only one thing stopped it from being Utopia, and that was the fact that an elephant never forgets.

Not ever.

No matter how hard he tries.

✿

When men finally landed on Neptune in 2473 A.D., the elephants were very apprehensive. Still, they approached the spaceship in a spirit of fellowship and goodwill.

The men were a little apprehensive themselves. Every survey of Neptune told them it was a gas giant, and yet they had landed on solid ground. And if their surveys were wrong, who knew what else might be wrong as well?

A tall man stepped out onto the frozen surface. Then another. Then a third. By the time they had all emerged, there were almost as many men as elephants.

"Well, I'll be damned!" said the leader of the men. "You're elephants!"

"And you're men," said the elephants nervously.

"That's right," said the men. "We claim this planet in the name of the United Federation of Earth."

"You're united now?" asked the elephants, feeling much relieved.

"Well, the survivors are," said the men.

"Those are ominous-looking weapons you're carrying," said the elephants, shifting their feet uncomfortably.

"They go with the uniforms," said the men. "Not to worry. Why would we want to harm you? There's always been a deep bond between men and elephants."

That wasn't exactly the way the elephants remembered it.

✿

326 B.C.

Alexander the Great met Porus, King of the Punjab of India, in the Battle of the Jhelum River. Porus had the first military elephants Alexander had ever seen. He studied the situation, then sent his men out at night to fire thousands of arrows into extremely sensitive trunks and underbellies. The elephants went mad with pain and began killing the nearest men they could find, which happened to be their keepers and handlers. After his great victory, Alexander slaughtered the surviving elephants so that he would never have to face them in battle.

✿

217 B.C.

The first clash between the two species of elephants. Ptolemy IV took his African elephants against Antiochus the Great's Indian elephants. The elephants on Neptune weren't sure who won the war, but they knew who lost. Not a single elephant on either side survived.

✿

Later that same 217 B.C.

While Ptolemy was battling in Syria, Hannibal took thirty-seven elephants over the Alps to fight the Romans. Fourteen of them froze to death, but the rest lived just long enough to absorb the enemy's spear thrusts while Hannibal was winning the Battle of Cannae.

✧

"We have important things to talk about," said the men. "For example, Neptune's atmosphere is singularly lacking in oxygen. How do you breathe?"

"Through our noses," said the elephants.

"That was a serious question," said the men, fingering their weapons ominously.

"We are incapable of being anything *but* serious," explained the elephants. "Humor requires that someone be the butt of the joke, and we find that too cruel to contemplate."

"All right," said the men, who were vaguely dissatisfied with the answer, perhaps because they didn't understand it. "Let's try another question. What is the mechanism by which we are communicating? You don't wear radio transmitters, and because of our helmets we can't hear any sounds that aren't on our radio bands."

"We communicate through a psychic bond," explained the elephants.

"That's not very scientific," said the men disapprovingly.

"Are you sure you don't mean a telepathic bond?"

"No, though it comes to the same thing in the end," answered the elephants. "We know that we sound like we're speaking English to you, except for the man on the left who thinks we're speaking Hebrew."

"And what do we sound like to you?" demanded the men.

"You sound exactly as if you're making gentle rumbling sounds in your stomachs and your bowels."

"That's fascinating," said the men, who privately thought it was a lot more disgusting than fascinating.

"Do you know what's *really* fascinating?" responded the elephants. "The fact that you've got a Jew with you." They saw that the men didn't comprehend, so they continued: "We always felt we were in a race with the Jews to see which of us would be exterminated first. We used to call ourselves the Jews of the animal kingdom." They turned and faced the Jewish spaceman. "Did the Jews think of themselves as the elephants of the human kingdom?"

"Not until you just mentioned it," said the Jewish spaceman, who suddenly found himself agreeing with them.

✧

42 B.C.

The Romans gathered their Jewish prisoners in the arena at Alexandria, then turned fear-crazed elephants loose on them. The spectators began jumping up and down and screaming for blood—and, being contrarians, the elephants attacked the spectators instead of the Jews, proving once and for all that you can't trust a pachyderm. (When the dust had cleared, the Jews felt the events of the day had reaffirmed their claim to be God's chosen people. They weren't the Romans' chosen people, though. After the soldiers killed the elephants, they put all the Jews to the sword too.)

✧

"It's not his fault he's a Jew any more than it's your fault that you're elephants," said the rest of the men. "We don't hold it against either of you."

"We find that difficult to believe," said the elephants.

"You do?" said the men. "Then consider this: the Indians—that's the good Indians, the ones from India, not the bad Indians from America—worshipped Ganesh, an elephant-headed god."

"We didn't know that," admitted the elephants, who were more impressed than they let on. "Do the Indians still worship Ganesh?"

"Well, we're sure they would if we hadn't killed them all while we were defending the Raj," said the men. "Elephants were no longer in the military by then," they added. "That's something to grateful for."

✧

Their very last battle came when Tamerlane the Great went to war against Sultan Mahmoud. Tamerlane won by tying branches to buffalos' horns, setting fire to them, and then stampeding the buffalo herd into Mahmoud's elephants, which effectively ended the elephant as a war machine, buffalo being much less expensive to acquire and feed. All the remaining domesticated elephants were then trained for elephant fighting, which was exactly like cock fighting, only on a larger scale. Much larger. It became a wildly popular sport for thirty or forty years until they ran out of participants.

✿

"Not only did we worship you," continued the men, "but we actually named a country after you—the Ivory Coast. *That* should prove our good intentions."

"You didn't name it after *us*," said the elephants. "You named it after the parts of our bodies that you kept killing us for."

"You're being too critical," said the men. "We could have named it after some local politician with no vowels in his name."

"Speaking of the Ivory Coast," said the elephants, "did you know that the first alien visitors to Earth landed there in 1883?"

"What did they look like?"

"They had ivory exoskeletons," answered the elephants. "They took one look at the carnage and left."

"Are you sure you're not making this all up?" asked the men.

"Why would we lie to you at this late date?"

"Maybe it's your nature," suggested the men.

"Oh, no," said the elephants. "Our nature is that we always tell the truth. Our tragedy is that we always remember it."

The men decided that it was time to break for dinner, answer calls of nature, and check in with Mission Control to report what they'd found. They all walked back to the ship, except for one man, who lingered behind.

All of the elephants left too, except for one lone bull.

"I intuit that you have a question to ask," he said.

"Yes," replied the man. "You have such an acute sense of smell, how did anyone ever sneak up on you during the hunt?"

"The greatest elephant hunters were the Wanderobo of Kenya and Uganda. They would rub our dung all over their bodies to hide their own scent, and would then silently approach us."

"Ah," said the man, nodding his head. "It makes sense."

"Perhaps," conceded the elephant. Then he added, with all the dignity he could muster, "But if the tables were turned, I would sooner die than cover myself with *your* shit."

He turned away and set off to rejoin his comrades.

✿

Neptune is unique among all the worlds in the galaxy. It alone recognizes the truism that change is inevitable, and acts upon it in ways that seem very little removed from magic.

For reasons the elephants couldn't fathom or explain, Neptune encourages metamorphosis. Not merely adaptation, although no one could deny that they adapted to the atmosphere and the climate and the fluctuating surface of the planet and the lack of acacia

trees—but *metamorphosis*. The elephants understood at a gut level that Neptune had somehow imparted to them the ability to evolve at will, though they had been careful never to abuse this gift.

And since they were elephants, and hence incapable of carrying a grudge, they thought it was a pity that the men couldn't evolve to the point where they could leave their bulky spacesuits and awkward helmets behind, and walk free and unencumbered across this most perfect of planets.

✿

The elephants were waiting when the men emerged from their ship and strode across Neptune's surface to meet them.

"This is very curious," said the leader.

"What is?" asked the elephants.

The leader stared at them, frowning. "You seem smaller."

"We were just going to say that you seemed larger," replied the elephants.

"This is almost as silly as the conversation I just had with Mission Control," said the leader. "They say there aren't any elephants on Neptune."

"What do they think we are?" asked the elephants.

"Hallucinations or space monsters," answered the leader. "If you're hallucinations, we're supposed to ignore you."

He seemed to be waiting for the elephants to ask what the men were supposed to do if they were space monsters, but elephants can be as stubborn as men when they want to be, and that was a question they had no intention of asking.

The men stared at the elephants in silence for almost five minutes. The elephants stared back.

Finally the leader spoke again.

"Would you excuse me for a moment?" he said. "I suddenly have an urge to eat some greens."

He turned and marched back to the ship without another word.

The rest of the men shuffled their feet uncomfortably for another few seconds.

"Is something wrong?" asked the elephants.

"Are we getting bigger or are you getting smaller?" replied the men.

"Yes," answered the elephants.

✿

"I feel much better now," said the leader, rejoining his men and facing the elephants.

"You look better," agreed the elephants. "More handsome, somehow."

"Do you really think so?" asked the leader, obviously flattered.

"You are the finest specimen of your race we've ever seen," said the elephants truthfully. "We especially like your ears."

"You do?" he asked, flapping them slightly. "No one's ever mentioned them before."

"Doubtless an oversight," said the elephants.

"Speaking of ears," said the leader, "are you African elephants or Indian? I thought this morning you were African—they're the ones with the bigger ears, right?—but now I'm not sure."

"We're Neptunian elephants," they answered.

"Oh."

They exchanged pleasantries for another hour, and then the men looked up at the sky.

"Where did the sun go?" they asked.

"It's night," explained the elephants. "Our day is only fourteen hours long. We get seven hours of sunlight and seven of darkness."

"The sun wasn't all that bright anyway," said one of the men with a shrug that set his ears flapping wildly.

"We have very poor eyesight, so we hardly notice," said the elephants. "We depend on our senses of smell and hearing."

The men seemed very uneasy. Finally they turned to their leader.

"May we be excused for a few moments, sir?" they asked.

"Why?"

"Suddenly we're starving," said the men.

"And I gotta use the john," said one of them.

"So do I," said a second one.

"Me too," echoed another.

"Do you men feel all right?" asked the leader, his enormous nose wrinkled in concern.

"I feel great!" said the nearest man. "I could eat a horse!"

The other men all made faces.

"Well, a small forest, anyway," he amended.

"Permission granted," said the leader. The men began walking rapidly back to the ship. "And bring me a couple of heads of lettuce, and maybe an apple or two," he called after them.

"You can join them if you wish," said the elephants, who were coming to the conclusion that eating a horse wasn't half as disgusting a notion as they had thought it would be.

"No, my job is to make contact with aliens," explained the leader. "Although when you get right down to it, you're not as alien as we'd expected."

"You're every bit as human as *we* expected," replied the elephants.

"I'll take that as a great compliment," said the leader. "But then, I would expect nothing less from traditional friends such as yourselves."

"Traditional friends?" repeated the elephants, who had thought nothing a man said could still surprise them.

"Certainly. Even after you stopped being our partners in war, we've always had a special relationship with you."

"You have?"

"Sure. Look how P.T. Barnum made an international superstar out of the original Jumbo. That animal lived like a king—or at least he did until he was accidentally run over by a locomotive."

"We don't want to appear cynical," said the elephants, "but how do you *accidentally* run over a seven-ton animal?"

"You do it," said the leader, his face glowing with pride, "by inventing the locomotive in the first place.

Whatever else we may be, you must admit we're a race that can boast of magnificent accomplishments: the internal combustion engine, splitting the atom, reaching the planets, curing cancer." He paused. "I don't mean to denigrate you, but truly, what have you got to equal that?"

"We live our lives free of sin," responded the elephants simply. "We respect each other's beliefs, we don't harm our environment, and we have never made war on other elephants."

"And you'd put that up against the heart transplant, the silicon chip, and the three-dimensional television screen?" asked the leader with just a touch of condescension.

"Our aspirations are different from yours," said the elephants. "But we are as proud of our heroes as you are of yours."

"You have heroes?" said the leader, unable to hide his surprise.

"Certainly." The elephants rattled off their roll of honor: "The Kilimanjaro Elephant. Selemundi. Ahmed of Marsabit. And the Magnificent Seven of Krueger Park: Mafunyane, Shingwedzi, Kambaku, Joao, Dzombo, Ndlulamithi, and Phelwane."

"Are they here on Neptune?" asked the leader as his men began returning from the ship.

"No," said the elephants. "You killed them all."

"We must have had a reason," insisted the men.

"They were there," said the elephants. "And they carried magnificent ivory."

"See?" said the men. "We *knew* we had a reason."

The elephants didn't like that answer much, but they were too polite to say so, and the two species exchanged views and white lies all through the brief Neptunian night. When the sun rose again, the men voiced their surprise.

"Look at you!" they said. "What's happening?"

"We got tired of walking on all fours," said the elephants.

"We decided it's more comfortable to stand upright."

"And where are your trunks?" demanded the men.

"They got in the way."

"Well, if that isn't the damnedest thing!" said the men. Then they looked at each other. "On second thought, *this* is the damnedest thing! We're bursting out of our helmets!"

"And our ears are flapping," said the leader.

"And our noses are getting longer," said another man.

"This is most disconcerting," said the leader. He paused. "On the other hand, I don't feel nearly as much animosity toward you as I did yesterday. I wonder why?"

"Beats us," said the elephants, who were becoming annoyed with the whining quality of his voice.

"It's true, though," continued the leader. "Today I feel like every elephant in the universe is my friend."

"Too bad you didn't feel that way when it would have made a difference," said the elephants irritably. "Did you know you killed sixteen million of us in the twentieth century alone?"

"But we made amends," noted the men. "We set up game parks to preserve you."

"True," acknowledged the elephants. "But in the process you took away most of our habitat. Then you decided to cull us so we wouldn't exhaust the park's food supply." They paused dramatically. "That was when Earth received its second alien visitation. The aliens examined the theory of preserving by culling, decided that Earth was an insane asylum, and made arrangements to drop all their incurables off in the future."

Tears rolled down the men's bulky cheeks. "We feel just terrible about that," they wept. A few of them dabbed at their eyes with short, stubby fingers that seemed to be growing together.

"Maybe we should go back to the ship and consider all this," said the men's leader, looking around futilely for something large enough in which to blow his nose. "Besides, I have to use the facilities."

"Sounds good to me," said one of the men. "I got dibs on the cabbage."

"Guys?" said another. "I know it sounds silly, but it's much more comfortable to walk on all fours."

The elephants waited until the men were all on the ship, and then went about their business, which struck them as odd, because before the men came they didn't *have* any business.

"You know," said one of the elephants. "I've got a sudden taste for a hamburger."

"I want a beer," said a second. Then: "I wonder if there's a football game on the subspace radio?"

"It's really curious," remarked a third. "I have this urge to cheat on my wife—and I'm not even married."

Vaguely disturbed without knowing why, they soon fell into a restless, dreamless sleep.

☼

Sherlock Holmes once said that after you elimi-nate the impossible, what remains, however im-probable, must be the truth. Joseph Conrad said that truth is a flower in whose neighborhood oth-ers must wither.

Walt Whitman suggested that whatever satis-fied the soul was truth.

Neptune would have driven all three of them berserk.

☼

"Truth is a dream, unless my dream is true," said George Santayana.

He was just crazy enough to have made it on Neptune.

☼

"We've been wondering," said the men when the two groups met in the morning. "Whatever hap-pened to Earth's last elephant?"

"His name was Jamal," answered the elephants. "Someone shot him."

"Is he on display somewhere?"

"His right ear, which resembles the outline of the continent of Africa, has a map painted on it and is in the Presidential Mansion in Kenya. They turned his left ear over—and you'd be surprised how many left ears were thrown away over the centuries be-fore someone somewhere thought of turning them over—and another map was painted, which now hangs in a museum in Bombay. His feet were turned into a matched set of barstools, and cur-rently grace the Aces High Show Lounge in Dal-las, Texas. His scrotum serves as a tobacco pouch for an elderly Scottish politician. One tusk is on display at the British Museum. The other bears a scrimshaw and resides in a store window in Beijing. His tail has been turned into a fly swatter, and is the proud possession of one of the last *vaqueros* in Argentina."

"We had no idea," said the men, honestly appalled.

"Jamal's very last words before he died were, 'I forgive you,'" continued the elephants. "He was

promptly transported to a sphere higher than any man can ever aspire to."

The men looked up and scanned the sky. "Can we see it from here?" they asked.

"We doubt it."

The men looked back at the elephants—except that they had evolved yet again. In fact, they had eliminated every physical feature for which they had ever been hunted. Tusks, ears, feet, tails, even scrotums, all had undergone enormous change. The elephants looked exactly like human beings, right down to their spacesuits and helmets.

The men, on the other hand, had burst out of their spacesuits (which had fallen away in shreds and tat-ters), sprouted tusks, and found themselves convers-ing by making rumbling noises in their bellies.

"This is very annoying," said the men who were no longer men.

"Now that we seem to have become elephants," they continued, "perhaps you can tell us what elephants *do*?"

"Well," said the elephants who were no longer el-ephants, "in our spare time, we create new ethical systems based on selflessness, forgiveness, and fam-ily values. And we try to synthesize the work of Kant, Descartes, Spinoza, Thomas Aquinas and Bishop Barkley into something far more sophisticated and logical, while never forgetting to incorporate emo-tional and aesthetic values at each stage."

"Well, we suppose that's pretty interesting," said the new elephants without much enthusiasm. "Can we do anything else?"

"Oh, yes," the new spacemen assured them, pulling out their .550 Nitro Expresses and .475 Holland & Holland Magnums and taking aim. "You can die."

"This can't be happening! You yourselves were el-ephants yesterday!"

"True. But we're men now."

"But why kill us?" demanded the elephants.

"Force of habit," said the men as they pulled their triggers.

Then, with nothing left to kill, the men who used to be elephants boarded their ship and went out into space, boldly searching for new life forms.

☼

Neptune has seen many species come and go. Microbes have been spontaneously generated nine times over the eons. It has been visited by aliens 37 different times. It has seen forty-three wars, five of them atomic, and the creation of 1,026 religions, none of which possessed any universal truths. More of the vast tapestry of galactic history has been played out on Neptune's foreboding surface than any other world in Sol's system.

Planets cannot offer opinions, of course, but if they could, Neptune would almost certainly say that the most interesting creatures it ever hosted were the elephants, whose gentle ways and unique perspectives remain fresh and clear in its memory. It mourns the fact that they became extinct by their own hand. Kind of.

A problem would arise when you asked whether Neptune was referring to the old-new elephants who began life as killers, or the new-old ones who ended life as killers. Neptune just hates questions like that.

Copyright © 2000 by Mike Resnick in Asimov's *magazine.*

Alvaro Zinos-Amaro is a Hugo- and Locus-award finalist who has published fifty stories, as well as over a hundred essays, reviews, and interviews, in a variety of professional magazines and anthologies. These venues include Analog, Apex, Lightspeed, Beneath Ceaseless Skies, Galaxy's Edge, Nature, The Los Angeles Review of Books, Locus, Tor. com, Strange Horizons, Clarkesworld, The Year's Best Science Fiction & Fantasy, Cyber World, This Way to the End Times, The Unquiet Dreamer, It Came from the Multiplex, Shadow Atlas, *and many others.*

THE RHINOS ON JUPITER

by Alvaro Zinos-Amaro

For Mike.

◆ ◆ ◆

On their return trip to Earth, the men and women who had once been elephants on Neptune felt inexplicably drawn to Jupiter.

Everyone knew that Jupiter was a gas giant. Of course, everyone had known that Neptune was a gas giant too. The first error in judgment didn't make the second any easier to accept, but the force of precedent is nearly as strong as gravity, and it helped to bend the travelers' perceptions into accepting that Jupiter's interior was far from what they had expected.

Savannas, plains, shrublands and rivers floated atop idyllic clouds, which drifted against a glorious blue backdrop. In these oases the plains, carpeted by grasses ten inches high, were peppered by bountiful waterholes, and all was awash in a perpetual apricot glow that tapered off with calibrated smoothness into azure horizons.

In one rich muddy waterhole fed by an artesian spring, a group of rhinos calmly bathed.

Here the travelers paused.

From their former lives as elephants, they remembered their dealings with rhinos. From their current lives as humans, they remembered very different sorts of dealings with rhinos. As humans who had once been elephants, they were able to relive both sets of memories simultaneously. Perhaps in this moment the travelers were the most alien they had ever been.

When the rhinos saw the travelers approach, they stopped bathing and climbed out of their magnificent waterhole. The rhinos talked amongst themselves in infrasonic frequencies beyond the range of human sensitivity. But these humans, having once been elephants, retained the ability to hear them.

They heard, and thought they understood.

"We want nothing from you," assured the travelers.

"Of course you don't," said the rhinos.

"Listen," said the travelers. "We always tell the truth."

"We were agreeing with you," said the rhinos. "When fifteenth-century Albrecht Dürer made that ridiculous drawing of us, the one that led to so many misunderstandings, he didn't want anything from us. When poachers slaughtered half a million of our kind a few hundred years later, *they* didn't want anything from us. When your predecessors ground the keratin of our severed horns into powders, *they* didn't want anything from us."

"We didn't realize that rhinos were capable of sarcasm," the travelers observed without irony.

"Indeed, we are not," said the rhinos. "You never really did want anything from us—you only thought you did. All along, you were seeking something within yourselves that we could not provide."

The travelers made a funny face and flapped their ears. If they had been elephants, the gesture would have been considerably more impressive. "Times are different now," the travelers said. "We are different."

The rhinos thought on this. Jupiter had taught them certain lessons. "Times are always different," the rhinos said. "That's how time works."

"What we mean," said the travelers, advancing toward the waterhole, "is that that wasn't *us*. That was the humans. We just look like them."

"Do you remember the time before you were human?" the rhinos said.

"Yes," the travelers said. "We are masters of remembrance. Do you recognize us?"

Without coming any closer, the rhinos sniffed the travelers.

Identifying the travelers' ancestral smells, the rhinos' demeanor did not improve.

The travelers stayed where they were, which under the circumstances might have been going one step too far.

"Yes," the rhinos said at last. "You were once elephants. In that form, you raped and killed us."

The travelers fretted. What did they have to do, exactly, to prove that they didn't intend harm to these lifeforms? First they had been judged for their actions as humans, and now the verdict on their elephant deeds was no more flattering.

"We can explain," the travelers said, summoning their patience. It was possible to see, from a certain angle, how the rhinos might be a bit touchy, and so the travelers edged into this perspective as much as they could. "The raping and killing of your kind was a temporary madness that afflicted us *because* of the humans. The humans attacked and hurt our tribes just like they did yours. Some of our kind went insane as a result. They weren't responsible for their actions, and they do not represent us as a whole."

"When you were thriving," the rhinos said, "well before the humans arrived on the scene, you were not ever possessed by an ecstasy of generosity that made you forage for us or care for our sick."

"We never bothered you."

"When life was good for you, you ignored us. When it wasn't, you didn't."

"Look here," the travelers said, "the memories of our crimes against you are very disturbing. They make us feel great shame." The lush greenness of the shrublands around them did nothing to dispel sudden gelid needles in the air. "We are deeply sorry for our actions. We live with the torture of knowing our own cruelty. Let that be our punishment."

Said the rhinos: "Punishment is the answer to a human question, and memories are the response to an elephant quandary. Neither are our concern."

The travelers couldn't exactly follow this, but the tone was not encouraging. "Nevertheless," they said, trying to regain firm footing, "you grasp the weight of the past, or you yourselves wouldn't be bringing it up."

The rhinos pondered these statements. "Observe the oxpeckers that ride along on our backs," they said.

The travelers, tired and hungry, were tempted to get closer to the rhinos to look at the oxpeckers. Straining their necks to make out the small birds was not foremost on the travelers' list of desires. Yet a lingering prudence kept them at bay.

"We see the oxpeckers," the travelers said a few moments later. The yellow and red from the birds' bills seemed to hover in place as the oxpeckers remained unnaturally still. There were no ticks, flies, maggots or larvae on the skins of these rhinos for the oxpeckers to eat, but their immobility could not be explained by such an absence. It went deeper. They appeared possessed of a strange placidity, and seemed to look right through the travelers. That was preferable, the travelers supposed, to screeching or any other kind of ruckus.

"These oxpeckers used to live on our skins too," the travelers remembered, "when we were elephants. That brings our two peoples closer together."

"These birds are like the memories of your atrocities," the rhinos said. "You carry them along with you, but they're not truly a *part* of you. There's no weight to speak of. And in time, when the memories have no more guilt upon which to feed, they will simply flutter away."

As though forming an exclamation mark at the end of this statement, all the oxpeckers shot up into the air in tandem and flew about in vertiginous pathways. Eventually they settled back on the hides of the rhinos.

After the rhinos' presumptuous words and aggressive display, the travelers knew they would be justified in taking offense. But they decided to rise above their now-human-yet-former-elephant natures. "That wasn't a very nice thing to say," they replied. "You don't really know us, so you shouldn't speak about what we will or won't experience." The best option for the time being, they decided, was to retreat and deliberate among themselves.

As elephants they had been able to communicate through a psychic bond, but they had lost this particular gift when they took human form, and so at a time like this were relegated to the limitations of verbal speech.

"A very strange planet," one of the senior travelers said. "Everything looks warm, but there's a piercing chill in the very fabric of this world."

"I feel it," said another.

"Do you hear that music?" someone asked.

"Like a heartbeat," one of the younger travelers said. "It's slowing down."

"I can hear it," said another.

"What do you think the rhinos are really up to?" the elder said. "Do you think they're hiding something valuable in that waterhole?"

"I think the rhinos themselves are probably the most valuable thing on this planet," someone else replied.

"You might be right," said another traveler pensively.

One of the group who normally stayed quiet said, "I don't think they've planned anything. They didn't know we would come here. They're simply being who they are."

"Nothing good ever comes of that," admonished the veteran.

"That's true of humans," the other said. "But perhaps it's different for rhinos."

"We should consider leaving," the quiet traveler said, and at this suggestion several folks booed, urging him, in less than kind terms, to return to his usual laconicism.

"No, we won't be made to leave," the elder said, "whether actively or passively. If we go, it shall be because we will it so." He did not speak for all, but the certainty of his pronouncement intimidated those who had doubts, so that presently he did in fact speak for all.

"My legs are starting to tingle," another veteran traveler said. "My toes are going numb. I don't like it."

"Me too," the once-quiet traveler said, earning further glares of disapproval.

"Let's ask the rhinos what's going on," the self-appointed leaders said.

They marched forward and called out. "Several among us are experiencing the onset of hypothermia," the travelers said. "Do you know anything about this?"

The rhinos advanced in unison. The travelers remembered that a group of rhinos is called a crash, which was not a helpful thing to think about at a moment like this.

"Jupiter is a cold place," the rhinos said, "but it takes a long time for the truth of its temperature to be felt. Like the human heart, it reveals the beauty of its cruelty in stages. By the time the full truth is exposed, it's always too late."

The travelers could see a certain logic to this, but they also wondered if it might not be a ploy to get them off-world, away from whatever treasure might be stashed in the waterhole.

"You seem to be doing okay," the travelers pointed out. "If what you're saying is true, why haven't you yourselves frozen to death?"

A great sadness permeated the rhinos' response. "We discovered Jupiter's awesome power too late, alas. We are trapped here. No longer warm enough to leave, and not yet cold enough to die. But you might still save yourselves."

The rhinos descended dejectedly back into the waterhole.

The travelers retreated and spent a while taking a vote. The decision to depart was made, but a small cohort insisted that the customary rules of vote-taking had not been followed precisely, and thus a recount was required. Since the entire procedure had been admittedly informal and spur-of-the-moment, the majority consented to taking the vote a second time. While all this happened, Jupiter's heartbeat continued to pulse more and more slowly, and an increasing number of the travelers was pierced by its sapping chill.

Huddling together for heat, the travelers said, "We'd invite you to join us, but we're not sure we have enough room for all of you." Their assessment of the ship's size vis-à-vis the rhino population was admittedly an estimate, so they were not technically lying. One of the charms of self-deception is that it can preserve truth-telling by dulling truth-seeing. "Perhaps you wish us to take the most endangered groups of your kind," the travelers went on. "Black rhinos, Sumatran rhinos and Javan rhinos, for example, were all near extinction back on Earth."

"Here," one of the rhinos said stoically, "we are all Jovian rhinos. You should also probably know that the difference between black and white rhinos was an artifact of man. Both were in fact gray-brown."

"It was merely a practical suggestion," the travelers said with haste. "We meant nothing by it. In reality, we would hate to have either us or you choose who among you lives and who dies."

The implications of those words clung to all like a fine spray of jade-white snow.

"Do you hear Jupiter's heartbeat?" the rhinos asked.

"Yes," the travelers said. "It became audible to us a short while ago."

"Then it's too late for you as well," the rhinos said. "The slower that drum beats, the colder you'll become. The colder you become, the more slowly you'll move."

"And yet—" Again, the travelers did not wish to be indelicate by casting possible aspersions of deceit on the rhinos, who were already lukewarm in their reception, and quite possibly their skins. "And yet," they managed to get out, "you move at ordinary speeds."

"The first time you saw us move, Jupiter's veil clouded your vision. When you see us move now, your own slowness distorts our speed. The more normal we appear, the less so you are."

"Wait a second," said the travelers. "You've been here a long time. Years maybe, probably decades. If you're still moving after all that time, why are we experiencing our decline so quickly?"

"It begins fast, and then proceeds ever more slowly," explained the rhinos. "As you cool, entropy decreases. Time is measured by molecular motion, and so time itself slows down. It too, if you will, cools. The more slowly time passes for you, the more slowly you continue to freeze. Our best philosophers believe that death on this world is an asymptote."

The travelers began to fret in earnest. "We're very sorry about everything," they said. "Despite your proclamations of defeat, we must attempt to reach our ship. We wish you only the best in your future endeavors."

The rhinos smiled. "Safe travels to you."

The travelers turned around and walked at their briskest clip toward the ship. When they felt that they were out of the rhinos' visual range, and that decorum might therefore be shed, they ran, some of them whimpering with pain at the gnawing cold. Their lungs burned with each exhalation, and for every two feet covered by their pumping legs, the ship seemed to somehow recede from them by four more. After pushing on to the brink of exhaustion, they reached a literal edge, for they discovered that they were on a cloud that had broken off from the cloud on which they had originally landed. These two cloud masses were drifting away from one another, rent asunder by a vast precipice of sky.

"They tricked us," one of the elders said.

"Why would they do such a thing?" wondered another.

"To steal our ship, of course!" spat out the elder.

"But the rhinos are on this cloud with us," rejoined the skeptic. "The ship is equally out of their grasp."

"Perhaps that's another illusion being fed to us by this godforsaken planet," said the elder.

Now that the group had stopped their mad dash, the stalking cold was really starting to reach deep within. As the rhinos had predicted, the travelers' movements as they backed off the edge of the cloud became more sluggish. This seemed to slow down the advancement of the cold, so they moved even more slowly as they continued on their trek back toward the rhinos.

The journey might have taken hours or weeks, the travelers could not be sure. By the time they returned to the waterhole, they heard Jupiter's heartbeat only once every many hours, so on that day each time it thudded it seemed to mark a whole new day rather than a new moment.

"You knew this would happen to us," the travelers said upon sighting the rhinos once more. "You let us fall into the same trap as you."

"Why did you come to Jupiter?" the rhinos asked.

To this, there was no good answer. "We felt called here," the travelers said. "It was in our nature to follow the call."

"Then your nature is the one who laid the trap," the rhinos said.

"You could have warned us," complained the travelers.

"Would you have believed us? You didn't believe us even after you were experiencing Jupiter's effects for yourselves."

"This is pointless," one of the travelers said. He had been holding his tongue ever since the expedition had landed, but too much was too much, even for one as conflict-averse as he.

"We cannot disagree," the rhinos said.

"What we need to do," the disgruntled traveler said, "is to pool our resources. Then perhaps we can get off this world—together."

Some travelers groused, but no one raised any outright objections. Even those who believed the rhinos had acted in bad faith didn't have it within them to hold a grudge.

"Very well," the rhinos said. "In order to formulate a common plan, we must first get to know each other."

One of the rhinos climbed out of the waterhole and made its way to a specific spot south. When it had reached this destination the rhino said, "You may approach."

With wariness the travelers bridged the distance.

As they got closer, a pungent smell assailed them.

"This is your excrement," one of the elders said. "What is the meaning of bringing us here?"

"This," said the rhino, "is our midden. It is a communal area. It says a lot about us. With one whiff of this dung heap you can know our ages, our sexes, even our reproductive states."

"Perhaps this works for rhinos," the elder said. "But we're humans."

"You used to be elephants, with a more advanced sense of smell. All we ask is that you try."

The elder grunted in irritation, but came closer to the midden and let its odors infiltrate his lungs. Others, including the disgruntled traveler, soon followed suit. Everyone closed their eyes and took deep breaths. The olfactory sensitivity they had once possessed as elephants returned, at first in little whispers of significance, then flourishing into fuller comprehension. The travelers appreciated that the rhinos had shared this information as a symbol of goodwill in their budding relationship, and also as a practical way of speeding up introductions.

"To understand someone you can look at who they are in the present, or you can study what they leave behind," one of the rhinos said.

"You *do* have a sense of humor," said the disgruntled traveler, now visibly less disaffected.

"Only for those who know us," replied the rhino. "Come, join us for a mudbath."

The travelers followed this cue, and through the mudbath learned more about the rhinos' history, their personalities, relationships and worldview.

After this they joined them in the waterhole.

"Fear for your lives has made you less fearful of us," the rhinos said in the shared waterhole. "We, in turn, fear you less. It is a start."

The travelers discovered that speaking of fear like this did much to dispel it. It was indeed a start.

"The only thing we ask," said the rhinos, "is that you know us through our identities, but judge us by our commonalities."

To the best of their abilities, the travelers did just this.

The ensuing conversation ranged far and wide, and soon the larger collective began brainstorming ways to escape the planet's pernicious grasp.

A solution presented itself with relative ease. The rhinos, having been trapped here longer than they could remember—it was a good thing they weren't elephants—had taken to recording the movements of the clouds within their visual range. They had determined that over short periods of time these large floating worlds moved in erratic patterns, but over longer timescales followed paths amenable to prediction. In a sense, they were like miniature planets following elliptical orbits, with some micro-zigzagging along the way. The travelers helped them identify which specific cloud was carrying the ship. With this data in hand, it was straightforward to determine when this cloud would once more be within reach. To pass the time until said rendezvous, the group exchanged stories, sharing their thoughts and feelings as freely as they could.

At last, on the appointed day, the rhinos said, "A very long time ago, before you knew us, you said your ship would not have enough space for all of us."

"We will make the space," the travelers assured, and so the matter was put to rest.

The cloud appeared in the sky almost exactly on schedule. "It is time," said the travelers.

"Allow us one final moment to grieve," the rhinos said.

The travelers paused. Before spending time with the rhinos, they would have questioned how these beings could grieve for the place that had ensnared them. Now they understood that the rhinos had ensnared themselves, and despite its frosty nature, this world had become their home.

A few instants of solemnity passed, and the travelers and rhinos boarded the ship together. In order to accommodate the rhinos, the travelers ejected the former crew's belongings. In truth, they were human possessions that the travelers, having once been elephants, had never truly loved, and had only kept

out of a sense of guilt. The ship thus enlightened, the unified crew took off from Jupiter.

"We were originally going to head to Earth," the travelers said, "before we heard Jupiter's song. But Earth no longer speaks to us."

"For us it is likewise mute," the rhinos said with a hint of slyness, "and therefore moot."

"In that case," the travelers replied, "to honor the kindness you showed us on Jupiter, we would like you to experience our old stomping grounds on Neptune. It is a paradise."

"We are honored," said the rhinos.

They reached Neptune in 2491 A.D. Though the world was cold in appearance, and lacked the acacia trees and euphorbias they enjoyed foraging on, time passed pleasantly for both groups: the travelers delighted in memories of yore, and the rhinos were fascinated with their discoveries regarding the travelers' old ways of life.

Many years passed in peace and tranquility.

One day, a baby rhino was born, the first on Neptune. Both herds celebrated as one. When the calf turned six, he asked his parents why they were so friendly with the travelers. The calf had learned that humans had been cruel to rhinos in the past, and it wondered why these humans should be any different now.

"They were elephants once," the parents explained. "And we helped each other back on Jupiter. We have been friends ever since."

The calf nodded. Forgiveness is often forged in simple gestures, which nevertheless require a new generation to be birthed.

When the calf turned eight, he asked his parents how the elephants that had turned into men had acquired a ship.

"When we became men," the travelers said, "we behaved as men."

This time the calf was slower to nod, but assented in the end. The arsenic of the past, if allowed to rise up, can poison the ground water of the present, so that a filtration of the truth is sometimes preferable to its untreated consumption.

As time passed, the rhinos appeared to fully embrace the ways of Neptune. One day the travelers said: "There is a unique and enigmatic property to this planet you have yet to experience. It is the gift that allowed us to become human, ward off our former oppressors, and take up the exploration of the heavens. With the same insistence that Jupiter demands *stasis*, Neptune bursts forth with the desire for *metamorphosis*."

The rhinos congregated and reflected on the matter, after which time they announced: "Neptune has been a most gracious host, allowing both of our tribes to thrive. Whatever transformation it wishes to confer upon us, we willingly accept."

The travelers were curious to discover what might be in store for the rhinos. Being changed from elephants into humans was the only time they had undergone a transformation; the possibilities seemed endless.

The rhinos fell into a dreamless void of sleep, and when they awoke, they felt strange urges they had never before experienced, like the desire to create a byzantine set of taxation laws in order to immediately deregulate them.

"You look like us now," the travelers said, with perceptible chagrin.

The rhinos' change into humans struck them as anticlimactic. Didn't Neptune have anything more fun in its repertoire than turning all species into humans? Then again, there was some old adage about strength in numbers that might conceivably be undergirded by this development.

"We might say the same of you," said the rhinos.

Where once elephants had lived in bliss and rhinos had dwelled in chilly near-immortality on different planets, now a single cadre of humans stood bemused, playing an unstated game of spot-the-difference.

"What now?" the former elephants asked the former rhinos.

"We are all travelers," the former rhinos said. "We should venture into the cosmic beyond."

Everyone boarded the ship. They began at once to study the computer's navigational charts, but before they could make any real progress the ship's com channel bleeped to life.

Dialing up the volume, the travelers heard an exchange of human voices coming from a ship in the vicinity of Jupiter.

After the transmission ended, everyone sat in glum silence for several minutes.

"There's no ambiguity there," a traveler said with a pained expression.

"Agreed," replied another. "The humans are going to perpetrate one of their typical acts of barbarism. They call it 'helium-3 extraction,' but we all know what it means. Helium-3 mining on Jupiter will only be the start. They will plunder our former world, and as their ships and technology become more advanced, they will not hesitate to pillage whatever other worlds they encounter—this one included—for fuel and resources."

"This can't be permitted to happen," decreed many voices.

"Let us set a course to intercept their ship," said a second chorus. "We must stop the United Federation of Earth, at any cost."

So it was that these two tribes of ancient creatures, recently minted into men, headed out to kill their human brethren. Outwardly, they donned an armor of unimpeachable moral justification. The more introspective among their number quietly wondered, however, if a secret revenge motive might lurk deep within. Such thoughts were best cast aside, though, in the interests of justice and freedom for all.

Their real motivation, of course, was more basic than altruism or revenge. If anyone had cared to solicit Neptune's opinion, the planet would have emitted it unhesitatingly, and without a smidgeon of judgment, for it too operated under the same compulsion afflicting the men.

Simple habit, Neptune would have said.

And that would have been correct.

But incomplete.

Neptune's opinions are to be trusted only as far as its own self-knowledge, which is to say, no farther than a stone's throw from the travelers' ship. It would have taken Neptune a transcendent level of discipline and rumination far beyond its current capacity to peer through its own atmosphere, past the hydrogen of homage, the helium of hubris, the methane of metaphor, and the ammonia ice of allegory, to see, all the way in the deepest subatomic levels of its metallic core of catharsis, the primordial vibrating force behind its motivation and that of everyone else: the inexorable drive of story.

Sword of Fire, a new Deverry novel, is available from DAW Books and HarperVoyager. She is on Twitter as Kit_Kerr, Facebook as Katharine Kit Kerr, and Patreon as Katharine Kerr.

A LEAF IN THE WIND

by Katharine Kerr

I saw the case first on the local news websites. "Prominent Bay Area Developer found dead!" the headline ran, above a picture of Albert Harlander from the files: bald, chubby, smiling, little pig eyes gleaming with corruption. My dad had worked in construction for years in San Francisco, and we all knew that if Harlander could save a buck by cheating his illegal immigrant labor, or using sub-grade materials and slapdash construction methods, he would. Among the permit and oversight departments at various cit y halls, he wasn't known as "Baksheesh Bert" for nothing. The news article stank of murder with its vague hints about mysterious circumstances and unexplained details, but it lacked concrete information.

I remember that his cheese-paring way of working had killed a roofer not long before. If the guy's relatives had returned the favor, I couldn't blame them. My main reaction: thank god the case wasn't mine to solve! When the police began digging into Harlander's business dealings, a lot of influential people in San Francisco and San Jose were going to do their best to make their official lives miserable. Lullabies would have nothing on the "hush, hush" that the cops were going to hear.

My name is Nola O'Grady. I do work in law enforcement, but for a federal agency so secret that not even the CIA knows of its existence. Even if I could tell you its name, you wouldn't believe me. Our mission: fight the forces of chaos that threaten our world and others throughout the multiverse. While Bert was as slimy as a stick of margarine on a summer day, a Chaotic he wasn't. Not my pigeon, I thought.

The universe answered, "Oh yeah?" and led to me a café on upper Fillmore Street for lunch the same day I'd seen the news. I'd ordered a salad and a cup of coffee when a tall, grim guy in a navy blue suit strolled over to my table—Lieutenant Sanchez of the San Francisco police. He sat himself down across from me before I could even say hello.

"O'Grady! Just the person I wanted to see. Where's your partner?"

"Ari? At the Hague on Interpol business. They need him as a witness in a deposition. Human rights violation, but that's all I can tell you because that's all he told me."

"That's like him, yeah. How overworked are you these days? I'd like your opinion on a case that's more than a little weird."

"Weird, huh? What made you think of me?"

He grinned, very briefly. I'd been involved in a couple of cases with Sanchez before. He'd always done his best to disbelieve in my psychic talents, but the man wasn't stupid.

"Heard anything about the Harlander case?" Sanchez continued.

"It was all over the web. Not that there was a lot of hard information in those stories. Like how he died."

"He was strangled." Sanchez paused for effect. "With some kind of vine."

"Vine? Like ivy?"

"Stronger than that, but that's the idea, yeah. We didn't find the weapon, but in the deep abrasions on his throat our experts found traces of plant material." He paused to take a smartphone out of his pocket and open a note app. "He was found lying a hundred yards or so from his car in Golden Gate Park. From evidence at the scene it looked like he'd tried to run away from his assailant and been overtaken. He was strangled with this plant material, whatever it was, and then—here's the weird detail—crowned with a wreath made out of dandelions and crab grass."

"It's pretty clear what the killer thought of him, then."

"Yep." He closed the app and put the phone away. "Mr. Weed."

"Do you think it was the roofer's family that did it? The Chu murder case."

"Huh? No. He'd settled plenty of cash on them, and he donated to the Buddhist temple they went to, too. His one good deed." Sanchez rolled his eyes. "His last stunt is just so damn typical. Did you hear about the tree?"

"Er, no."

Sanchez explained it to me. Harlander owned a big corner lot out in the Seacliff neighborhood, upper middle class ritzy, that is. The old house had burned down, but the firemen had saved the enormous heritage tree, a cypress, that graced the property. Bert wanted it cut down so he could build a McMansion. The neighbors objected. They had their own pull at City Hall. When Harlander couldn't get a permit, he had the tree axed anyway, on the Sunday before the murder—Sunday, when the permit offices were closed and no one could stop him.

"That tree he had cut down," I said. "Revenge on the part of the neighborhood? Treehuggers on the warpath?"

"They hugged him pretty hard if that's the case. It sure looks like that, but for chrissakes, no one murders a man over a dead tree! Beat him up, maybe, but not kill him. I'm guessing that we're supposed to waste time thinking about the tree, but the real motive's something else."

"Yeah, that's reasonable."

"There was a woman in the car with him, we think. Traces of lipstick, a few long blond hairs, a tissue on the floor that smelled like cheap perfume. The scent was still fresh, which makes us think she was there right before the kill."

I wanted to say I'm sorry, I can't help you. But one of my irritating intuitions, as mbiguous as always, nagged at me. If Sanchez the consummate realist could admit he wanted my help, the Agency needed to get involved.

"Can you take me to the scene?"

He grinned. "Sure can. Where's your car?"

Thanks to budget cuts, the western end of Golden Gate Park has fallen on hard times, at least in the areas where the tourists don't go. Although strips of lawn line the roads, just beyond them weeds, underbrush, and blown trash lie thick among unpruned Monterey pines and head-high clumps of juniper. A jogger had found Harlander's body stretched out on one of the strips of lawn with his head pointing toward the thick cover.

"Just after dawn, and the grass had dew all over it," Sanchez told me. "The kid had his cellphone with him, so he took pictures, bless his little heart, of the footsteps around the corpse before the dew burned off. Two pair—Harlander's, and then someone wearing high heels came after him. Or I should say, she was wearing them for the first few steps. She kicked them off at one point. One of our women officers tells me you can't run worth crap in heels."

"She is so right. I take it your mystery woman left his car behind."

"Assuming she was in it with him, yeah. My first thought was he'd picked up a hooker who didn't like what he had in mind. But if she killed him, she didn't rob him, and he had three hundred bucks in his wallet when we found him and a couple of credit cards." Sanchez frowned at the grass. "Another weird point. Her footsteps left the corpse and turned toward those trees over there." He waved at at a thicket of half-grown cypress trees, bent and twisted by the constant sea wind. "But they disappeared before they reached it. She still had about five feet of wet grass to go when her footsteps vanished."

"Is that where she got the murder weapon? Looks like there's ivy growing on at least one of those trees."

"Maybe. But judging from her footprints, she swerved around his body to head toward the trees. He must have been lying on the ground already."

"That doesn't make sense."

"I know. That's why I wanted to bring you into this."

Logical enough, I supposed. I took a couple of steps toward the trees and ran an EPIS, an Exploratory Psychic Input Scan, the official Agency name for the talent more usually known as 'second sight'. I received a faint impression of Harlander's mind, only a faded fragment since he'd been dead for some time. With it came the sensation of the touch of the putative vine on his throat, the rough surface, the sudden tug and choke. I felt the expected surge of terror, but I also received surprise, a sheer staggering disbelief in what was happening to him. I shut the scan down.

"Okay," I said. "This is definitely weird. Y'know, it takes a lot of muscle power to strangle someone who knows you're there and can fight back. Are you sure he didn't pick up a male hooker? Someone in drag?"

"Not sure at all. It could be, yeah. Don't you have an associate who—"

"I do. Let me consult him and get back to you."

As we turned to go back to the car, the slanting afternoon sun caught the grass at just the right angle to reveal the faint, blurred imprint of the body. I noticed something crushed down among the stalks and stooped to pick it up.

"What's that?" Sanchez said.

"A leaf."

"Oh. Yeah, we found a couple others under the victim." He shrugged. "The park is lousy with trees."

True, but I slipped the leaf into my pocket, because thanks to its scent I thought it might have come from a European laurel tree, and you don't find that species among the Monterey pines and local shrubbery in this section of the park. From the killer's garden, maybe—a slender clue, probably valueless, but better than nothing.

When I got back to my flat, I phoned the associate Sanchez had mentioned, Jerry Jamieson, one of the three people I work with in the San Francisco office of the Agency. He's technically a part-time stringer. For his other job he works the streets as a specialized kind of male prostitute, which means he sees and hears plenty of interesting things, some of which concern the Agency. When I asked him if he'd heard about the Harlander case, he had information to pass on.

"Lots of buzz on the street, darling," Jerry said. "Wondering who she was."

"You're sure it's a she?"

"Oh yeah. I know my competitors in the drag department. This dangerous little bitch is new on the street, very new, as in no one had ever seen her work before. One of the doormen at one of the fancy hotels saw her get into a car with Harlander."

"Has he told the cops?'

"Oh please! Of course not. He'd never get a percentage again."

"Can you describe her for me?"

Jerry could and did, because in his mind the Agency doesn't count as "cops". A blonde, all right, tall but not slender -- she had a Marilyn Monroe type of figure, or so the doorman called it. She wore a short green dress under a silk coat. The doorman had particularly noticed her hands because she had long, delicate fingers but wore her nails cut straight across.

"Not a trace of polish, and he didn't think she was wearing any make-up, either. No costume jewelry."

"That's very strange for a sex industry worker."

"Which is why I'm making a point of telling you, darling. What's more, the doorman was kind of freaked by her, even before the news hit the Net. He couldn't say why, just that she had a creepy vibe. Not helpful, I know."

"But Harlander went for her, creepy vibe or not?"

"He wasn't the sensitive type." Jerry paused for a laugh. "I never serviced him, but he was known on the street. He'd fuck anything."

"Did the doorman think this woman was strong enough to strangle Harlander?"

"No, he didn't. Which is another reason he didn't tell the cops."

I thanked him and ended the call. Possibilities: she was stronger than she looked or someone had hired her to lure Harlander to a good spot for murder. The pattern of footsteps ruled out an accomplice, unless he could hover in mid-air. In my line of business, you never know who or what you're going to find, but a giant wasp or a demon seemed unlikely in this case. Harlander had committed his crimes against other human beings and their property in an all too earthly way.

When I contacted Sanchez to pass along Jerry's information, the lieutenant gave me a quick summary of a few of Harlander's shady practices, those that seemed like they might provide a motive for murder.

"I'm putting my money on blackmail," Sanchez said. "We've got three instances of code violations that were never prosecuted. In one, the person who should have nailed him admitted to being paid off. The other two cases involve a different official, but no one could find any evidence of a pay-off, so he was allowed to quit without any kind of action against him. I wonder if Harlander had something on him."

"Sounds logical, yeah."

Too logical, actually, to fit in with the disappearing footprints and the lingering trace of shock from Harlander's recently deceased mind. A properly illogical idea was beginning to form in my mind. Although I couldn't give it words just yet, I felt it floating into my consciousness from the CDS, the Collective Data Stream of knowledge that permeates our culture.

I found a good site on the Internet for plant ID and learned that the leaf I'd found came from a European laurel tree, not the local bay laurel—another clue for my illogical idea. When I finished, I still had a couple of hours before sunset, just enough time for me to revisit the scene in daylight. Out at the site, the fog was just beginning to roll in from the ocean a few blocks away. Long tendrils of gray reached across the sky and cast a shroud of shadows over the strip of lawn. I parked, then walked over to the spot where the body had lain. All traces of Harlander's mind had disappeared as thoroughly as if the chilly west wind had blown them away. I saw no one, but I felt a presence nearby. I ran a Search Mode: Location scan. Whatever it was stood among the trees beyond the lawn. A Search Mode: Personnel confirmed my guess: not human.

I began to gather Qi with a small circling motion of my right hand. In serious circumstances, such as self-defense, I have a license to ensorcell, that is, to blast whatever's threatening me with so much life force or Qi that its normal functioning shuts down. Only temporarily, I hasten to add— I'd hate to use psychic talents to kill someone. The karmic burden would be enormous. In the midst of so many green and growing things, with the ocean itself so near, Qi was mine for the taking. I swept it from the air and wrapped it into a silver sphere around my hand.

Armed and ready, I waited. I felt the presence watching me. The wind blew steadily. Trees bowed and quivered with a sound like waves on a gravel beach. Overhead the fog grew thicker, darker, and colder. I hate being cold. I decided to try a long shot.

"Okay, Daphne," I called out. "Want to talk about this?"

No answer.

"I could make things hot for you in there. Ever hear of matches?"

I felt her fear, just tinged with respect. Among the trees a pale light flashed. A being in the form of a young woman with long blonde hair and a voluptuous figure strolled out of the underbrush. Instead of evening clothes she appeared to be wearing a long tunic made of green laurel leaves. She kept her gaze on the softball-sized globe of Qi.

"My name isn't Daphne," she said, "but that'll do."

"I didn't expect you to tell me your real name, no."

"You're pretty smart, ape girl, fingering me like this." She set her hands on her hips. "What are you going to do about it?"

"Oh come off it! You're perfectly safe. There's nothing the cops can do to a dryad these days."

"You expect me to swallow that?"

"Yeah, because nobody on earth believes your people still exist. Well, except maybe for a few left-over hippie types."

"What about you? Going to avenge that murderous little swine?"

"No. I agree with your opinion, is why."

As a sign of good faith I allowed the Qi I carried to scatter. She sighed in profound relief and looked me in the eye at last.

"That tree he paid to have cut down," I said. "I'm thinking that one of your people ensouled it."

"You're right. She was wonderful, one of the oldest of us, wise and noble." Her voice shook with tears. "She was over four thousand years old, too old to move fast. By the time we heard her cry for help, it was too late. We couldn't get her transferred to a new tree in time."

"So it was murder in your eyes."

"He didn't have to axe her. He wanted wood? There's all kind of trees in that garden he owns that are—well—just trees. He could have taken any of them. Why her?"

"She was in his way. He was a greedy, impatient little soul. He wanted to build a house where she was standing, and he didn't want to change his plans."

Daphne flung her arms in the air and moaned, the sound of a high wind in a spreading tree. Her illusion wavered. For a brief moment I saw bark instead of skin and hair like a spray of green leaves. With another moan she returned to human form.

"I chased you down because I'm curious," I said. "What did you use to kill him? An ivy vine?"

"No. These." She held up one hand.

Her long fingers shimmered, grew longer, became the pale gray-brown of twigs or rootlets, long and tough and moving, searching through the air for something to cling to, to twine around, to strangle. I took a step back and began to gather Qi again. She laughed and shook the hand into human form.

"No wonder he was shocked," I said.

"Oh yeah. I let him see what he was in for. She had to watch the axemen. She had to tremble in terror when they fired up their horrible screaming stinking saw." Daphne took a deep breath to steady her voice, then smiled. "And so did he tremble. Like a leaf in the wind."

With that she made a graceful bow in my direction and disappeared. I drove home.

You can doubtless guess that I told Sanchez nothing about this conversation. Still, I didn't want to leave him dangling. "I've got a little bit of useless information," I told him over the phone. "The woman in the car was Greek. She disappeared the next day. If she went home, you've got a problem. Trying to pry a witness out of the Greek government would be a bigger headache than it's worth."

"Assuming she's run for home, that's true. I'll follow this up, though, check the airlines, all the usual routine."

"Okay. She might not have run far, but I bet she wants to keep out of sight. She might be afraid that someone's going to shut her up permanently."

"She might be right about that. Nothing else?"

"My associate told me she was new on the street. Looks to me like she didn't like it here."

"She got herself into some real trouble is probably why. Well, thanks for looking into it. I'd better get back to work."

Not long after, pressure from above derailed his investigation into the various well-heeled people who had possible reasons to want Harlander dead. The police case went colder than an August day in San Francisco. Just as well, really, since they didn't have a hope in hell of arresting a dryad, much less convicting her!

But I filed a full report with the Agency. We have ways of dealing with the weird. If "Daphne" ever kills again, we'll be on her trail.

If you'd like to read more about Nola O'Grady and her world, there are four novels available from DAW Books: *License to Ensorcell, Water to Burn, Apocalypse to Go, and Love on the Run.*

Copyright © 2022 by Katharine Kerr.

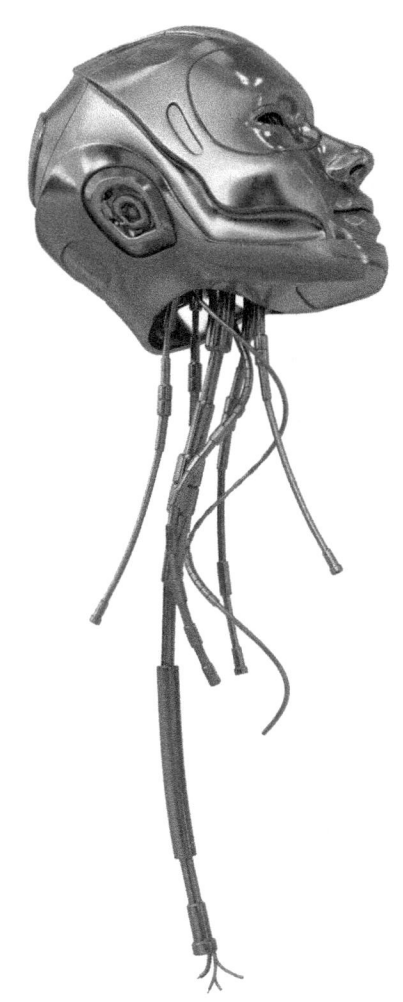

J.R. Troughton is a writer of fantasy fiction who lives and works in Essex, England. After graduating from the University of Leicester in 2007, he moved to Seoul, South Korea, where he worked in language academies for three years before returning to the UK. He now works in Primary education. He likes cats.

WITH OUR SONGS OF SCARS AND STARLIGHT

by J.R. Troughton

Stories are told about my daughter and the day she vanished into the ocean. On my trips to the mainland I hear them; tales of the violent storm she called down on our island and the lightning that came, fierce enough to split the ocean in two and burn the sky black for a month and a day. These stories don't mention the details of her disappearance; not the curses she screamed until her throat ran red, nor the torrents of starlight that burst from her pores as she became one with the white foam of the sea.

If she is still out there, in whole or in part, I hope I can find her and tell her it is okay. That it was never her fault and that I should have been kinder, and wiser, and, perhaps, less ambitious. If she is still alive, I want to apologize. It should never have been her.

I simply chose the wrong daughter.

I lean over the railing of the lighthouse, shielding my eyes from the ferocious blue of the sky, and watch the summer gulls dance above the surf as the tide rolls in. The ice in my glass rattles as I shakily raise it to my lips and sip the whisky; I roll it around my mouth and savor the familiar smoky taste, then the hints of vanilla and toffee that follow. Jagged rocks reach out of the water below like wild claws, desperately searching for purchase. Each evening I return here, hitch my skirt up above my knees, and weakly climb the spiraling steps, my bones brittle, legs ironcast. Then I wait.

Each evening, my heart brims with hope once more.

Not a day goes by that I don't miss my daughters, both. It has been too many years to bear. Perhaps even a decade already? The years appear like an amateurish watercolor; out of focus and unclear. Individual memories blend together, almost beyond recognition.

⬡

Icante, then

In the distance, cutting through the crystal water, is a pearl-white schooner. White as the swans of the lake at the center of our island. Yet it's even more graceful, carving a wide arc around the island at impressive speed. I narrow my eyes; there are several figures on the boat. They come no closer than a hundred meters from the shore before the schooner turns and heads back in the direction of the mainland. I watch until it vanishes into the horizon, then turn my attention back to the gulls.

Boats come most days, though none ever make landfall. Icante is a dead island now; a curio for those brave enough to still set sail in these waters, or rich enough to think themselves beyond danger. Nobody else is left but me.

Not that anyone knows that for sure.

Nobody but my children.

I taught the twins to sing to the wind when they were six and to the rain when they were ten. Only simple songs, melodies their young minds could remember and repeat.

It was a few days after their tenth birthday, and a burning hot summer's eve, when we stood at the top of our lighthouse—Isla, Caitlin and I—and sang to the sky together. High above the rolling green hills of the island, the clouds bulked, grew bulbous and dark, then burst over the town and drenched the townsfolk. We cried with laughter and the children rolled around my feet like drunks, cackling and whooping; I had always enjoyed a joke, and they did too.

They'd taken on all my best qualities, and a handful of my worst. What more could a mother dream of than for her daughters to be better than she was?

The governor of the time was a man so thin it was as if he were built of twigs, with a round head like an egg and a most unfortunate haircut—the style of the time, I gathered, though I thought it left him looking like a battered crow (and remarked as such to raucous guffawing from the girls). He sent soldiers to speak to me, and they spoke most unkindly, demanding I show him the appropriate respect and turn the weather at their beck and call. So each day I carved the weather into unkind shapes with my tongue and spat it at them angrily. I gave them a month of floods and blistering winds; apologies came after, transported by boat with the sheepish governor at its helm.

They didn't trouble us for several years after that.

We lived well, practicing our songs, our magic, and talking of dreams and ambitions. I had always felt a hunger to change the world, to make it a better place. During my youth I had seen such poverty and sickness and I had myself barely escaped their smothering grasp. While rich folk ate greedily, my family clawed about the corners of the city for a loaf of bread. This did not leave me bitter, nor hopeless, as it did to so many who grew up in such circumstance, but with an understanding of the world; there simply wasn't enough to go around.

The girls were fourteen when the latest governor (they changed as often as the wind) sent a new envoy to speak with me.

He offered gifts of silk, gold and the finest deer meat on the island, as well as words of deference and respect. I took these with a smile and a promise that I could grant their request of fine weather for the following years. My powers were waning by now, but I still held the strength for such simple magic.

The next few years were blissful. We ate well, gorging ourselves on the finest veal and turtle soup. We dressed finely, adorning ourselves in the red and blue silks sent to us by the governor; expensive, ornate garments from both sides of the ocean. The girls' singing voices grew more intricate and adept, and they had a hunger for learning that matched the hunger of any shark. Caitlin bubbled with enthusiasm for each new song, or verse, or true name-of-a-thing, smiling widely at every new lesson. Isla kept pace, but was never so engaged as her sister. Never as interested.

Not during my lessons, anyway, though I knew she practiced when I was not watching. I could see the hesitancy in her heart and doubt in her mind. She needed a spark to ignite the strength I knew she held inside.

And if there was one thing I knew, it was how to start fires.

Incate, now

I have spent too long back on Icante and now must move on again and begin my search. I have been south and east and west. North is next, as unlikely as it may be. Unlikely and hard-going. I study the cold gray sky; the delicate clouds; the blank ocean slate. It is with a sigh that I place my empty glass down. Bottle loosely in hand, I head inside.

I descend the stairs slowly.

Carefully, I step across those wild rocks. Amorphous sea-creatures built of blubber and slime moil around, sucking limpets off of rock faces. I take a final slug from my bottle and clear my throat, close my eyes, think of soothing words. I bend the air around my tongue and shape it in artisanal ways before sending it out alongside my song. One of the creatures shudders, then stalls, before waiting, expectantly. I depart. It follows across the shingle, undulating like a vast slug, as I stagger around the causeway to my rowing boat, *Birdcall*, which sits sullenly on the shingle, pale blue paint chipped and flaking. With a coarse rope I bind the thing—I shall call her Amb—with loops around two appendages and tie her tightly to the front of *Birdcall*.

I sing a few bright notes—dancing, summer notes—and Amb drags us out into the ocean. She carries me over the gentle roll of the tides, and we head north.

Icante, then

The twins were born on a warm evening on Blessday. I have forgotten many things over the years, but remember the exhaustion and elation well. Scars, both physical and mental, that bring me nothing but joy. My fifth spouse—my second husband—beamed at me and held my hand as I lay. We watched them for hours, marveling at each breath, wriggle and yawn; their small miracles bewitched us both. We were never happier than in those fleeting moments.

Sadly, it didn't take long for us to return to quarreling. It had been his lighthouse alone before he met me and he struggled to change with the blossoming of our pairing into a family. His complaints about slovenliness were bitter and spiteful, not to mention unfair. He had lived alone for too long and the girls and I were too much for him, close-minded and insular as he was. Set in his ways, too old of mind. Cleaning dishes in the morning is no different to the night before, once all is said and done. To say otherwise is a lie and I never had time for liars.

He didn't leave until the girls were nearly eight, which was an uncharacteristic feat of endurance for him. The last time I saw him he was leaning over the balcony of the lighthouse, sipping bourbon straight from the bottle, gazing out over the ocean. I heard he was seen near the docks on the day he vanished, but nobody could tell me what ship he had boarded, or if he had embarked at all. For all we knew, he had walked into the ocean with his pockets full of rocks.

It would have been just his style to take my curses so damn literally.

I raised the girls on my own and did a fine job of it too. He may have taught them to tie their shoes and ride their bikes down the hill toward the town, but I taught them to sing to the world and shape it with their words. How we could sing to the elements and to the wild things of the world, but that we must never try to sing to those greater powers. Not to time, the sun and stars, nor to death itself. Not until they were ready. Not until I was certain we had prepared enough and we would sing together and change the world.

And change the world we would. Once the girls had learned enough, once they had turned their voices into fine crafting tools, we would carve out a new world together, our strength combined. A world without darkness or fear or death. Together, once fully prepared, we would sing to the moon and the sun and take their magic. Use it to grant ourselves everlasting life and to end war, famine, and cruelty.

What better gift could they have had than this? What better purpose?

They adored my lessons. Caitlin, so full of joy and energy, visibly shook with anticipation of learning new names and tricks, thirstily drinking in new skills. Isla never showed her emotions. She always watched quietly and rarely wanted to practice with Caitlin and I. Caitlin was all aspiration and vigor for songcraft, yet Isla seemed so lackluster in compari-

son, so disappointing. I never let my feelings on the matter show, of course.

I would never have done that to her.

Northbound, now

I pull my scarf tighter and wrap my arms around my body. The sky is a ferocious blue. Bergs jut out of the water like teeth, and as I shiver I wonder if the North is going to devour me whole. Vast plates of ice surround me as I sail ever onward, pulled along by the diligent Amb. Foreign birds watch curiously, hop from foot to foot and caw to me. *Birdsong* has done well.

The journey has been long and cold, but I am confident. I sang words of inspiration to a school of dolphins and they told me of a girl who rode in a great wooden fish that cut through the waves and was chased by monstrous winds.

I rub my hands together and slap them against my thighs. My heart sings for the first time in years. It won't be long now until I can apologize and make it all fine once again. I don't blame her anymore. I realize now that I made mistakes too.

My dear Isla is here. I can feel it in the marrow of my bones.

Icante, then

"Mama! Mama!" Caitlin's voice bounced down the stairs of the lighthouse. "Come and see what I've made!"

As I reached the top of the lighthouse and stepped out onto the balcony, she was dancing from foot to foot and pointing to the sky. Isla stood in the shade of the lighthouse spire, watching. The clouds had been shaped into a fleet of galleons. My chest swelled with pride and I rested my hand on her back. "Beautiful, Caitlin."

"Watch," she laughed. She cleared her throat and began to sing. Familiar syllables, sung in a pitch I could never reach, cast out into the sky.

The galleons moved. Slowly at first, they slipped across the sky-sea and glided effortlessly toward the town, their white sails drifting apart in the wind. Caitlin raised her voice and they grew faster. Her voice took on sharp edges, full of hard geometry where it had been soft moments earlier, and the clouds quickly darkened. From their side puffed several dark rings of cloud, and rainfall burst over the houses.

"So boom, sung the cannons!" laughed Caitlin. "And the people did turn wet." She chortled and hopped from foot to foot, beaming at me. Her face was radiant. It was at times like this I saw just how similar to me she was. She looked just like I did as a girl, with long dark hair and wide features; not beautiful, but full of *life*. She also shared my sense of humor and wild imagination.

The ships continued to drop their payload, having moved across the town from the villagers' houses to the open-air market. Such clever magic. So creative. "Beautifully worked, my darling." I gripped her by the shoulders. "Such wonders. I adore the style of your ships. You'll have to teach me the song one day."

"I will, Mother," she grinned. Her eyes flickered to her sister. Isla's lips twitched, just slightly, but she remained silent, a glazed look on her face. She went indoors and disappeared down the stairs.

"Isla thought it was stupid." Caitlin's face crumpled like crushed origami. "Didn't she?"

"No, my dear. I'm sure that's not true. She is probably just feeling sad today." Or envious. Isla had never been an artist, not like Caitlin or I. She could sing to the world and form it to her will, but not with the craft that Caitlin showed. Long ago I had seen resentfulness building in her, but what could I do? Hold back Caitlin? I had made my choice. Caitlin wanted to learn and to grow her songcraft. I could sense the dormant power in her and together we would change the world for the better. If Isla couldn't give me her focus, that must not stop Caitlin from achieving all she was capable of. Isla could still sing in support of us, despite her weakness.

"Are you sure?" Caitlin nuzzled against my shoulder. The cloud-ships had almost dissipated now, though still cast heavy rain upon the town. The people would be most upset. Not that I care any longer.

The gifts from the town had dried up. The former governor's generosity had been an oddity; the new governess—a sharp-eyed woman with a nose like a fish hook and the instincts of a magpie—had returned to the ways of the old island rulers. And with that, we had also returned to our old ways, toying with the townsfolk for our own pleasure. I told the girls that this was just, hence Caitlin's rainfall song. They should have showed more respect.

"Do not worry, Caitlin. Isla just finds it difficult to see magic she cannot yet do herself. That's why she likes to practice on her own so much."

"Like when she goes down to the bay?"

"Exactly." In the distance, I could see Isla walking down the winding path toward the bay. She often went there to sing on her own and to practice magic without my discerning eye pulling her up on errors, or pushing her onward to greater heights. Seeing Caitlin's eyes wet, I pulled her tight to me and hugged her. Yet as I relished her closeness, my nose wrinkled; she smelled of sweat and smoke both.

I frowned and pulled her in front of me, gripping her shoulders firmly. "Why do you smell of smoke?" I had thrown my pipe into the ocean once the girls grew old enough to start imitating me. Their father had insisted. I hadn't started again, even after he left.

Caitlin's face turned pale. "We weren't smoking!"

I raised an eyebrow and shifted my gaze from steely to savage. She shuddered.

"It was Isla's idea…" she mumbled, her eyes dropping to the floor. "She said we could bottle the smoke and then shape it into birds…"

"Of course she did."

I glowered for a moment longer, then stormed inside and after foolish, selfish Isla.

The North, now

Isla is here. Whatever remains of her. I am so happy to have the chance to apologize for everything that I did, and for everything that I did not. How many mothers can say the same after making the same mistakes that I had? I make landfall and drag *Birdsong* onto the ice. There is no fear of someone stealing her here, so I do not try to hide my trusted boat. It is with warmth in my heart that I pat thanks across her bow.

I can tell Isla is within reach by the closeness and shapes of the aurora. Vast birds and horses and dolphins of vibrant blues and greens flicker across the black curtain of the night, dancing across the polar skies like carnival beasts. Just like the girls used to make out of the clouds, back on Icante. Isla had never been as powerful as Caitlin, but what she could now shape with her songs was resolutely beautiful. Her songcraft had blossomed in her isolation. Perhaps I should have believed in her more.

Of course I should have. That much is obvious now. But to see how strong she has become lifts my heart. Perhaps all is not lost. Perhaps we can still accomplish our destiny.

With a few quiet words, I shape the ice around me. I form a chariot, basic and lacking in the pomp I would once have insisted upon in my youth. It is enough to travel and that is all that matters now. No intricacy nor artistry is needed.

I just need to find Isla and say sorry. And ask her to come home.

Amb drags me forward, faster than one would imagine possible. Her many appendages clutch at the permafrost and drag us across the bleak and lonely icescape, toward the dancing circus of light that marks the whereabouts of Isla.

☼

Icante, then

It was summer. The sun had already melted away after a burning hot day where I did little but read and drink. The stars were brighter than ever and decorated the sky like jewels.

The world was content.

I sat on the balcony of the lighthouse and rattled the ice in my glass. The girls would be back from the town soon; they had gone drinking together to celebrate their nineteenth birthday. Privately I had told Isla to make sure her sister did not drink too much. She needed a clear head for practice.

Caitlin's training over the past years had gone well. Her voice reached notes mine never could and she always wanted to please me, so she worked hard and listened to my commands with infinite diligence. Watching her develop had been joyous. Isla had grown too, of course, though never quite showed the strength of her sister. She didn't have the courage, I suppose; it was as if she had leashed herself, kept her greatest strengths bound and tied. Something a true artist would never do.

An unseasonal wind blew across the eyrie. I shivered and took a swig of whiskey.

Fireworks crackled over the docks, showers of color and light bursting over the dull, limpet-strewn hulls of the ships, over the forest of their white masts. The distant merriment of the townsfolk reached me, a whisper on the breeze, and my lip curled with disdain. I finished my glass and poured another. I didn't mind the solitude; it gave me time to work on my wordcraft without distraction. Once the world was ours, and was saved, only then there would be time to be merry.

A streak of light caught my eye. It came from the east, over the secluded bay where the girls and I would go crabbing; where Isla liked to practice her singing alone. I clumsily stepped across the balcony to get a better vantage point, and as I did, the streak appeared again, running through the night sky like a stream of light and down into the bay. The moon glowed brighter than I had ever seen, and the stream of light quickly turned into a river. It fell for several seconds, disappearing into the bay, then faded.

Suddenly, the moon dulled.

There was another burst of light from the bay and I saw them, just for a moment. Two figures stood upon the rocks, holding hands.

Caitlin and Isla.

The river of moonlight ran into the bay once more and, carried by the rising wind, I heard distant song words. I dropped my glass but didn't hear it shatter, my mind already ablaze with worry as I rushed down the stairs, taking them three at a time despite my creaking knees and unsteady gait, out of the lighthouse, and flew down the path. It is a wonder I did not fall myself.

What were they doing? So foolish! They couldn't sing without me. Not to something so powerful as the moon!

My legs felt leaden and it was as if my lungs had been covered in steel webbing that grew tighter and tighter, yet I couldn't stop running toward the bay, couldn't slow even for a moment. Caitlin knew she should be resting for tomorrow, when we would sing together. Isla should have stopped her; why didn't she stop her?

As I half-ran, half-stumbled, I pushed past townsfolk who were also following the light show. They murmured excitedly, thinking it an extension of the Blessday frivolities. My elbows were sharp, my bellowed words still sharper. Any complaints they may have made fell on dead ears.

I rounded the corner and froze. Crowds lined the bay, jaws slack. The twins stood in the water, waves lapping at their ankles, hand in hand and facing the moon. They both sang different songs. I recognized neither the words nor the tune; this was something of their own creation. They were drenched in ferocious moonlight that fell from the sky in torrents.

"Caitlin, no!" I cried as I ran toward them.

It was Isla who spun to face me, her song lost in distraction. "Mother?" Her voice was full of disbelief and irritation.

As she turned, the light intensified, burned bright and scorched my eyes. It rushed into Caitlin, like water sucked into a whirlpool. I squinted and tried to keep my eyes on the girls.

Caitlin screamed as she was enveloped by the light. Isla screamed alongside her.

I realized I was screaming too as the girls both disappeared into an ocean of blinding white. I could no longer tell them apart, their shapes so similar, all individuality—every dimple, scar and pore—masked by the incandescence.

Caitlin—it must have been, I am sure, for she stepped forward with such confidence—took several steps closer to me.

"It was working!" she screamed. My insides shook. She had never spoken to me like this before. "Why did you interrupt? Why did you have to ruin this? It was working!" Her voice turned hoarse as she continued to bellow. "It was going to make everything better! Why couldn't you just stay away?! We were doing it on our own!"

And with that, she screamed a baleful cry that shook the blood in my veins and the sky tore open: moonlight streaming all around; stars burning furiously; gathered crowds fleeing, barging, stampeding. I couldn't make out the girls anymore, but I watched in horror as their silhouettes pulsed in the light. A final scream, so ferocious it made my heart weep, and Caitlin exploded in a firework of blood and brine and both girls disappeared into the waves.

The sky sundered and rain began to lash down like a thousand whips, tearing at my clothes as I rushed forward and dove into the red and white foam. I thrashed around the water, but of my daughters,

there was no sign. They had both melted away and become one with the waves, or the light, or perhaps even the dark of the bleak night itself.

I searched until the sun rose.

Both of my daughters were gone.

The North, now

Close.

I know she must be nearby now. The aurora continues to dance wildly above. Vast pillars of ice line the valley through which Amb pulls my chariot, like great sentinels created to watch and protect.

Then I see her. A hunched shadow. It can only be her, surely? She is facing away from me, watching a colossal horse made of sapphire light charge across the sky. I whisper the words and Amb immediately halts. She curls into a spiral, ammonite-like, and quietly waits. Stepping from my chariot, I approach, my heart full of joy at finding my daughter. I am almost fighting to keep the smile from my face, but as I draw close the words evaporate.

It is not Isla, but Caitlin.

My brow furrows and I think back to that night. Was I remembering it wrong?

"Caitlin?"

The girl starts, and turns. She looks up at me, her face black and charred, hair recently torn from her scalp, leaving sore red patches. Her cheeks are hollow and she is all rag and spindles. Her mouth opens but words do not come; eyes wide with surprise and writhing emotion. I try to decide what to say. All this time I had only considered the verse and script of what I would say to Isla, the damned daughter, the terrible influence that broke my pride and joy just when she was reaching her greatest triumph. Just as she was about to sing with me and change the world. I have never been one for improvising.

"My love, I've missed you," I start. She is shaking. "Why did you come so far north?"

Her face, as broken and hard to read as it is, sours. "I've been finding myself," she whispers and points at her grotesquely misshapen face with a three-fingered hand. "That night I was spread far and wide."

A question burrows its way through my heart. "Is Isla…"

"She's gone."

I nod. An idea comes to me. "Would you..." I continue, uneasily. "Would you like to sing together? As we had planned? Perhaps we can fix this together? Fix you." Even as the words fall, I know they were the wrong ones.

Impossibly, her eyes grow wider. Her irises are void black, the whites stark even amid the snow. Caitlin stands, staggers backward, and draws breath. She sings a song I do not know.

A snowstorm rises, violently.

That is not all.

Searing pain strikes me across the back and I cry out at the first stroke. Her song cuts—fervently cuts—like a hot knife. Not cleanly or precisely, but with uneven teeth that tear at my skin like a rusty saw. I fall to my knees and try to black out the pain as she flays my arms and legs and back, my cheeks, forehead and nose.

"Mother." Her voice ragged, but calm. "This is you. This is all you." She points at her ruptured face. "Isla is on you. Icante is on you."

Tears drip down my cheeks. "I'm sorry," I say. I am not sure why. I only wanted to help her.

Caitlin's song changes. From fast, guttural tones it shifts to something calmer, more serene. The searing pain that covers my body does not leave, though it is blunted, and I feel my skin tighten. I pull up my thick coat sleeves to see; my wounds are healing, sewn up neatly by lyric and verse, leaving thick, ugly scar tissue. I choke with shock and my tears fall faster.

Scarification: she has cut me open with words and sung them into permanence.

"Isla..." I read the name upon my skin, hot tears rolling down my cheeks. Caitlin has carved her sister's name across me and left it as an ever-cruel reminder of the past.

"Go home, Mother," she screams. "You ruined us all. You never cared about the right things. Not for Isla, or Dad, or anything but your own vision. For your own greed!"

And with that, she disappears into the snowstorm, her silhouette vanishing all too quickly as I stumble after, desperately reaching out for her. To have come so far, I cannot have lost her again!

I wail her name to no avail and when I try to summon up the words to break the storm, I cannot find them. I know a thousand songs and ten times as many verses, yet not one will come to my lips. Slumping into the thick snow, I hang my head and hug my coat close. The storm will subside, I am sure.

It takes longer than expected.

✧

Icante, latterday

I sit inside my lighthouse on Icante, a good book in my lap, a pitcher of water on the table beside me. I can no longer climb the stairs to the eyrie, and I have long stopped singing. Since I returned to the island, I have not offered a word to a soul since Amb delivered me home and I said goodbye. My molluscan friend has stayed at the island, finding a dwelling amid those wild rocks, even though her brethren are long gone. I am beyond grateful for the company.

Many years ago, stories were told about my daughter and the day she vanished into the ocean. I remember my trips to the mainland where I heard them, tales of the violent storm she called down on our island and the lightning that came, fierce enough to split the ocean in two and burn the sky black for a month and a day. These stories don't mention the details of her disappearance; not the curses she screamed until her throat ran red, nor the torrent of starlight that burst from her pores as she became one with the white foam of the sea.

I know she is still out there, in part, and I only wish I had told her it was okay when I had the time. That it was never her fault and that I should have been kinder, and wiser, and, certainly, less ambitious. I should have trusted in her talent, as her twin obviously had.

I want to speak with Isla one more time, and I want to apologize. It should never have been her. It should never have been either of them.

It wasn't just that I chose one over the other, but the choosing itself that was wrong.

And, girls, I am sorry for that.

ZZ Claybourne is the author of The Brothers Jetstream: Leviathan and its sequel Afro Puffs Are the Antennae of the Universe. Other works include By All Our Violent Guides, Neon Lights, and Conversations with Idras. His stories and essays on sci fi, fandom, and howlingly existential life have appeared in Apex, Galaxy's Edge, GigaNotosaurus, Strange Horizons, and other genre venues, as well as the "42" blog at https://www.writeonrighton.com. He is the 2021 Kresge Foundation Literary Fellow. He grew up watching The Twilight Zone and considers himself a better person for it.

GIANT MECHS IN THE DISTANCE, FOREVER FIGHTING

by ZZ Claybourne

Birdsong, of the few birds that hung around, barely carried in the omnipresent haze. Behemoth mechs—some shaped like spiders, some like angry giants, others like pieces of war held together by magnets—fought along every horizon. They always fought and always in the outlying areas, as there was no point fighting inside a city meant to be taken over. Even the lowliest taggers didn't spar for turf if the turf was unusable rubble.

Birdsong came short and swift; each tiny, fragile winged body had a point to make and made it without waiting to be felled by a drone or eaten by whatever feral animal was nearest; they twittered for a moment hoping for a mate. They took off before a rival answered the call instead.

Life in general was primarily chaotic as mechs fought. The mechs were glorious. War had never been so aspirational until the first two rolled off the line two continents away from each other. Seeing that much science, ingenuity, and high expenditure brought to bear for killing genuinely stirred folks. Up close, the neighborhoods fought about water, they fought about air, they fought about footsteps and living space. They fought at all hours of the day and night. Even the people with jobs fought, but not as often.

Marshall had a job. Marshall usually stayed indoors. Fighters heard him playing now and then when they were quiet, which wasn't often. He played each day in his rundown home with the shiniest guitar in the world. It was played for however long a tune needed, polished after each use, and replaced carefully as a babe on fur when done.

Marshall peered outward, but not at the giant mechs along the horizon of the flat barren land stretching forever away from his border home. He observed a group of fighters in the middle of the street. The group got bigger and bigger the longer he peered between the slats of his blinds. Half of them wore masks to protect themselves from the ash of nearby warfare, half did not. All were angry, nearly feral, except for the fact that they worked in organized groups with rules and roles, but Marshall had long since supposed feral cats acknowledged hierarchy and structure. The fight was going to be ugly since it was about absolutely nothing. Those fights usually ended with lots of blood for loud, crazed gulls to land atop, leaving strange, red art on the broken roads. The municipality took care of the bodies; ash rain eventually washed the gulls' prints away.

Scavengers, all. One day the gulls would learn that there was never food following these deaths.

He couldn't tolerate a fight today. He was too old for it. He was too frightened for it. That morning he'd said the customary prayer to remake the world, but had done so in front of the glow of a monitor showing three pre-determined pictures over and over. The house computer forever asked him if he'd like it to import additional images. He never responded to it. Marshall Monday-nee-Wellis always hated the day the world's spy machines had been made cheap enough for poor people to be able to buy their conveniences. The lovely Anna Monday said she'd marry him if he took her name—after kissing his ear while they cuddled against a gray, rotted tree—to which he'd mellifluously sang yes. Anna had loved the idea of things being done for her for a change.

The first 3-dimensional image showed Anna holding tongs; smiling and grilling before the ash had become an everyday thing.

The second photo was one she'd taken at his birthday twenty-three years ago. Pre-ash again. They were all pre-ash. Photography had died after that first intercontinental bomb. A part of her hand was in the photo, owing to her laughing at the expression on his face at the misshapen cake guitar she'd attempted.

In their locked home it had tasted wonderful.

Lemon and butter, not at all like the bitter taste of being old and alone.

The last picture was Anna's face up close, each freckle and blemish a sun on honeyed skin, with the real sun—that now permanent smudge behind haze—haloing her gray twists brilliantly.

Life now was nothing but peering between blinds and working. He never left the house on this day—this anniversary—not even for the nightly cleaning of the air vents at the various municipal offices he toiled. Today had been his day for ten years, no matter what clanked on the horizon. He'd fought for it tooth and nail, wearing the bosses down year after year.

"I just need this one day off, sir—"

"I never ask for anything at all—"

"I don't make trouble, sir, I just—"

The municipality no longer even docked his pay.

He narrowed his eye at the fighters. Hven gave a disinterested glance toward the mechs. One—at this distance just a confluence of lines and angles—toppled in a huge cloud of cartoon dust. The other fired another rocket at it.

In the middle of his street, several people shoved each other. Marshall was inured to the shouting. That was background noise—that and the random bursts of gun fire. This, though, was the type of gathering that gained strength, like the old hurricanes used to do. Its threat potential leaving people wondering if it would become a one, a three, or a five—

"Just go away," he muttered. He was grumpy and old enough to have muttered "Get off my lawn," had there been any lawns left under the constant haze of warfare.

It was merely a matter of time before the flash of an ancient blade or the glint off a silver-painted printed gun made its way through the quarter inch view of the world he allowed. Every light in the home was turned on, except for this closed-off room. The living room. It was the smallest room in the house, but it faced the street, and Anna had claimed the space as their place of daily respite.

He didn't want them to see or notice him.

He just wanted to sit on his stoop and play his guitar without wondering who was coming to fight him for it.

Marshall's tight breath displaced motes on the blinds. The fighters jostled far enough away that they wouldn't see the slat vibrating from his nervous heartbeat shaking his wrinkled fingers.

Still, the hurricane category worsened. The sounds of escalation were invading his personal space. *Their* personal space.

"Not today!"

He dropped the blind and rushed to his polished guitar.

He pulled his mask off the nail by the door.

He yanked the door open so angrily it frightened him at the same time.

The fighters didn't notice at first. They shouted, pushed, and were probably about to kick or punch. Kicks and punches led to weapons being drawn.

He played as he walked.

It stopped everything.

The notes, even though they didn't fly far, took to the air.

He kept his eyes closed and played to calm them. It was an impromptu arrangement, a melody of awakening and creation, a G chord which wandered the crowd like a small bystander. He stopped inside a wide, shallow pothole while the fighters stared at him. He played as if there was no one but him, his guitar, and music for Anna Monday at the curb of that city street, keeping his eyes closed because otherwise the reality of the world would have knocked his music from the sky and eaten it.

The fighters stared at him. He didn't want to feel their stares. They murmured. He didn't want to hear their noise. This strange concert kept everyone's hands away from knives and guns, and when they realized he wasn't going anywhere—that he was going to stand there with eyes closed and continue playing music—several fighters went away.

He'd done this before. He hated it each time.

Neighbors told Marshall Monday he was going to get killed doing that. He agreed it was likely.

But today was Anna's day. He had fought this ragged city to hold this day away from the hungry world. If he had to fight a mech along the border too, he would. Getting smooshed wouldn't matter. What was life but blood under a thumb anyway.

He played in the pothole that would never be repaired. After a short time, everybody left, disappearing into the gloom of ash to put on spyglasses to see which mech toppled another. There was always fighting, whether it was man or machine.

Marshall Monday kept playing until all he heard was his music. He opened his eyes. Even all the neighbors had gone inside. He played a little more, then he stopped strumming only long enough to carry his guitar to his cracked stoop. He sat on the top step where the rusted awning placed him in deeper shadow, and played the tune out to the end. Then he too disappeared inside. He locked his front door and glanced out one last time. He thought of Anna, her face in what used to be the sun.

In the distance, soundlessly and surely, a toppled mech righted itself to begin again. Marshall didn't care. He carefully placed his guitar on the table and went to get polish to wipe dust and ash from it yet again.

No more fighting today.

Torion Oey holds a B.A. in Creating Writing and Psychology and has attained an M.S. in Psychology. He dedicates his free time toward writing, and has participated in National Novel Writing Month for six consecutive years since 2014. Stories he has written range from romance and fantasy to thriller and mystery.

FEEL

by Torion Oey

"Your top two cervical vertebrae fractured and your spinal cord was injured in the ski lift accident. Most feeling is absent from the lower half of your body."

Leslie grimaced, having heard this so many times before. "I know. Can't we just skip to the exciting part?"

"Please be patient. I'm sorry to be bringing this up again. This is just to recap the progress your body has undergone since then for the recording." Dr. Patton pulled his bottom-rimmed glasses off his nose to let them hang from a neck chain below the collar of his shirt. He placed the clipboard with Leslie's medical information on a counter behind her bedside. "Despite the biotherapeutic administration of AST-OCP1, progenitor cells, you're aware the injuries are profound and beyond full recovery?"

She sighed, resigning herself to the questions. "Yes."

"Does this hurt?" he asked, pinching a spot on her upper arm.

"Yes. Yes! Ow!" She flinched, her face expressing the pain the rest of her paralyzed body could not.

Dr. Patton smiled tightly. "It's been two months. It seems your sensory nervous system has healed enough for us to improve your condition."

Leslie looked up at the doctor, startled. "You mean, more surgery, now that I can feel more?"

"No, that's not what we mean…" Dr. Patton rose from his rolling stool and paced to the foot of her bed. He turned and gripped the metal rail that her feet numbly rested against. "We've told you your injury is similar to Christopher Reeve's, the man who played Superman a century ago?"

Leslie nodded.

"He needed assistance breathing and was unable to walk again, but medicine has come quite a ways since then. Surely you have heard of the innovative research team working on projecting dreams?"

Leslie shook her head. "Why would I know that?"

"I thought your parents might've—never mind. Technology based on their work has been made that can…well…you know computer games, right?"

"Yes," she responded, trying to hide her exasperation. "How does this conversation relate to—"

"Bear with me. In computer games you play a character that isn't you, but that you control." He paused, considered her for a long moment. "Have you thought about feeling what your character experiences yourself?"

She blinked, frowned. "No, not really."

Dr. Patton smiled, releasing the rail on her bed to stand up straighter. "Let's say there's a device that can help you experience things without leaving this room. Would you like that?"

Her eyes jumped from his to look out the square window overlooking a flat roof, pigeons sunbathing to the window sill beside a row of sterilizers and medical equipment. "What about leaving the room myself?"

Dr. Patton's smile froze. Slowly, he brought his hands together. "That will take some more time, I'm afraid."

Leslie's eyes flicked back to stare out the window, trying to hold back her emotions.

"It's miraculous you're able to feel more at all," he continued. Seconds of silence passed. "I know it is difficult, but we've talked about this. Healing takes time."

She didn't acknowledge his attempts to mollify her. His statements were just one time too many.

Dr. Patton sighed. "Mirror neurons."

Leslie glanced at him, before looking back out the window. "What?"

"Through observing others, mirror neurons activate in a sort of mimicry. They mirror what is observed. The technology I was talking about would use mirror neurons to help you experience the sensations another is experiencing…without you actually doing what they do."

She frowned, confused. "Please explain."

"Look at me," Dr. Patton instructed, and he smiled.

"I don't want to," Leslie replied, although her glaze flicked towards him briefly, instinctively.

"I'm demonstrating something. Do you see that I'm smiling?"

"Yes, though I don't know why."

"When babies see someone smile, they tend to smile as well."

Leslie's brow furrowed in frustration. "I'm not a baby."

"I know." Dr. Patton moved to the counter and picked out a cotton ball from an ovular glass container. "Okay, how about this." He put it in his mouth. "Ew!"

"Exactly," Dr. Patton said, spitting it out. Using his foot on a trashcan pedal to open it, he tossed the cotton ball in. "You recognized how it would feel for you to put a cotton ball in your mouth, by seeing me do it. It enabled you to react to a sensory experience without having to do it yourself. That's what the technology using mirror neurons does."

Leslie was still confused. "I don't want to play a video game."

"You won't be." Dr. Patton waved a hand to the door in the far corner. "Some people are here who can tell and show you more about the technology based on mirror neurons. I wanted to make sure you're all right with that before I invite them in." He waited for her hesitant agreement before turning and knocking on the door. Two others wearing matching gray attire stepped in; a man with sunken eyes and holding a briefcase gave Leslie a tired smile; a woman whose face was remarkably pale stared wide-eyed at Leslie, her expression unreadable. "This is Matthew and Erika, two of the researchers who've been studying dreams for a while. They'll explain—"

"Then," Matthew interrupted, "she accepted?"

"Accepted what?" Leslie asked.

"Undergoing a transference trial." Matthew took up the rolling stool and lay the briefcase atop his lap to unclasp its latches. The corners of his mouth lowered as he appraised what was inside. "You're aware how dreams are more or less a simulation?"

Stop asking me questions as if I don't know anything! "Yes," Leslie said, trying to keep her voice even. "But I already said I don't want to play a video game."

"This trial isn't going to be a virtual reality, where you wear a headset and pretend you're somewhere you're not," Matthew continued, his voice almost a drawl. He pulled out a headset from the briefcase, as if to illustrate his point.

"I don't want to simply be *in* a dream either."

"You'll be awake. And *you'll* be moving." A lilt of enthusiasm raised his voice briefly.

Leslie looked dubiously from the intricately-wired headset to Dr. Patton. "I'll be able to move, just by wearing that?"

Dr. Patton looked at Matthew. The other man asked, "Where does your sense of feeling end?" He touched his callused finger to her shoulder and slowly ran it down her arm.

"There," Leslie said when his finger came near her elbow.

"And you can't feel me holding your hand?"

"No."

Matthew nodded. "Would you like to?"

She blinked. "Yes, but how?"

The woman—Erika—stepped up to the bedside finally. "It'll be easier if we showed you." She brushed her long blonde hair back and softly added, "Your parents have already agreed. All we need is your consent."

"Where are they?"

"Outside, waiting for you."

Leslie's breath caught. "All right, then."

Matthew lifted the headset and gently set it onto her head while Erika took position on the other side of the bed by the window. "It'll be disorienting at first, but there's no risk involved. You'll be awake but you'll need to keep your eyes closed."

"How will I go anywhere if I can't see?"

"With these," Matthew said, procuring two translucent contacts. "We will put them onto your eyes, which you will then keep closed. They'll project what you'll be seeing."

"I thought you said this wasn't a video game."

"It's not. Here." He waited for Leslie to be ready before he deftly placed the contacts over her corneas. "Dr. Patton and Erika will be here with you the whole time. Follow Erika's instructions, and you'll see me in a bit." He got up and exited the room.

"This feels weird," Leslie said. The headset didn't come down over her eyes, though she felt it coiling all around her scalp. She blinked, getting accus-

tomed to the lens between her eyelids and eyes, trying to keep them closed. "Will I really—?"

Erika pulled out her phone that'd begun ringing to silence it. "It's time," she said. Gingerly, she placed a hand on the part of the headset above Leslie's forehead. "Close your eyes, please. Keep them closed for the entirety of this trial."

Blinking several more times, Leslie finally shut her eyes. "Okay." She felt slight pressure over her forehead when Erika pressed something. Then warmth extended from the places the headset touched her, like water rippling against the top of her head from a warm shower.

"You'll feel a slight warmth," Erika said. "Your instinct will be to open your eyes, but please keep them closed. You'll see soon."

A dim image came into view. At first she wasn't sure if it was her imagination placing it there against the back of her eyelids. Seconds passed and the image became more defined. It was still dim, though the impression she got was that she was sitting upright, facing something like the interior of the back doors of some kind of cargo truck. *Sitting.* As soon as she thought it she felt the sensation of cushiony leather pressing against her legs and back. "I'm sitting!?"

Leslie's eyes flew open and the image of the truck's back doors faded slightly and clashed against the view of her hospital room.

Erika leaned in front of her. "Please keep your eyes closed," she reminded the girl.

"But I'm…" Leslie shut her eyes again, letting the image of the truck's back doors refocus. "I'm still in my bed."

"Yes."

Leslie heard Erika, though her voice was distant now.

"You are also elsewhere. Dr. Patton and I will stay quiet for the rest of the trial."

"How does it feel?" Matthew asked, suddenly entering the image, moving in front of the truck's back doors.

Without reopening her eyes she tried looking around. The image changed as she mentally glanced around. The side of the truck came into view. This was too precise not to be real. "I *feel* myself sitting," she said.

"Good. Do you still feel the headset?"

Leslie paused. She could, though it also felt diminished. Distant, somehow.

"We'll try not to interrupt any of the sensations you feel during this trial."

"You can hear me talking? Where is this?"

"The parking lot outside the hospital," Matthew replied. "I'll open the doors when your eyes and body adjust further. For now, try moving your hands and feet."

Leslie did. Her fingers lifted and felt the texture of the leather chair armrests her arms were resting on. Her feet pressed against the fabric of socks, which she felt pressed against the soles of shoes, which she felt pressed against the floor of the truck. And her clothes…snugly fit black jeans and a pale gray T-shirt. She couldn't suppress her shock. "This is real."

"Yes," Matthew said. "The feelings you're having right now in this van are being transferred to your body in the hospital. This body you are sensing these things from is virtually real—that is, not in the virtual sense, but it is easier to think of it as actually being you since you are very much in control of it."

"This is…"She looked down at the hands—her hands?—and saw the perfection in form. "I am a robot, then? How?"

"Artificial sensory nerve systems integrated with prosthetics. The senses of it are far more generalized than what a human's nervous system is capable of. You may feel some difference at first with how localized or specific the senses of this body are. Here." He reached out and poked her shoulder.

Leslie felt the same callused finger, though it came from a wider area than he was actually touching. "It feels like you put your hand on my shoulder."

"Yes," Matthew said. "While you're still adjusting, you'll notice the senses become more localized, but it will still not be perfect. That's one reason for this trial, to test how precise we can make artificial nervous systems."

"How?" Leslie repeated in wonder.

"This is cutting edge research." Matthew's tired eyes grew wider as he smiled. "I've always wanted to say that."

The pressure on her hands built as she pushed. She found her body—her other body—rise from the chair.

"Slowly," Matthew said, carefully guiding her into a standing position.

Leslie glanced down at her artificial hand, which Matthew was holding. She appraised how realistic her fingernails and skin looked. "This is really a robot?"

"Basically, though we don't think of it that way since you're in full control. It's all you."

She gasped and quickly unclasped his hand to feel her face. "It's an artificial me?"

Matthew laughed slightly. "No, that'd be weird. This body looks unique—it's not your clone."

Pulling strands of hair in front of her face, she saw that the hair was black rather than her dirty brunette. She let go of the hair and gazed at the truck's back doors. "I'd like to walk."

"Then let's try it."

He gripped and swung the doors outward. Sunlight painted the metal interior in bright color, reaching the tips of her shoes. She squinted, partially aware of her own eyes still being closed. Matthew jumped down, the lifted weight unsettling the truck briefly. Though it was a minimal shift, Leslie focused on moving her balance between her feet. She held her arms out. Slight strain ran along the tops of them. The pull of gravity. Then, she took a step. Her body moved forward. She took another. The sunlight fell upon the cuffs of her jeans and rose up her pants as she progressed. The fabric quickly absorbed the heat and warmed her legs. *My legs are warm.*

Her left hand brushed the side of the truck and took hold of its edge. Gazing out, she saw her parents standing in empty spaces of the parking lot, watching. Excitement bubbled within her. *Excitement.* Her heartbeat—*her* heartbeat—pumped moderately within her chest. Tingles spread around her body as her attention fell to her stomach subtly expanding and contracting with her quickening breaths. Excitement felt incredible.

She leapt down from the truck and landed on her feet. Still a little stiff, but feeling the hard jolt run up her legs was also incredible.

"Easier than you think," Matthew said. He shut the truck's doors and gestured for her to follow him over to her parents.

"Leslie?" her father spoke. His rosy face had grown since the accident. His mouth shivered once while his eyes sparkled.

Leslie walked right into him and pressed her face against his chest. He stumbled back a step before catching himself and her. She brought her arms around and held him. She felt his body convulse as he sucked in a breath. Her mother's arms touched Leslie's back as she wrapped them around the two in a hug. "I can feel," Leslie murmured.

They remained there for several seconds before finally pulling apart.

"You may've already noticed other feelings beyond the usual numbness of internal processes," Matthew said. "That's the work of mirror neurons. They took quite a bit to adapt from specially responding to actions with clear goals…" He trailed off, rubbing the side of his face as the three looked blankly at him. "I'll quit with the jargony jargon." He pointed at a cooler lying beside her parents' feet. "Ready for the first test?"

"What is it?" Leslie asked.

Matthew knelt and opened the cooler. He snatched up a Coca-Cola can, the displaced ice rattling around inside. "Catch."

"Whoa!" Leslie's hand flew out, her fingertips managing to snatch onto the rim around the top of the can before it slipped away.

"Good hand-eye coordination. Drink that," he instructed.

"But you just threw it. It's gonna fizz all over the place if I open it now."

"That's the idea."

With intense focus, she lifted the can's metal tab using an index finger. A satisfying *tsssskah* sounded and fizz overflowed around the small basin at the top. She quickly brought the can to her mouth and tipped it. The soda flowed toward the back of her throat, sourly bubbling across her tongue as it went. "Mmmm!" she exclaimed, quickly swallowing the liquid. "I can taste it! It's pretty much the same as what I've tasted."

"Excellent," Matthew said. "Go ahead and have some more."

She sipped some more before holding the can away from her.

"What's wrong?" her mother asked.

"It's…filling my stomach." She looked at Matthew. "Does this—do I use food and water to get energy?"

"No, your body is battery charged."

"Then, where does this go?"

"Don't worry about that. I'm going to make sure the computers are picking up the data we're gathering." Matthew stepped away toward the truck.

"Leslie," her father said. "I'm so sorry."

"What?" She saw his face tremble again. "What's wrong?"

"Don't," her mother said. "It's not your fault."

"What's not his fault?"

"I shouldn't have scheduled that stupid lodge vacation." He clenched his hands into fists. "It's my fault…"

"Hey!" Leslie objected. "Shut up."

Her father blinked. "What?"

"Don't blame yourself!" she said, her voice trembling. "Is that why you've let yourself go?"

"Leslie," her mother said disapprovingly, though her mouth betrayed a slight smile.

Clenching her fists, Leslie breathed in and out while her muscles tightened. *This is anger.* "It's *my* fault I fell the way I fell! I couldn't even sit with you at the table for Christmas dinner! It's—"

"So," Matthew's drawling voice interrupted. He was leaning against the driver's side of the truck. "This is what's happened that day."

Leslie felt herself blush and was startled her robot form could even do that.

"Your medical records stated there was a malfunction with the lift," he continued. "Nothing any of you could account for." He gazed among the three. "I'm no therapist, but when this type of thing happens, people often search for blame. I think it gives them meaning, which is in its own way comforting, even if it means someone undeserving becomes the bad guy."

"Leslie…" Her mother put a hand on her shoulder. "It's not your fault."

"That's what I just said," Matthew muttered.

Leslie swirled the can around, feeling the circling momentum of the liquid within as the tightness in her chest dissipated. "Are there more tests?"

"Yes." He pulled out a mobile phone and checked it. "The charge will last for more than an hour, so we can keep going until that time."

"Only an hour?"

"Running this, ah, body takes a lot of energy," he said.

Leslie patted her own pants pocket out of muscle memory, only to find her phone not there. "What time is it?"

"One oh-four"

"What are the other tests?"

"Well, we have several more physical exercises to—"

I've had enough of tests. Leslie took off running toward the entrance of the parking lot. As she ran her instincts during P.E. classes kicked in. Glancing back, she saw her parents and Matthew watching her with puzzled expressions.

"She's running," Matthew commented with a frown. "Where is she going?"

"It looks like she's heading for the school," her father said.

They quickly moved, Matthew going to the truck and her parents to their car.

Leslie looked ahead as she leapt over a curb and stretch of dirt separating the lot from a sidewalk. She knew the hospital was down the street from her school. Would her friends be there? It'd been since before winter break that she'd seen any of them. None of them visited her, though she was somewhat thankful they didn't see her as she was now. *Do they remember me?*

Her breathing picked up as she ran faster along the road. Oncoming cars drove by, sending intermittent gusts of wind to ripple along her clothes and body. While her muscles strained from the exertion, she also savored it. Something touched her shoulder and she cast her gaze back. Nothing was there. Then a distant voice talked.

"Leslie, what are you doing?"

She recognized it to be Erika next to her real body in the hospital room. "Can you still hear me when I talk?" she asked between panting.

"Yes."

Embarrassed that Dr. Patton and Erika had heard everything before, she said, "I'm going to my school."

"Most kids would be running the other way. Why?"

The school name atop an LED billboard cropping out of grass came into view ahead of her. "I want to see my friends!"

"It's the weekend."

She braced her legs to stop abruptly and watched as the billboard displayed SATURDAY, 1:06 p.m. with decorative light flashes. *Of all the days to finally leave my room.*

Matthew honked his truck as he pulled up on the other side of the street. He leaned out the window, raising a phone to his ear and beckoning her over. Her parents' car pulled up behind his.

Erika's voice came again, saying, "Matthew is telling me to tell you that you'll like the next test."

Sighing, she looked both ways before jogging across the road to him.

"Get in the passenger's seat," Matthew said somberly, stowing his phone somewhere.

She obeyed, rounding the front of the truck and pulling the door handle. "Are you mad?" she asked as she buckled the seatbelt and settled in. He silently changed the gear and started driving. Her panting faded, although her body remained tense. An unsettling sensation ran up her arms. It wasn't specifically physical.

After a few seconds he briefly looked at her, then back to the road. "There're a lot of things you must want to do."

"Yeah…" Her eyes shifted away. "Will this be the only time I get to do this?"

She felt his gaze return to the road. More silence. I'm sick of silence.

Matthew leaned over. He reached to press a button along the dashboard. A rapid drumbeat reverberated from speakers all around her. She felt the vibrations against her right leg which rested beside one of the speakers. And then electric guitars, a bass, and a synth blasted a bright rock melody, sending chills cascading through her body.

Without thinking she started moving. It started with her head nodding. Then her shoulders swayed. Her fingers tapped against her lap and she lifted her heels to thump back on the floor. The vibrations of the truck pulling onto the freeway were overwhelmed by the music and vocals. She hummed along.

Beside her, Matthew grinned. They continued driving before he pulled off onto the side of the road and the view turned into an expanse of shimmering blue.

"What are we going to do at the beach?" she asked.

"Sand, sea, and air are perfect for testing the limits of sensory ability. I also hear you swim?"

"I played water polo." Leslie stopped swaying as the music faded and the memory of loneliness surfaced. "Do you know why people stop talking to you?"

Matthew frowned, started driving again. "What do you mean?"

"Like, ghosting. I get that something like what happened with me could prevent them from staying in contact. But they can't all also be paralyzed."

Matthew turned the steering wheel to bring the truck down a road paralleling a beachfront. "Has no one outside your family been in contact? Visited?"

"My parents use my phone for me, and I've seen friends' posts about me on Twitter, Instagram, and Facebook. Only on some of my replies to them have I gotten responses—though mainly likes or heart emojis."

Matthew pulled the truck into a parking lot and stopped in an empty corner space. "It's one of the biggest ironies of our times, isn't it? The more access we have to communication, the less we truly connect. There've been some theories in psychology that attempt to explain the effects of an online social world. The Toussaint-Martin 'Online Singularity' theory suggests that with every decade the online world deepens, grows, and replaces more aspects of what humans historically have done in real life. An older, more popular theory is Bronfenbrenner's ecological model." He unbuckled his seatbelt and exited the car.

Leslie did the same and quickly got out. She rounded the hood and stood beside him while they waited for her parents to pull into an adjacent space. "Bronfa-what?"

"The name isn't important. His theory is used to understand individuals as being within multiple different environmental systems, from micro to macro. For example, peers would typically be in your immediate surrounding, or microsystem. But cultural attitudes regarding online use, or the macrosystem, may be influencing them which in turn influences you. But I have a more simplistic idea of why people don't communicate well."

"Why?"

Matthew looked sideways at her. "People are idiots." He moved around to the back doors of the truck while her parents parked.

"It's been a while since we've been to the beach," her mother commented, getting out of the car.

Leslie nodded. She turned her gaze to the ocean. Her hair danced with the light breeze while she shaded her eyes against the stinging sun. Not many people were out. A few figures bobbed among the waves, and further off a sailboat floated.

"You two should get back," Matthew said when he returned. He carried what looked to be a faded lunch bag.

"We just got here," her father said, halfway to shutting his car door.

"When we're done here the trial will be over."

Already? Leslie clenched her fists but remained silent.

"We'll want to be at her bedside, for when she's back," her mother agreed. They looked at her with small smiles. "We'll see you in a bit." Her parents got back in their car while Matthew beckoned for her to follow him down a sandy stairway leading from the parking lot to the beach.

At the bottom of the steps, she planted her feet and felt her footing sink as the sand shifted under her weight. Without being told, she bent over to take off her shoes and socks. Her bare feet burned against the sand's hot surface. She wriggled them until they were submerged in a cooler layer of sand.

"Come a little bit farther," Matthew said.

Stuffing the socks into her shoes, she carried them in a hand while he led her closer to the shoreline. They stopped where the sand got firmer and he plopped himself down. "Your clothes," she said.

"They're just clothes. Have a seat." He unzipped the lunch bag and took out what looked to be a microfilm reel.

"What's that?"

"Artificial skin grafts," he replied.

Sitting down, she watched as he pulled a tan panel away from the plastic like it was a sticker.

"I'm going to put this on your index finger," he said. "Hold it out, please…thank you. It's interesting you brought up communication before, since it's somewhat related to our research."

Leslie turned her finger toward her, staring at the panel now meshed and almost indistinct from the rest of her skin at the tip. "Mirror neurons?"

He moved his head in a yes-no fashion. "Perception in general. Among the other pessimistic things I said was that we tend to communicate less when we have more means of communicating. It's not entirely true. Do you feel anything different on your finger?"

"Uh. It feels cooler."

"Try touching the sand."

She put her finger down and ran it slowly against the grains, leaving behind a subtle line. "Oh! Before when I opened the soda can it felt like the pressure was all through my fingers, but now I feel it more clearly on a specific fingertip!"

"Good. You may also be able to feel something as little as air displacement if you wiggle your finger back and forth."

She tried it, though mainly felt the movement of her finger.

"It's kind of hard when there's already wind," he said, running a hand through his hair after a breeze left it disheveled. "These grafts were made to increase perceptual ability. They're not quite long-lasting, but they work."

"What were you saying about perception?"

"So…when you're focused on one thing when there're more things going on than you're aware of, that's called selective attention. Like when you focus on the senses in your finger, you're ignoring other sensations like the wind in your hair or your breathing. There's also failing to see something in plain sight due to focusing on other things, like a driver not noticing a car moving into their lane, which is called inattentional blindness. It could be the endless distractions of an online world and overstimulation in addition to different, nonreciprocal ways of communicating…. I'm not saying it's an excuse, though it can explain why people don't keep in touch sometimes."

Leslie nodded and rubbed her fingers together to clear away clinging sand. Apparently the graft really wasn't long-lasting, as she again felt a general sensation along the majority of her fingers. "Can I go swim?"

"Of course."

Leslie stood up quickly, then stopped herself. "I'm not going to sink and break, am I?"

"Nope. Your body has the same buoyancy as any other person. The waves are calm right now, but I'll be nearby if you have any trouble."

Leslie went to the shoreline, the moist, compact sand mushing under her feet. A gentle, inch-high wave lapped against her toes and the sides of her feet. It was cold. *It's always coldest when you get in.* Bemusement warmed her cheeks, though she didn't smile at the saying her friends always repeated before going in the pool. Soon her feet and ankles were submerged. As she moved forward, the water's surface rose, the cuffs and the rest of her jeans began to weigh her down. Suddenly, she bent her legs and let herself fall under the beginning of a cresting wave. The rest of her clothes were completely soaked by the time she stood up again, her body shivering from the chill. Wading in deeper, she kicked off the ground and let her lower body rise into a horizontal position. She swept her arms in a breaststroke, pulling herself over another wave before it crested. Then, she turned herself over to lie on her back and bob with the waves. Their quiet crashes and gentle rocking lulled her into a relaxed state. It almost felt like her bed, except the bobbing water was far more comfortable to feel beyond the tenseness in her upper body, which eventually faded to nothing. She felt *everything*, the water rippling under her and the wind rippling over her.

On the shore Matthew pulled out his phone, getting a call from Erika. She sounded excited. "Hey, what's happening there?"

"She's swimming," Matthew replied, pacing a few feet closer to the shoreline. He watched her start to do a backstroke parallel with the surf and he slowly followed along, avoiding the waves every time they approached his feet too closely. "Is something wrong?"

"No. There is something unusual happening, though we'll need to run some more tests."

"Unusual, how?" A lone seagull's caw echoed as it circled a rocky outcrop. He stopped walking and turned to look at Leslie, who had turned over and begun freestyle strokes. "Leslie!"

She heard his call just before both her ears submerged. Treading the water, she shouted back. "What? I just got started!"

"Huh?" Matthew said quietly into the phone. "Oh. Keep swimming!"

Thinking nothing more of it, she started her freestyle stroke again. She had missed the gentle resistance of the water before it filtered around and between her fingers. Behind her, the water sloshed as it got kicked up by her legs, light spray tickling her calves through the fabric of her pants. The one thing that felt different was the absence of stinging in her eyes. Because her real ones were already closed, she figured the robotic body's eyes would remain open to keep giving her a visual of what was happening around her artificial form. She realized she had only just noticed now not needing to blink since she started the trial. It would be a pain to always feel like her eyes were dry, even if it was more realistic.

"Leslie!" Matthew called again.

She'd just finished swimming around a hundred yards and was turning back to go the other way.

"Come here!"

Reluctantly, she waded back out of the water. The cool of the wind against her damp skin felt just like she remembered it. "Are we done already?"

"I've got good news, and normal news. Which would you like to hear first?"

"No bad news?" she asked, dubious.

"There is none, though I could think of something if you give me a moment."

She shivered and paced farther away from the shore to rest her feet in the warmer sand. "What's the good news?"

"Dr. Patton and Erika observed your real body moving during this trial."

Her eyes widened. "Is that normal?"

"Partly. We've conducted similar trials with others who are paralyzed, and the participants shifted while using the robot. But it was always parts of their bodies that *hadn't* lost motor control that moved." He paused. "You're currently unable to move your hands and feet?"

"I've tried, but yeah."

"Apparently you've been moving them since you started swimming."

"What!" She could feel the hope swelling up.

"Not completely," Matthew said quickly. "It's more like involuntary twitches. But it does indicate a po-

tential breakthrough in our research, and your recovery. We're going to need you to do this again."

Leslie stayed motionless, not daring to believe. "I'll get to do this again?"

Matthew nodded. "The normal news is that we were going to let you do this again anyway. At least once a week."

She looked out across the beach slowly. "Why didn't you tell me when I first asked?"

"Sorry," he said. "That was strategic manipulation to get you feeling disappointed and see how the emotions influenced you physically. This was a trial, after all."

She didn't know what to say. Thankfully, she didn't have to say anything.

"Erika's shortly going to turn off the headset and you'll no longer be connected here. Are you ready?"

Leslie absorbed all the feelings she could: the soaked clothes clinging to her skin, the wind still mercilessly causing her to shiver, and the warmth of the sand surrounding her feet. She took a deep, calming breath. "All right."

There was a subtle pressure on her forehead and the bright beach began to fade from view. She opened her eyes and blinked rapidly, taking in the dimmer room with Dr. Patton sitting on the stool to her left and Erika leaning over her to her right.

"Matthew told you everything?" Erika said, smiling lightly. She gently took out the contacts and stowed them, along with the headset, in the briefcase.

"I'll really get to do it again?" Leslie didn't dare believe. Not yet.

"Yes. This was possible largely due to your parents," Dr. Patton said. As he did, the door opened and they entered. Behind them, a group of faces she hadn't seen in months also followed.

Leslie sucked in a breath. "What—what are you all doing here?" Her parents beamed at her as Samantha, Ruby, and Jessica approached the bed. She blinked, feeling her eyes get watery at the sight of her friends, as well as the deluge of feelings of a successful trial hitting her at once.

"I'm so sorry I didn't come sooner," Sam stammered.

"Your parents contacted us, saying we should get together to surprise you and celebrate."

"Celebrate?" Leslie questioned, her shoulders shivering but not from the cold. "You guys know I'm getting movement back?"

"Movement?" Her parents looked at me, and then to the doctor, surprised. "She'll recover her legs?"

"It's nothing conclusive," Dr. Patton interjected, rising from the stool.

"You're going to recover!?" Her three friends gripped the side of her bed and shook it excitedly. "They only said you'd be able to feel things through a robot or something! But to feel more in your real body—that's amazing!"

Feeling her lips tremble, she broke into a smile. "It's been so long…!"

"I can't imagine!" Ruby said. "Being unable to swim would be the worst."

"No. I mean…since I've experienced this. You. Friends. It's been so lonely." Finally tears escaped and slowly fell down her face.

Her three friends froze. Her parents shifted their feet, looking down. "Oh, Leslie…" her father said.

Dr. Patton stepped over to the counter and pulled a tissue from a Kleenex box. He handed it to Sam who lightly brushed away the tears.

"I might *not* recover," Leslie said when Sam pulled her hand away.

"That's also not decided," Dr. Patton added, gently.

"But even if I don't—"

"You will!" Ruby interrupted.

"—and even if I can no longer use the robot—"

"You'll always have access to it," Erika interrupted.

"—can you promise to visit me again?"

Her friends' faces showed a wide array of emotions, and they gripped the bed harder. They each sniffled. "Yes!" Sam cried. "We should have come before—we just didn't know what to say. It felt insensitive, that our lives could just continue on, while yours had effectively…frozen."

Leslie shut her eyes, waiting until she was in control of herself again, feeling her heart begin to thaw. The image of the beach was still in the back of her mind. Opening her eyes, she smiled. "I'm ready to feel again."

Copyright © 2022 by Torion Oey.

YANG FENG PRESENTS: A *GALAXY'S EDGE* TRANSLATION EXCHANGE

Tai Yi is a Chinese science-fiction writer born in the 1980s. He mostly writes works set in Japan. In 2016, he published his first science-fiction story, "Sound," in Science Fiction World. In 2017, he won the 28th China Science Fiction Galaxy Award for Best Newcomer. In 2020, he won the 31st Galaxy Award for Best Short Story for "Hibana." His stories can often be seen in magazines such as Galaxy's Edge and Science Fiction World.

The recommended story, "The Moon is Beautiful," was originally published in the third edition of the Chinese version of Galaxy's Edge. In the beautiful summer season of the Bon festival in Japan, Haruichi experiences a lingering sense of regret upon returning to his former home. Please enjoy.

◆ ◆ ◆

THE MOON IS BEAUTIFUL

by Tai Yi, translated by Roy Gilham

ONE

Haruichi was dreaming of the summer holidays he spent at his grandfather's house as a young child.

In the living room spread with tatami mats, he sat cross-legged beside sister Shoko, his neighbor and friend. Shoko, who was a year older than him, wore her hair in a ponytail and sat with her bare legs sticking out from her white dress, stretched out under the low wooden table. Thin smoke trails curled up from the mosquito coil on the veranda, and the wind chimes sounded crisp and sweet in the summer breeze.

Dark clay teacups, set on the low table in front of them, exuded an aroma of barley tea. Also on the table was a clay plate filled with Haruichi and Shoko's favorite sweet cakes. Haruichi's grandmother, Miki Ishihara, often made these cakes, which the whole family loved. Haruichi and Shoko, however, were too obsessed with the game Haruichi's grandfather had made for them to pay much attention to the food.

Before he retired, Grandpa Koichiro had been a professional game designer. Skilled in both graphics and programming, he was a mainstay of the game development team at his company and often worked on traditional Japanese games. After his retirement, he used VI (virtual interface) technology to create his own games and programs, and Haruichi and Shoko were his regular game testers.

This was the era when VI devices first became popular. Worn on the pupil, in the same fashion as contact lenses, the devices enabled people to experience augmented reality. Simply by moving their hand, they could activate a virtual keyboard in their field of view and use various software based on global positioning technology.

Though Haruichi and Shoko were sitting in the living room, it seemed like they were in an aquarium. The sound of the sea came through the shared sound register associated with the VI. Corals were layered over the tatami mats. Now and again, clownfish emerged from between the soft corals and swam around Shoko's hands. Slowly, she raised one hand, and the clownfish followed. In the depths, ugly anglerfish used natural lures, like hanging lanterns protruding above their mouths, to catch their prey. Hidden in the fine sand of the seabed, a flounder waited for the anglerfish to pass by before stirring from its hiding place, sending up a cloud of sand. A golden arowana swam lazily around the house's outer corridor as a school of sardines emerged from the ceiling, changing course with the current.

Suddenly, the light in the room dimmed, and Haruichi and Shoko ran excitedly toward the veranda, their footsteps sounding noisily on the wooden floor. Looking up, they saw an enormous humpback whale swimming through the blue sky, blocking out the sun.

"Grandpa Koichiro," Shoko cried in astonishment, "how did you do that?"

"It's simple, really," said Grandpa Koichiro, smiling proudly. "I just reduced the light transmittance of the virtual interface."

"These models are so realistic!" exclaimed Haruichi. "Can I touch them?"

He reached out to touch a passing dolphin, but his hand passed right through the dolphin's body. It was still impossible to simulate the sense of touch using VI. Though Haruichi knew this already, he couldn't help but try.

"Oh."

With a lingering sense of disappointment, Haruichi awoke from his dream. He walked out onto the balcony of his room wearing a short-sleeved shirt and blue jeans, and stood in the sunshine of the midsummer season. While waiting for his parents to get up, he stretched out his body.

He heard a click, and the second-floor window of the neighboring Tachikawa's house opened. But as soon as he looked back, the window immediately closed again. *Sister Shoko*, he thought sadly. She was still hiding from him.

The year before, Haruichi's father had been assigned to the company headquarters in Tokyo, an offer that was too good to refuse. Haruichi had wanted to remain in his hometown with his grandparents—after all, his classmates were here, and it never felt good to be the new kid at school. But his grandfather was getting old, and his grandmother had already passed away many years ago. His parents had been worried about leaving him behind and insisted that he join them in Tokyo. Things had happened so fast. Haruichi had wanted to say goodbye to Shoko, who had been his closest friend since childhood. But Shoko was upset when she learned that he was leaving and did not appear on the day of his departure. Instead, Haruichi received a farewell message through his VI that read simply, "Don't contact me again."

Before they left, Haruichi complained to his grandpa, but the old man did not object to Haruichi's father leaving his hometown. "Although I'm getting older," he said, "I don't need anyone to take care of me, at least for the time being."

This much was true. The VI system was very convenient. If there was any kind of emergency, Grandpa Koichiro could contact the nearby hospital. And if he felt he could no longer handle the housework by himself, he could place an order with the housekeeping service company. The transfer was an important opportunity for Haruichi's father, and Grandpa Koichiro was glad to hear of it.

As for Haruichi's situation, although Grandpa Koichiro understood that Shoko held a special place in his heart, there was nothing that could be done.

In Tokyo, Haruichi's father was very busy with his work. They had only returned now, during the *Bon* festival, to pay their respects at Grandma Ishihara's grave.

Shoko, who Haruichi had not seen for a long time, followed her family wearing a pale blue dress. She said nothing when she saw Haruichi. She hurried past him, and Haruichi had to quicken his pace to catch up with her.

"Sister Shoko," he said, trying to break the frosty atmosphere between the two of them. "It's been a long time."

Shoko didn't answer. Haruichi said nothing more, but he watched Shoko as he followed behind her. He didn't understand why she was sulking. After finally returning to his hometown, he hadn't expected her to be so indifferent.

Suddenly, Shoko stopped dead in front of him, staring intently at a bus stop on the side of the road. Haruichi followed her gaze but saw nothing except the empty bus stop. Only then did he remember that he had raised the filtering function of his VI to a high level.

When walking the streets of Tokyo, a whole lot of information would appear before your eyes as a result of wearing VI. Especially in the central business district, a flood of information constantly rushed into your face, completely overwhelming your vision. For this reason, many people turned up the filtering function in their VI. Users filtered content according to tags embedded in the information itself, such as "ad," "video," or "message board." Government regulations required advertisers to label their posts as advertisements which, with the exception of the ads for his favorite games or bicycle brands, Haruichi mostly blocked. But advertising wasn't the only annoying kind of information. Tokyo's streets were filled with cryptic graffiti—and some horrible fakes. Only once he had filtered out everything posted by anyone except his relatives, friends, and the classmates listed in his VI contacts, was Haruichi able to walk the streets of Tokyo without being overwhelmed by information.

"Sister Shoko," asked Haruichi, about to turn off the tag filtering function. "What are you looking at?"

"It's a spirit, a *yokai*," said Shoko.

Haruichi was taken aback, and his hand froze in mid-air. *Perhaps the filtering function is better left as it is*, he thought. Shoko never used any kind of filters in VI, and Haruichi could hardly even imagine the bizarre world she saw every day.

Before long, they came to a nearby hill. The entrance to the shrine was through a red *torii*, an old traditional gate set amidst several large trees hung with sacred ropes. Climbing the stone steps, the sight of the midsummer sunlight shimmering on the lush trees made Haruichi feel full of life, as though something magical was about to happen.

After borrowing wooden buckets and ladles from the shrine's caretaker, the two families each went to pay their respects to their ancestors at their respective graves.

When they came to his grandmother's grave, Haruichi and his parents gathered up the fallen leaves and twigs into a garbage bag, ladled water from the bucket over the tombstone to wash it clean, then wiped it dry with a cloth. Haruichi placed two bouquets of lilies on the grave, along with his grandmother's favorite rice cakes and a jar of sake. He set down the miniature cucumber horse (*shoryouma*, spirit horse) and the cow made from eggplant (*shoryoushi*, spirit cow), and finally a watermelon. His father lit a joss stick and fanned the smoke with his hand, and the family clasped their hands together to offer a prayer before the grave.

Grandma Ishihara had passed away more than five years before, due to a sudden myocardial infarction.

With his eyes closed, Haruichi recalled the scene of his grandparents' home when he was a child. Grandpa was romantic by nature, and he loved Grandma very much. Although he had mild diabetes, Grandpa Koichiro was constantly pestering Grandma Ishihara for sweets. In front of her, he would act like a spoiled child, but she couldn't help but make him some of his favorite cakes stuffed with pumpkin. Every time she watched him eat, she would smile again.

Regardless of how he acted in front of Grandma, Grandpa Koichiro was actually very determined and persevering. Even after his retirement, he insisted on going jogging every morning. In the past, his colleagues would often come to the house to talk things over. Although Haruichi was very young at the time, he remembered these things clearly.

"Ishikara-san is very serious in his work and familiar with emerging programming software," said an old associate of his grandfather's, who was a little overweight. "He knows how to create characters that people love."

"That's true," said the old man sitting opposite, giving a slight bow, "but he also takes care of his health. He often goes jogging in the park and exercises on the office roof. He even changes into his running shoes at the end of a shift, then gets off the train a few stops early and runs home on foot."

"Right, right. Ishikara-san knows how to look after himself," everyone chimed in.

"After all," said Grandpa Ishikara with a smile, "our work takes its toll on our bodies, so it's important to take care of our health."

As for Grandpa's technical ability, that was hardly in doubt. He had made a lot of games and software for VI at home, and Haruichi and Shoko had grown up playing these games. Sometimes the house became a giant aquarium; at other times, it was a campsite in the waning autumn. The two of them worked through the games he created for them together.

He had also created a housekeeping system for the home. After putting on VI, visitors could see the housekeeper in the shape of a little fox, following their footsteps. The little fox's name was Kon.[1] As soon as Shoko set eyes on the lifelike little fox, she began pestering Haruichi's grandfather to create a virtual housekeeper for her own family. Grandpa created a seven-year-old boy in a red kimono, and everyone called him Zashiki-Boy.[2]

Haruichi thought back to those summer evenings when the garden at his grandparents' house was filled with the scent of jasmine, Grandma Ishihara's favorite flower. Haruichi and Shoko would sit with them on the veranda under the moonlight, eating watermelon cooled in the freezing spring water. But the good times didn't last long. After Grandma died, Grandpa Koichiro walked to her grave, leaning on Haruichi's father for support, with tears in his eyes. He clasped his hands together as he said goodbye to his life's companion. Ever since that day, Haruichi's grandfather had seemed in a daze, sitting at his desk for hours upon end, devoting himself to developing new games.

After the prayers, the family gathered up the food and garbage, leaving only the joss sticks in front of the grave. As they prepared to descend, the two families met up again. After completing the ceremonies, everyone's mood was a little more relaxed. This time, Haruichi and Shoko walked at the front of the procession.

"Did you speak to your brother?" asked Haruichi.

"Yeah," said Shoko, nodding.

They walked side by side. Haruichi sensed that Shoko was not so distant as before. After walking for a while, she pointed to his back.

"Kon has been jumping around excitedly behind your back. How come you're ignoring him?"

"Is Kon following us?" Haruichi turned and looked around but saw no sign of the little fox.

"Can't you see it?" asked Shoko.

"Um…" The sweat stood out in beads on Haruichi's forehead. He didn't want to admit to Shoko that he'd switched on the filters on his VI.

TWO

Haruichi and his parents had arrived at his grandfather's house the afternoon before the visit to the grave. Grandpa's gout had returned and his knees and ankles were aching, so the next day he could only mourn his wife from home instead of going to the cemetery with everyone else. As Grandpa Koichiro lay in bed, Haruichi's father talked to him briefly about his work. Meanwhile, Haruichi's mother was in the kitchen, cooking some of her specialties.

Before leaving for the cemetery, Grandpa Koichiro beckoned Haruichi back. "Is Shoko still ignoring you?" he asked.

"Yeah," said Haruichi, with a sigh.

"It's so good to be young," said Grandpa, smiling.

---

1 The Chinese character 痕, means scar, trace, or mark. In Japanese, it is also used to represent the cry of a fox, "kon-kon."

2 *Zashiki-warashi* (parlor-child) or *Zashiki-bokko* are a form of *yokai* that take the shape of small children. They are said to live in strange rooms and perform pranks. It is considered good fortune to see one in Japan.

"I don't get what's so good about it," Haruichi muttered.

"I think back then, Midori was also pretty bad-tempered. I must have suffered a lot." Remembering the past, Grandpa smiled and shook his head. Then, looking Haruichi straight in the eye, he said, "Seize the opportunity tomorrow."

At the time, Haruichi had thought his grandpa was only trying to give him some encouragement. But now, on the way back from the graveyard, he felt a little nervous because of what Shoko had said. Although she liked to play harmless pranks on Haruichi, she would always smile her mischievous smile. However, their relationship was very delicate at the moment, and Haruichi didn't think she was teasing him this time.

He activated his VI control screen and turned off all the filtering functions. His field of vision was immediately flooded with information, from advertisements and bizarre images to traces of other people's doodles and graffiti.

Kon hopped around, turning circles around Haruichi. Now that he could see the fox, it stood before him and gave a formal little bow.

"Did you screen Kon out by accident?" asked Shoko.

"I just checked the filter labels. Nothing was shielding Kon. Could it be a bug in the system?" Haruichi also had a lot of questions.

Kon walked ahead of them, turned around, and raised a paw to beckon them forward. The fox's pose reminded Haruichi of the lucky cat figurines found on the counters of the noodle restaurants. The two of them followed quickly.

After walking for a while, the little fox paused at the bus stop.

"This is where I saw the yokai before!" said Shoko, pointing to a figure standing in front of the shop. Haruichi approached slowly, then carefully observed the yokai's appearance. She wore a gorgeous red kimono and had a charming face, with fox-like ears on her head and nine furry tails peeking out behind her.

Kon jumped into her arms and nestled there. As she stroked its head, the little fox closed its eyes contentedly.

"Little brother, you're finally willing to look at me." The yokai's smile was seductive and soul-stirring. Haruichi wasn't sure, but he suspected she might be modeled on the legendary fox spirit, Tamamo-no-Mae.

"Well…" Haruichi wasn't sure how he should answer.

He used the VI's virtual buttons to interact with the character in front of him, then checked the creation content. Sure enough, it was Tamamo-no-Mae.

"Who created her?" asked Shoko curiously.

"My grandpa." After confirming the information, Haruichi closed down the production interface. "And that little fox following us isn't Kon, it's Kon 2.0."

"If your grandfather made them, you should be able to see them directly. After all, your VI doesn't filter out things from your relatives." Shoko was a little puzzled.

"That's true. But the creator is listed as Green. It's one of Grandpa's old pseudonyms. I didn't think he was still using it, so I didn't add it to the whitelist."

Haruichi searched the VI for any hidden information on Tamamo-no-Mae and Kon 2.0, but found nothing. It looked like he would have to interact with them if he wanted to learn anything more.

Haruichi looked at Tamamo-no-Mae, then asked her, "Why did Grandpa tell you to come here?"

"This is a game," said Tamamo-no-Mae. "Your grandfather wants you to test it together. It might take a whole day to play through the game." The fox spirit smiled at him. "Haruichi is too dumb to clear the game by himself, so he'll need Shoko's help."

So, it was like that.

"What game is it?" Haruichi asked the fox spirit.

"This is the first game your grandfather made under the pseudonym Green." Tamamo-no-Mae raised her right hand, blue flames dancing at her fingertips.

Using the VI interface, Haruichi selected the blue flames and downloaded the game into his VI.

"Can you tell us anything else?"

"This is the only message I carry," said Tamamo-no-Mae, smiling regretfully.

"Okay."

Tamamo-no-Mae was similar to a non-player character, and Haruichi guessed she wouldn't lie. The two of them were on their own. He watched as Tamamo-no-Mae and Kon 2.0 gradually retreated from view before disappearing into a rock.

"Grandpa Koichiro is really cunning," Shoko murmured.

"Sister Shoko, you don't have to help if you don't want to. I—"

Shoko cut him off. "I'll help you. As Grandpa Koichiro said, Haruichi is really too dumb."

She looked confident and eager to get started.

"Why do I feel like I'm getting the cold shoulder?" Haruichi shook his head helplessly.

By now, it was approaching noon. The two of them went to a nearby family restaurant for a quick meal. After eating, Haruichi ordered a soda, and Shoko ordered a strawberry sundae. In the restaurant, they began to study the game that Tamamo-no-Mae had given them.

First, Haruichi examined the game information. His grandpa had created the game before VI was invented and had only recently transplanted it into the virtual interface. The game was a branching decision-based game about a teenager obsessed with programming who falls in love with a girl in his class after entering high school. The game itself was very simple, and the sound and graphics were nowhere near the level of his more recent work. But even in this early game, his grandfather's talents were already evident. Save for a little help from his friends in recording the music, he had created the story and graphics entirely by himself.

There wasn't a whole lot to the game, and they played through it very quickly. At the end, the background changed to a library scene, and the boy walked up to the girl with her hair in pigtails. Outside the window it was dusk, and the cherry blossom flower was falling from a giant cherry tree. Although the pictures and music were somewhat childish, they blended together perfectly, creating a warm feeling.

When the boy approached the girl, two options appeared:

1. Confess your love to her.
2. Pass her by.

"Shall we try B first?" asked Haruichi, glancing at Shoko. He wondered if he was just being shy.

"Sure." Shoko saved their progress, then nodded.

The boy passed by the girl. He didn't cry, but his heart was filled with emptiness. The surrounding scenery gradually dimmed, and the world returned to its normal state. When the words "Bad End" were displayed on the final screen, the two of them couldn't help but sigh.

Haruichi reloaded the saved game, and this time they selected the first option. The boy walked up to the girl and whispered to her, "Will you go with me?" The girl smiled at him, her lips opened slightly, and she whispered something, but a sudden wind stirred the curtains and the boy couldn't hear her voice. The game came to an abrupt end, leaving Haruichi feeling that something was left unfinished.

"Is this the end? I thought it was supposed to take all day."

"It's strange," Shoko answered, a little puzzled. "The game seems so simple."

"But who declares their love to a girl in a library?" said Haruichi, mocking the game's plot.

"Huh? Didn't Haruichi know?" Shoko tilted her head, tapping her lips with her fingers.

"Know what?"

"The library was where Grandpa Koichiro first confessed his love to your grandma. Grandma Ishihara told me once that he asked her to play this game, then confessed his love to her." Remembering this romantic anecdote from so long ago, Shoko couldn't help but smile.

The game's final cutscene was brief, mainly showing information about the creator and developers. But in the lower right corner of the final screen were displayed the words "to be continued."

Haruichi turned to Shoko. "It seems like the game's not over yet," he said.

"Right, but how does it continue?"

"I guess we should go to the library. The big cherry tree in the game is in the atrium of the city library."

"That's it!" Shoko suddenly realized what he meant.

They left the restaurant and walked toward the municipal library. To ensure they didn't miss anything, Haruichi switched off the filtering system on his VI. However, that meant that a lot of information which was usually invisible flooded his vision. There were advertisements all over the place, along with the subtle messages that people leave behind for one another. A bench was marked "Lost and Found," yet appeared conspicuously empty. Under a tree, someone had scrawled "Ant's Nest" in what looked like a child's hand. On the seesaw in the park at the intersection was written, "Taro is the best in the world," a reference neither of them understood. And at the bottom of the slide, something was written in small, almost illegible letters—and the letters were glowing.

Tortured by curiosity, Haruichi had to find out what it said. As he moved closer, he saw that it was a love umbrella.[3] Yet, though the message was a public declaration, the writer had written the names of the lovers using the Latin initials. Haruichi wasn't sure whether to laugh or weep.

"Obviously, they meant to communicate their feelings to others but didn't quite dare go all the way." Haruichi shook his head.

"It takes a lot of courage to tell someone how you feel," Shoko retorted, sounding a little angry.

Much to Haruichi's surprise, the library's interior was also filled with a lot of useless information. "All this weird stuff gets in the way of the useful books," Haruichi complained to the young female librarian.

Using VI, registering at the library was very convenient. You only had to drag your personal information into a designated space on the library's private network, and the loan card could be processed immediately.

"I know," said the librarian. "In the beginning, we applied for high-level clearance from the VI's chief technical officer so we could clean up all this junk. But it's too much work, and since most people have their filtering systems set up, we don't deal with it anymore." Frustration was written into her face.

"Don't tell me you also block most of it out?" Haruichi asked her.

"Well, if you don't, it's impossible to see anything once you enter the library."

Haruichi looked back at Shoko with a wry smile. Shoko was used to living with the plethora of unfiltered information, and was wandering around with interest. Haruichi sighed and hurried to catch up with her, careful to avoid a bookshelf obscured by the dense flood of information. With all this data around them, how would they find the messages left for them by Grandpa Koichiro?

---

[3]Just as American sweethearts might carve their names into a heart on the trunk of a tree, Japanese sweethearts often write their names under drawings of small umbrellas.

"That's it!" Haruichi suddenly thought of something and tapped Shoko on the shoulder.

"You have an idea?" Shoko asked in a low voice.

"Yeah," replied Haruichi, equally quietly. "We set the tag filtering permissions to maximum, then list the creator name Green as an exception."

"In other words, we won't see anything unless it's labeled as Green, right?"

"Exactly," said Haruichi.

THREE

Five years ago, Shoko's younger brother Tada-kun had died. He was just seven years old. It was the summer holidays, and Tada-kun met secretly with his classmates to play in a nearby river. Swimming without adult supervision, he had accidentally drowned.

Shoko hid away after that and refused even to attend her brother's funeral. No matter how her parents tried to persuade her, she would not leave her room. She had doted on her little brother, and they had been very close. To lose someone so close at such a young age was a shock from which she never fully recovered.

One night, Haruichi climbed from his balcony onto Shoko's and tiptoed into her room. "Shoko," he pleaded with her then, "you have to say goodbye to Tada-kun; otherwise he won't find rest in the other world."

"He can't hear anything. What's the use in saying goodbye? What do all these pointless rituals mean to Tada-kun?" Shoko was hostile toward her uninvited guest.

"I don't know, Sister Shoko. Maybe you're right, and Tada-kun can't hear us. Maybe it doesn't matter to him. But I think it means something for your parents, and I'm sure it's important for you."

"If you don't say goodbye to Tada-kun now," Haruichi continued after a pause, "you'll feel even worse in the future. I know how much you loved him. You can't let him go like this."

With that, he climbed back to his own balcony. He walked downstairs, then entered Shoko's house from the front entrance. In the hall downstairs, Buddhist monks were quietly performing the rites for Tada-kun, who lay silently in his coffin. It all seemed so small: the coffin, the shroud, and little Tada-kun's face.

After a while, Shoko came downstairs, still wearing her pajamas. Those present watched as she wept in front of her brother.

Looking at Shoko then, Haruichi couldn't help from crying.

✿

Haruichi began his search from the lending room on the library's top floor, working his way down, while Shoko worked her way up from the first floor. Before long, she discovered the message left by Grandpa Koichiro. Leaning against the windowsill in one corner of the third-floor room was a yokai.

Outside the window stood the large cherry tree, but it was already August, and there were no blossoms on the branches. The yokai puffed leisurely on an opium pipe, the smoke mingling with her white satin dress, as though the dress itself was formed from the haze of smoke. Her left leg rested on the windowsill, and her right leg hung down, her slender ankle peeking out through the skirt and the smoke.

It certainly looked like Grandpa Koichiro's style.

"A smoke and darkness spirit, an *enenra*, in the library. Maybe Grandpa's not so pure as he looks," Haruichi joked, keeping his voice to a whisper. After all, there was a yokai attached to all this smoke, and the library staff would surely feel uncomfortable should it be discovered. He stepped forward and scanned for information relating to the yokai's creator. Indeed, it was Green.

"Do you have a message for us?" asked Haruichi.

The yokai did not speak but pointed out a book with the handle of her long pipe. Haruichi looked at the name on the spine: *Love Letter*. It was a novel by Shunji Iwai, which Haruichi hadn't read. He turned the pages slowly, searching for information about his grandfather.

"I didn't expect it would be this book," said Shoko, leaning forward.

"You've read it?"

"Of course. It's a beautiful story, and the movie is also good. Especially the ending—no matter how many times I read it, I always feel warm."

Haruichi turned to the end of the book and read aloud:

The students appeared shy and hesitant, but Haruka spoke up. "We found something," she said, lifting the book for me to see. It was Marcel Proust's In Search of Lost Time*—the book he had left behind. The students were yelling at me, "Look inside! The library card is inside!" I did as they said and found the library card inside, with Fujii's signature on it. But the students were still yelling, "On the back! The back!"*

Without understanding, I turned the card over. I didn't know what to say. On the back of the card was a portrait of me from my high school days. Returning to my senses, I turned back to my students. They were enjoying my confusion. Pretending to be calm, I tried to slip the card into my pocket. Unfortunately, my favorite sleeveless dress doesn't happen to have any pockets.

Indeed, it was a heart-warming ending.

"Oh, right!" exclaimed Shoko, suddenly remembering something. "Haruichi, look at the lending card inside the cover."

Haruichi turned to the inside cover, removed the library card, and studied it. Due to the filtering effect on his VI, Haruichi saw a love umbrella linked to the card, with Green on one side, and Midori green on the other. Midori was his grandmother's first name.

Was this what Grandpa wanted them to find? Haruichi asked himself. Just then, the Enenra spoke to him again.

"It's not over yet."

Haruichi walked up to the spirit, awaiting her new clue. This time, the Enenra forwarded Haruichi a digital map. After a little analysis, he recognized it as a map of the park where Grandpa Koichiro used to go jogging in the mornings, come rain or shine. As soon as he raised his head, the Enenra faded into smoke, dissipating before his eyes.

✿

It was around three o'clock in the afternoon when Haruichi and Shoko arrived at the park. The trees were lush and green and the summer breeze stirred the branches, setting the leaves rustling.

The two of them searched separately, and before long, Haruichi spotted a dog-like Japanese demon, *tengu*, standing on a thick branch.

"Hey!" Standing under the tree, Haruichi called up to the tengu standing above him, but the demon completely ignored him. He wasn't sure what to do.

"It looks like we'll just have to climb up," said Shoko, joining him under the tree.

"Well…" Haruichi circled the tree, studying its thick trunk, which was a half-meter around. "I'm not sure I want to climb this tree in public."

"I'll do it," said Shoko, stretching her arms. She looked completely at ease.

"Don't. I mean…I'll do it." Haruichi said awkwardly. He remembered how he used to climb trees with Shoko back when they were still children. He would always tear his clothes or scratch his hands, and would be reprimanded when he got home. But it was always worth it, because the view from the trees was always so different from the view from the ground. As he got older, these memories had gradually faded from his mind.

Touch the rough trunk with your palms. Wrap your arms around it. Try to keep your shoes on the bumps in the bark. Haruichi climbed up little by little, the unique pain slowly reviving his memory. Fortunately, no one noticed him, least of all the park rangers.

Feeling a little guilty, Haruichi tried to climb faster. But the bark caught on his clothes, and he didn't dare strive too hard. It was nearly ten minutes before he reached the tengu, though it felt like it took him at least half an hour.

"I don't know why Grandpa had to put you all the way up here," he said to the tengu, treading carefully along the branch.

The red-faced tengu turned his long nose toward Haruichi. Somewhat haughtily, it released an audio file. When Haruichi clicked on the file through his VI, it was downloaded automatically. The creator of the audio file was Green, but the recording device was listed as a decades-old mobile phone. It appeared the file had been recorded a long time ago.

Haruichi shared the file with Shoko, standing under the tree. After entering the shared sound register, they listened to it together:

Two weeks ago, I broke up with Midori…

The man's voice, young as he was, sounded like Grandpa Koichiro.

Midori and I had been dating for six months. Before I knew what was happening, the love that was so sweet initially had become a burden to me. I want to become a game designer. I've been studying programming and graphics and need a lot of exposure to new games made by different development teams. The days were always too short, so I was always playing games late into the night, sometimes the whole night through.

In her eyes, I was overextending myself with this irregular schedule, but it was annoying having her try to take care of me every day. After all, there was nothing I could do about it.

We argued about this all the time until, two weeks ago, I finally broke up with her. The night of our breakup, I felt free at last. I ordered myself a midnight snack, ready to play through a game I had bought earlier. But, in the dead of night, when I looked at the imagery in the game, all I could think about was Midori. It dawned on me that even if I could beat the game, I would never be able to share my joy with her again.

At this thought, I couldn't restrain my tears. I lost the mood for gaming and lay on the bed, tossing and turning. When I woke up the following day, I was still deep in chaos. Looking at the text messages we exchanged before, saying good morning, I wanted to send something to Midori, but I just couldn't do it.

For the next two weeks, I spent every day in confusion, as though my soul had slipped into a body that had nothing to do with myself, living out a life that had nothing to do with me. I thought I'd get used to it, to being without her, but it didn't get any easier.

I realize now how important Midori is to me. Today, I came to the park, where we often came together. After recording this, I'm going to call her. I need to hear her voice again. I want to tell her how much I miss her.

I just hope she can forgive me.

Here, the recording stopped abruptly.

The tengu turned to Haruichi. "When the moon comes out," it said, "come here to dance the Bon dance." With that, the tengu spread its great wings and soared toward the sun.

FOUR

One day, four years earlier, Haruichi and Shoko were walking home from school together. The setting sun was sinking slowly in the west, elongating their slanted shadows. The traffic lights at the crossroads turned to green, to the melody of the "traffic light song:"

> Pass through, pass through
> Where does this path lead?
> It leads to the Tenjin shrine.
> Please allow me to pass through.
> First, you must tell me what for.
> The child is now seven years old,
> We've come to make our offering.
> Going is easy, but returning is scary
> If you think you are ready,
> Pass through, pass through.

Shoko had begun to hum along to the song's melody. But recalling the words, the song gave her a chill.

"Haruichi," she said then, "do you think the Zashiki-Boy really exists?"

"I don't know," said Haruichi. "Does Sister Shoko believe in him?"

"I don't know," she replied. "I just hope it's possible, so maybe I can see Tada-kun again."

By that time, VI technology had spread. Based on his own training, Haruichi's grandfather had quickly created little Kon. With VI on, you could see the cute little fox jumping around. Before he retired, Grandpa Koichiro had liked to base the characters in his games on legendary Japanese yokai. After becoming more skillful in using VI technology to develop games, he learned how to achieve a more realistic effect. Any kind of yokai seemed to be within his grasp, and the boundary between reality and virtuality was slowly disappearing.

"Haru-kun," Shoko had said after a long silence.

"What's the matter?" Haruichi tilted his head.

"I want to ask Grandpa Koichiro to make a housekeeper in the form of a Zashiki-Boy."

Later on, Grandpa Koichiro agreed to Shoko's request. From then on, the seven-year-old boy in a red kimono accompanied her whenever she was at home. In the eyes of Shoko's parents, this was more than a little strange, but they didn't want to hurt Shoko's feelings. At the same time, in Japanese mythology, the Zashiki-Boy is said to guard the home against danger. They decided to let it go.

When he saw how well Shoko recovered from her distress, Haruichi felt that the boundary between life and death had also become blurred due to the existence of VI.

✿

As the Bon festival progressed, the festive atmosphere grew stronger and stronger. Haruichi and Shoko arranged to meet at the park gate that evening. When he arrived, Haruichi was still in his day clothes. The children, dressed in colorful summer kimonos, *yukatas*, and wooden clogs, romped around the makeshift stalls. Bright lights were strung up around the park as more and more people arrived to join the celebrations.

Haruichi remembered attending these summer festivals with Shoko when they were children. Back then, they had both worn yukatas, and Shoko had always pestered Haruichi to buy her candy apples to eat. Haruichi never refused because he thought it was fun to see her tongue dyed red.

"I'm here!" Shoko ran up to Haruichi, her wooden clogs tapping out her footsteps.

Shoko was wearing a pale green yukata decorated with a pattern of white long-tailed butterflies. She carried a small handbag with little blue fishes painted on it, and she looked very beautiful. The wooden clogs on her bare feet left her slender ankles and tiny toes exposed. Almost in a trance, Haruichi felt like he had fallen back into the past.

"Do you like my yukata?" Shoko smiled a lovely, sly smile. The Sister Shoko he knew so well was back again.

"It…it suits you," he said. Shoko's beauty made him feel a little nervous.

"Then treat me to a candy apple!" Laughing, Shoko took Haruichi's hand and led him into the park.

The stalls selling octopus balls and fried noodles were overcrowded, and children shouted in delight in front of the shooting galleries and goldfish fishing stalls. Not wanting to be swept away by the crowd, Haruichi held tightly to Shoko's hand, just as he used to when they were children.

After searching for a while, they found an older man selling candy apples beside a stall selling masks.

"Thanks for your business," said the stall owner with a smile, handing Shoko a bright red candy apple. Shoko licked the icing lightly with her tongue, just as she always did as a child. They wandered through the celebrations together, looking for clues left by Grandpa Koichiro. However, they couldn't see anything related to Green anywhere.

After a while, they walked out to an open space in the middle of the park. The space was brightly lit, and musicians stood on a two-story wooden platform, playing the *taiko* drums. Men, women, and children formed a circle and danced to the rhythm of the drums. The dance involved no jumping or other intense movements, only a subtle changing of gestures and postures. It was suitable for all ages.

"The tengu said we should dance the Bon dance together," said Haruichi, remembering the clue.

"Okay." Shoko nodded.

They joined the group dancing the Bon dance. The older women danced at the head of the procession while the children followed with clumsy movements, which made everyone laugh. Everyone had a smile on their face, and the warm atmosphere complemented the summer evening perfectly.

Everything was just like before. Haruichi followed behind Shoko, unable to take his eyes off her. Her long hair swayed as she danced, and her yukata showed off her slender, attractive figure. But amidst people's laughter, Haruichi felt a deep sense of melancholy. When the Bon festival was over, he would have to return to Tokyo with his parents. Maybe in the future, only during the Bon festival would he be able to return to his hometown to see his grandpa—and Shoko.

At this moment, the view in Haruichi's VI suddenly darkened, and a huge figure appeared on the ground in front of them. Looking up, Haruichi saw the great tengu with its wings outspread, standing in the bright moonlight, like a god.

"Sister Shoko, look!" *Surely*, he thought, *this is Grandpa's masterpiece.*

Following the tengu's flight, they left the festivities, heading toward the foot of the hill beside the park.

Haruichi was shocked by what appeared there. *The night parade of one hundred demons!*[4]

Countless yokais holding dim lanterns climbed slowly up the stone steps leading to the top of the hill. Haruichi recognized the *Jorōgumo* (spider woman), the *Kappa* (amphibious river boy), the *Hashihime* (the jealous bridge maiden), the *Hone-onna* (the deceptive bone woman), the *Dodomeki* (cursed girls), *Aobōzu* (the blue priest), and the *Yuki Onna* (snow woman), along with the other yokais they had encountered during the day and a whole host of spirits and demons that Haruichi didn't know the names of. They marched quietly, wearing the bright moonlight like an insignia.

The two of them followed the great procession of yokais, walking slowly up the hill. The yokais stopped and whispered with every step, and Haruichi and Shoko followed their beat.

"Grandpa Koichiro's work is still impressive," Shoko exclaimed in a low voice.

"It sure is." Haruichi nodded.

"Don't speak aloud unless you want to be eaten," threatened Aobozu viciously.

Haruichi and Shoko stuck out their tongues, but kept silent.

When the procession reached the top of the hill, the lights went out one by one, as the spirits entered through an invisible door and disappeared. After Aobozu vanished into the air, Haruichi and Shoko stopped. Their eyes were still adjusting to the darkness, and Shoko held on to Haruichi's hand again. The ground at the top of the hill was paved with stone bricks, and the view was superb. Looking down, they could see the colorful celebrations spread out before them and, looking up, a sky full of stars. The beauty took their breath away.

"Haru-kun, look at that!" Shoko pointed to a stone bench, where a jasmine flower lay, its petals gleaming white in the moonlight.

They walked over and examined the creator's ID using their VI. It was Green.

---

4 *Hyakki Yagyō* (The Night Parade of One Hundred Demons) refers to a parade of thousands of supernatural creatures that march through the streets of Japan at night. A terrifying eruption of the supernatural world into our own, it is similar to the original concept of pandemonium in English.

"Bingo! We found it!" Haruichi and Shoko exchanged a high-five.

Activating the message carried by the jasmine flower, they discovered a letter inside:

Dear Midori,

I haven't seen you for a long time, such a long time. I've been thinking lately, what would I say if I saw you again. I have so many words in my heart, words that I've bottled up for a long time. But when I think about it, I forget what I want to say. I feel like I've been talking all my life! No matter what I say, you would only listen quietly, without saying anything. In that case, I might become even sadder, sadder than if I never saw you at all. So, I decided, the next time I see you, I'll just say, "Isn't the Moon beautiful?"[5]

Please don't laugh at me. Because the moonlight yesterday was truly beautiful, and today the Moon is beautiful too. And this is absolutely true.

The day I see you again, the Moon will still be beautiful, just like you.

Thinking of you always,
Green.

After reading this letter, Shoko began to weep. Her tears fell softly onto her yukata, making a small sound.

"Sister Shoko—" Haruichi wanted to comfort her, but he didn't know what to say.

"Stupid Haru-kun!" Shoko shouted suddenly.

"Huh? What did I do?" Haruichi was completely confused.

"You're really too stupid," Shoko said, looking at Haruichi's face in the moonlight. "Tada-kun was stupid, and so are you. Why did you go and leave me all alone?"

"You know I wanted to stay, but—"

"Soon, you'll forget me, won't you? You'll have a new life in Tokyo; you'll have new friends. They'll be new things happening every day. You'll be happy about things I know nothing about, sad about things I've never heard of. Every time I think about it, I feel so lonely…" Shoko trailed off.

"Sister Shoko, I'll never forget you." This time, Haruichi's words had more courage.

"But you can only come back once or twice a year. Maybe this year you'll still remember me, maybe next year too. But sooner or later, you'll forget me."

Even as Shoko spoke, her tone revealed a sense of unwillingness.

"I was afraid I would never see you again if I said goodbye. That's why I ignored you. Besides, I thought if I made you angry, maybe you wouldn't forget me. But when I heard you were coming back, I was overjoyed. When I saw you standing downstairs this morning, I rushed to pick out the right clothes to wear, afraid you would think me unworthy."

Hearing this, Haruichi understood why Shoko had suddenly closed the window. Now, observing the moonlight reflected in her eyes, he felt a pang of regret.

"Shoko sister," he asked suddenly, "do you know the language of the jasmine flower?[6]

"No, what is it?"

"Grandma always loved jasmine, so I looked it up before. The words of the jasmine flower are, 'You are my life.'"

Shoko was taken aback for a moment. She tried to speak but felt like she was going to cry.

"Shoko."

"Haru-kun."

"The Moon is beautiful tonight."

Haruichi kissed Shoko gently on the mouth. She didn't refuse him. He felt her soft lips, breathed in the fragrance of her body. The two of them held their breath and did not separate for a long time.

Shoko took Haruichi's hand, intertwining her fingers with his.

And the jasmine flower bloomed quietly under the Moon.

---

[5] This phrase is a poetic way of saying *I love you*. The Japanese writer, Natsume Soseki (1867–1916), during his teaching years, supposedly overheard a student translating "I love you" using the literal translation *"Ware Kimi o Aisu,"* which sounds very awkward in Japanese. Soseki suggested the subtle, more nuanced translation *"tsuki ga kirei desu ne"* ("The Moon is beautiful, isn't it?"), believing this better suited Japanese sensibility.

---

[6] In Japanese, *hana-kotoba* ("flower words" or "flower language") is a symbolic system, using various flowers to represent different words or ideas.

New York Times *and* USA Today *bestselling author Kristine Kathryn Rusch writes in almost every genre. Generally, she uses her real name (Rusch) for most of her writing. Under that name, she publishes bestselling science fiction and fantasy (including the Fey series, the Retrieval Artist series and the Diving series), award-winning mysteries, acclaimed mainstream fiction, controversial nonfiction, and the occasional romance. Her novels have made bestseller lists around the world and her short fiction has appeared in more than twenty best of the year collections. She has won more than twenty-five awards for her fiction, including the Hugo, Le Prix Imaginales, the* Asimov's *Readers Choice award, and the* Ellery Queen Mystery Magazine *Readers Choice Award.*

KILLER ADVICE (PART TWO)

by Kristine Kathryn Rusch

Richard managed to escape Janet Potsworth's room just as Lysa woke up from what Janet was calling Lysa's faint. It wasn't a faint, because Lysa had enough time to scream before passing out, but she had slipped into unconsciousness very quickly, and he had a few ideas as to why.

But he wanted to think about them first, and that required him to get away from the conversation, and from Janet Potsworth who had grabbed his ass when he bent over to make sure Lysa was comfortable. Potsworth was a menace, and he would be glad to get rid of her—although he wasn't sure when that would happen, especially now that Agatha Kantswinkle was dead.

He hadn't expected her to die, probably because she had always been the first person on the scene of the other deaths aboard the *Presidio*. He'd come to see her as a stout little angel of death, and had found himself wondering more than once if she hadn't done something to cause them.

He still hadn't ruled that out even though she had clearly been murdered herself. Maybe her death was in retaliation for one of the others…?

He sighed. He had no idea. And he was going to need one, because it was clear—at least to him—that a murderer lurked on this station.

He tread lightly as he hurried down the stairs—he didn't want to call any more attention to himself than he already had. He'd shown a bit more expertise in these matters than he wanted to, and someone had noticed.

That someone was the hotelier, Hunsaker. Hunsaker was refined and organized, not the kind of man you'd normally find in this shabby place at the edge of nowhere. Usually the proprietors of places like this were down-on-their luck drunks who couldn't be bothered to wait on a customer even if the customer offered five times the normal room rate. Or the proprietors were well-meaning spouses of someone on staff in maintenance, some handy person with cooking skills and an ability to take the drabbest room and make it just a tad gaudy.

Hunsaker seemed like he had training in hotel management. He certainly took his time checking everyone in, which meant that he looked up their identification as well as debiting their accounts.

He'd noticed Richard and he'd understood what Richard had said when Richard had closed the door on Agatha Kantswinkle's corpse. Often Richard made those snide little comments for his own edification, knowing that no one else would catch his meaning. But Hunsaker had and Hunsaker had looked momentarily put out. Not panicked. Put out. Like any good hotelier.

Richard passed the landing where Lysa had passed out. The door to Agatha Kantswinkle's room was closed and no one stood outside of it. He wondered if anyone was inside, and if Hunsaker had dealt with the corpse yet.

He almost stopped—he had a few suspicions he wanted to confirm—but he didn't. He was afraid that if the old lady's body hadn't been removed, then he would make himself even more of a suspect than he already was.

And he knew he was a suspect. Everyone from the *Presidio* was.

The first death had occurred two days out, when they were in the deepest of deep space—an area the captain had called no man's land because there were no settlements within landing range and no outposts. The trip from the Dyo System through the Commons System was dicey no matter what, but there was a section that was just plain empty. Humans weren't welcome at any of the stops for two full days of the trip. The captain had warned the crew—all three of them—that the first part of the run had nowhere safe to stop until Vaadum Station, and even then he liked to avoid the place because it was so small and so rundown. He preferred the extra day to Commons Space Station, where everyone could get off the ship and relax in style.

Richard braced himself for the extended run on a relatively small ship. He was particularly susceptible to cabin fever because he'd been the only survivor of a murderous rampage on a cruise ship as a boy. He'd been taking a trip with his father, who had died right in front of him. Everyone on that ship had died except Richard and the shooter, who had left in an escape pod before the ship docked at one of the many Starbase Alphas, this one nicknamed the NetherRealm.

And that had just been the beginning, of course. He'd seen a lot of death on small ships. Just never in quite such an odd manner as the three deaths on the *Presidio*.

He had argued that the *Presidio* shouldn't stop until it got to Commons Space Station, which had a security team and was in a sector with a real government, one that would actually look into the killings. There was no government here, even though technically, Vaadum was in the same sector as Commons. Vaadum was too far off the beaten path and too small to have so much as a leader, let alone some kind of official who would report back to the various governments presiding over the Commons System.

The captain had listened too, even though the three murders had terrified him—nothing like that had ever happened to the man, and of course Richard hadn't confessed his own history. Richard was only working the *Presidio* to gain passage across the sector. He was out of money and out of options, something that hadn't happened to him before. So he took one of his identities and used it to get work on the first ship that would take him.

Of course, that ship had to be the *Presidio*.

If the fire hadn't happened, if the ship hadn't had to stop here, Richard would've quit when they reached the Commons Station. He would have cited the killings as a hostile work environment and no one would have had second thoughts about his departure.

He couldn't leave here, now. There was no reason to stay on this station, since ships rarely stopped here, and he did need to keep moving. But he really didn't want to get back on that ship, provided the people in maintenance could actually fix the thing.

He let himself out of the "resort," through the double doors, past the restaurant. The smell of simmering beef—or was it lamb?—made his stomach growl. He wasn't sure when he last had a real meal.

Although he wasn't sure how anyone could serve real food here, either. He doubted supply ships made a huge profit coming in and out of Vaadum. But they probably got paid well to stop.

He hurried down the corridor toward the maintenance area. Clearly, the maintenance area had once been the entire station. The corridor proved it. The corridor was grafted on, little more than a tube with an environmental system, leading to the second part of the station, the resort, which someone had built on at least a century ago—and not from the best materials.

This part of the station felt very fragile. He could almost feel the corridor bounce with each of his footsteps, even though he knew that the thing wasn't built that way. It was his very active imagination, something he had failed to shut off for years now.

Finally, he got out of the corridor and into the maintenance area. It seemed huge, although it wasn't. He knew the sense of vastness was an optical illusion caused by the emptiness. The maintenance area was the oldest part of Vaadum, built two centuries ago to house at least six large ships in various states of disrepair.

Apparently, the station's owners throughout the years hadn't wanted to chop up the area, imagining, probably, that there might come a time when all seven repair bays were being used.

The *Presidio* had the center bay. It looked odd in here, since the ship wasn't built to be inside any kind of bay. Once it had been assembled, it remained outside buildings. But the station's tiny ring made it impossible to repair ships docked to it.

Richard was glad he hadn't been onboard when the captain had had to maneuver the *Presidio* in here.

That must've taken some white-knuckle flying, particularly since the ship was so damaged.

Richard could see the damage from the entry. The fire had burned its way through one entire wing of the ship. The wing had remained intact, but here someone had knocked the exterior off. Through the hole—large enough to hold at least five men—he could see the scorch-marked interior.

He shuddered.

He'd been afraid on ships before, starting with that cruise with his father, when the assassin had stood up, a laser rifle in his hands. He'd aimed it at Richard, and Richard hadn't cringed. He'd been twelve, too young to understand—too sheltered to understand—that the man who aimed the laser rifle at him meant to kill him.

Only the assassin hadn't meant to kill him. He'd left Richard—who was then known as Misha—alive, as a warning to Richard's mother, who had worked as some kind of double agent. Richard had never tried to understand the politics of it. All he ever knew was that his father and so many others had died because one government hired an assassin to warn his mother away from some job.

He wasn't even sure she had felt guilty about it, although she had been angry. And angrier at him when he had gotten his revenge on the assassin. She had wanted the assassin alive—for what reason Richard never knew.

He never tried to understand his mother. But her life, her decisions, had caused him to be here now, decades later, on the run for half a dozen killings, all of them he could say—he would have once said—justified.

Especially that first one.

"Help you?"

One of the maintenance guys came over. He was holding some fancy tools that Richard had never seen before. The maintenance guy was the first person that Richard had seen on this station who looked like he belonged. Whip thin, angular, sharp dark eyes and hair cropped close to the skull. He had a smudge along one cheek.

"I work on the *Presidio*," Richard said. "I was wondering if you'd found a cause for the fire yet."

"Why?" the maintenance guy asked.

Richard studied him for a moment. The maintenance guy seemed solid enough, although Richard wasn't the kind of man who trusted easily. Hell, Richard wasn't the kind of man who trusted at all.

But the maintenance guy had been on this station for a long time, and he would have had no involvement in the fire or the deaths. Not even Agatha Kantswinkle's death.

"I want to know if it was deliberately set," Richard said.

"What's it to you?" the maintenance guy asked.

Richard blinked at him, and nearly snapped, *What's it to me? If this outpost hadn't been nearby, I would have died on that ship. Murdered, if the fire was set. No one would have survived.*

"Three passengers were murdered on that ship," Richard said, "and another just died here."

The maintenance guy started. He hadn't heard about Kantswinkle then.

"So I want to know if that fire was a coincidence or deliberately set. Because I'm not getting back on that ship with someone who sets fires in space."

"But you'd get back on the ship if it had design flaws that made it catch fire?" the maintenance guy asked.

Richard almost smiled. He hadn't thought of that. Which showed that he was someone who didn't know much about ship mechanics, and knew too much about killers.

"Does it have design flaws?" Richard asked.

"All ships have design flaws," the maintenance guy said. "Some are deadlier than others."

"And this ship?" Richard asked, beginning to feel annoyed.

"This ship had some weaknesses that were easy to exploit," the maintenance guy said. "If you asked me to prove that someone deliberately set a fire, I can't. At least, not right now. If you asked me to guess how the fire started, I'd say that someone encouraged it. And I'd say you all were damn lucky to survive."

Richard felt a shiver run down his back. Two lucky survivals. If he were superstitious, he'd think that there was a third in his future.

"Can the ship be repaired?"

"It'll take us a few days," the maintenance guy said. "We have to rebuild a few things, replace even more, and then make sure that it's strong enough to handle space again. When we're done, it should be better than new."

He sounded confident. He actually sounded excited about the prospect of reviving the ship, of making it worthy to fly again. He probably didn't get challenges like this one often.

Or maybe he did. Maybe his job was all about cobbling ships together so that they would survive to the next port.

"Can you make it tamperproof?" Richard asked.

The maintenance guy gave him a sad look. "No ship is tamperproof," he said. "Especially not a ship as old as this one."

Richard must've looked unsettled, because the maintenance guy added, "We'll make it better than it was. If you have a problem out there, it won't be because of the ship."

"Yeah," Richard said, "I'm beginning to figure that out."

✧

Anne Marie Devlin still smelled of beer. Hunsaker wrinkled his nose as he stood inside Kantswinkle's room. Anne Marie had crouched over the body for only a moment, and then she started walking the parameter of the room as if the room were big enough to have a perimeter. She inspected every little thing. The walls, the chair, the bed, the floor.

Everything except Kantswinkle.

Finally, Hunsaker couldn't take it any longer. "What *are* you doing?"

Anne Marie didn't answer him. She stood on her toes, and peered at the small control panel he'd installed for the guests. The control panel didn't give them much control over anything, just the illusion of control.

You let them operate the heating and cooling in their tiny space, and they thought they had charge of the universe.

"Anne Marie," he snapped. "I asked you a question."

"You did, didn't you," she said, her back to him. He had never met such an aggravating woman. She'd be a marvel if she didn't drink.

"What. Are. You. Doing." He enunciated each word so that she would know just how annoyed he was.

"I. Am. Investigating," she said, mimicking his tone exactly.

His cheeks heated. Did he really sound that obnoxious? Not to his own ears, certainly. "Investigating what?"

Anne Marie turned. She looked at the door first, and then at him. He pulled the door again to make sure it was pulled tight.

"Don't do that," she said.

"Why not?" he asked.

She walked to the door and cracked it open just a little. "It's better this way."

"Don't tell me you're getting claustrophobic now," he said. He'd heard about her other ailments. The alcoholism she refused to treat aggravated the depression she refused to acknowledge which was caused by something in her past she refused to talk about.

All in all, the most infuriating woman he had ever met. And one of the most brilliant.

"I have a hunch I'll always be claustrophobic in this room from now on." She peered through the crack in the door as she clearly checked the hallway, then pushed the door open just a bit wider. "We're alone."

He had to check on that himself. Not that he didn't trust her, but he really didn't trust her.

"What's going on?" he said when he was satisfied no one lurked in the hall or the stairwell.

"This poor dear woman," Anne Marie said, thereby proving she had never met Agatha Kantswinkle, "suffocated."

He glanced at Agatha Kantswinkle's neck. No mottled marks, no sign of a struggle. If this woman had suffocated, she had done so without hands around her neck or something pressed against her nose and mouth.

He swallowed hard. "Even if the environmental system had shut down," he said, "she wouldn't have died this quickly."

"Yes, I know," Anne Marie said. "The problem is the environmental system hadn't shut down."

"Then how did she die?" he asked.

"I told you," Anne Marie said. "She suffocated."

"You can tell that from eyeballing her?" he asked.

Anne Marie smiled just a little. "I'll confirm with an autopsy," she said. "But I will confirm."

"No one touched her," he said. "And if it wasn't the environmental system, then what was it?"

"Oh, it was the environmental system," Anne Marie said. "That's why your other guest fainted. The door opened, she saw the body, she screamed, took in what she thought was a lungful of air to continue her scream, and passed out. Lucky girl. Had she been closer to the door inside the room, she would have died too."

Hunsaker was feeling dizzy. He realized he wasn't breathing either. He made himself take a breath, but it felt odd. He hadn't thought of breathing before. Maybe, like Anne Marie, he wouldn't want to be in this room alone with the door closed either.

"What did she breathe?" he asked.

"It wasn't pure carbon dioxide," Anne Marie said, "or her skin would be bright red. More likely a cocktail of gases, something that created the faint bitter odor that was in the room when we arrived."

He had been here earlier. The smell had been stronger. He didn't tell her that.

"How do you know?" he asked.

She held up one of her portable scanners. "I've been taking readings from various areas of the room. I'm getting a mixture of things that should never be in a residential area of a space station. I have the behavior of both women. I have the smell. And then there's the controls themselves."

She swept a hand toward them.

He walked past her and peered at them.

Someone had hit the override. The damn thing was blinking, asking for a manual code to confirm the oxygen mix, which was purer than it should have been.

Not only had someone tampered with the controls, but someone had tampered with them *twice*—once when Agatha Kantswinkle entered the room, and then again after she died.

"I would assume that these systems keep track of who touches them when?" Anne Marie asked.

He had no idea. The last time he'd used an override had been a decade ago. Since then, he'd replaced most of the guest room environmental controls, going to a simpler system—one that gave the guests two options—hotter or colder. Nothing as fancy as this little box, which even allowed the guests—with the override code—to mix their oxygen from thin to thick.

"I don't know," he said, feeling absolutely helpless.

"Well." Anne Marie smiled, clearly liking his discomfort. "I guess you'd better find out."

☼

Pounding, pounding, pounding.

Susan sat up, filled with adrenaline. She'd been dreaming. Not dreaming so much as trapped in a memory.

The slight banging noise, rhythmic, feet against the thin wall.

Her mouth tasted of bile. She got off the bed, rubbed her hand over her face, and went to her door.

Janet Potsworth stood outside. She looked more disheveled than Susan had ever seen her.

"Oh, you're all right then," Janet said with obvious relief.

Susan frowned. "Of course I'm all right. Why wouldn't I be?"

"Because you didn't come for dinner," Janet said.

Susan rolled her eyes. She had asked the chef—if that man could be called a chef—to give her a meal for her room. He had obliged, serving her some kind of stew that wasn't on the menu.

The staff will eat this, he said. *You will like it better.*

She had carried it upstairs herself, and she had liked it. She ate alone for the first time in a week. No angst, no speculation, no fear.

Just a quiet meal in her quiet room. Then she let her exhaustion take her, and she had fallen into a blissful sleep.

Until she dreamed of Remy's death. The man had hanged himself in his room—which had taken some doing. The sheet wrapped around his neck, dangling off some fixture. She hadn't seen it, but she had heard his feet, banging, banging, banging, which she hadn't thought odd until later.

He wasn't bumping against the wall when they found him. She must have been hearing him die.

In fact, no one thought he had done anything except kill himself. He was the first, after all. They'd said some words over him, looked at his traveler's contract, saw that his body didn't have to be returned to anyone, and slipped him into the darkness of space, along with a few of his possessions.

An act they all regretted when the second body turned up. By then, it had become clear that Remy hadn't killed himself and that banging she had heard was his attempt to get her attention. Or to kick his way free. Or to find purchase for his feet. Or to get to his killer.

She hated thinking about it, but she did think about it.

Often.

As did everyone else, it seemed. Including the killer. Who had to be laughing at them all.

She wasn't getting back on that ship. Not now, not ever. And she shouldn't have opened her door to Janet either. Janet was one of those obnoxious women who thought every man was a conquest and every woman was competition.

So there had to be another reason she was here.

"I'm fine," Susan said, and started to close the door.

"You can understand why we were concerned," Janet said, "considering what happened to poor Agatha."

Susan sighed. She was now supposed to ask, *What happened to Agatha?*…as if she cared. Agatha was the most obnoxious woman she had ever met. And that was saying something.

She didn't want to know what happened to Agatha. And if she took the verbal bait, she'd be regaled with some horrifying story of someone's rudeness to the most obnoxious woman she had ever met.

"Yes, I can understand," Susan lied. "Thank you for thinking of me."

And then she pushed the door closed.

"It started in this panel," said the maintenance guy. His name was Larry and he had been on the station for more than a decade. Larry loved his work. *Out here*, he said when Richard asked, *my job is a real challenge. You gotta be creative, you know? And you gotta be right. We've never lost any ship that's left here, and we've never gotten any complaints about our work later on. It's the best job I've ever had.*

Richard somehow found that enthusiasm reassuring. Reassuring enough to join Larry inside the burned-out section of the *Presidio*. It smelled of smoke and melted plastic. His nose itched with a constant urge to sneeze. He breathed shallowly through his mouth because he had a hunch if he started sneezing, he wouldn't stop.

"See right here," Larry said, pointing at a mass of blackened something-or-other, "there's one of those design flaws I mentioned. Nothing that would trigger on its own, but something that could be taken advantage of."

He explained it in rather technical language that Richard was surprised he understood. It sounded so simple, and yet he wouldn't have been able to do it.

"But this thing had been burning for hours when we found it," Richard said. "All the warning systems had been shut down."

"And the environmental system tampered with," Larry said. "The oxygen mix had to have been low here. There wasn't a lot of fuel for this fire, and there should have been. Also, this ship has a built-in system for putting out fires. It would have vented the atmosphere, and isolated the area. It did none of those things."

"Is that easy to tamper with?" Richard asked.

"For me, sure," Larry said. "For you, not so much."

"So someone who knew the ship's systems," Richard said.

"Most ships' systems," Larry said. "You have to know what's standard, what's unusual, what's expected, and what's normal."

"So someone who worked on the ship," Richard said.

Larry smiled. "Probably not. You guys were a week out, right?"

Richard nodded.

"That's plenty of time for someone to study the specs and figure out how this ship worked. Provided that he already had a base of knowledge on how ships in general worked."

"Could they time it?" Richard asked.

"Meaning what?"

"So that we were close to Vaadum when it happened?"

"Sure," Larry said. "That was the only smart way to do it. Unless your saboteur wanted to die along with everybody else. Or planned to take an escape pod. Of course, no one did. They're all here. I assume all your passengers are accounted for too."

"Yeah," Richard said. "They're all here. On the station. With us."

Nothing like murder to make a man stop procrastinating. After Hunsaker watched Anne Marie Devlin use one of the robotic carts to take Kantswinkle's body to the infirmary, he got his tools and finally fixed the lock on Kantswinkle's room. He couldn't shake the feeling that if he had done this before Kantswinkle had arrived, he would have prevented her death.

Then he would have had to deal with her the next two days while the *Presidio* was being prepared. That thought made him shudder—and made him feel guilty. It wasn't her fault that she was dead…

Except that no one seemed to like her, she was difficult to deal with, and if he had to pick someone to murder in this small group of stranded passengers, he would have chosen her.

Which made him shudder even more.

Had she died because of who she was?

Or because of how she acted?

Or because of the room he assigned her?

That last thought got him to find his staff (all two of them) and have them clean some of the other rooms, the ones with the limited environmental controls. Then he moved five of the passengers—Bunting and his roommate, Janet Potsworth and Lysa Lamphere, and Susan Carmichael.

The first four had left their rooms willingly. Then he had gone to see Carmichael.

He knocked, and she didn't answer. So he knocked again, harder. The door flew open, and Carmichael stood there, looking bleary.

She had struck him as the kind of woman whose hair was never out of place, and yet all the strands stood at odd angles with some kind of violent looking red mark on the side of her face. It took him a moment to realize that she had a pillow impression on her cheek, and her hair was mussed from the blankets. Clearly, Susan G. Carmichael was a messy sleeper, even if she never was messy awake.

She didn't want to be moved. She nearly slammed the door in his face, but he stopped her, and told her that if she stayed here, there was a good chance she'd end up like Agatha Kantswinkle.

Then Carmichael frowned.

"What happened to Agatha?" she asked.

He peered at her. She really and truly did not know. "She's dead," he said.

Carmichael closed her eyes for a minute, sighed, and leaned against the door jamb. "I suppose she was murdered," she said tiredly.

"Yes," he said.

Carmichael opened her eyes. They were a vivid blue. "I suppose it was too much to ask the murderer to stop killing once we got off that damn ship."

"I suppose," Hunsaker said, not knowing quite how to respond.

"He's going to run out of victims, and that will call attention to him," she said. She sounded angry, as if it personally affronted her that the murderer kept killing even though she didn't think it wise.

"I don't think he minds the attention," Hunsaker said. "Can I help you get your things?"

"There's not much," she said, indicating the purchases she had made earlier sitting on top of the chair. "I can get them."

Still, he took a pair of shoes and a blanket, just because he suddenly felt that he needed to be useful. Not that he hadn't been useful. He'd been more useful today than he had been in weeks, maybe months. He'd repaired locks on four doors, including Agatha Kantswinkle's (and then he sealed off that damn room, maybe forever), he'd gotten a whole bunch of rooms cleaned, he'd gotten the kitchen staff up and running again, and he actually had people in his hotel.

Until they murdered each other off, of course.

He left the door to her room open, since someone on his staff would be up here shortly to clean, fix this lock, and close off this room. No one was going to be in the older rooms, not while there were murderers on board.

"Did she suffer?" Carmichael asked as he led her down a flight of stairs, through a corridor, and into the newer—and, once upon a time, more hopeful—wing of his hotel.

He looked at her. She actually seemed concerned. No one had asked this question before. He hadn't even asked it when he'd been talking with Anne Marie, and he probably should have.

"I don't know," he said honestly—or as honestly as he dared. It took time to suffocate. If the death was merciful, she would have passed out like Lysa and then stopped breathing, but if it wasn't, she would have been gasping for air—

Although, he realized, had she had trouble breathing, all she had to do was step into the corridor and get far enough away from her door. She would have been able to clear her lungs, and maybe even get help.

"I suspect she didn't suffer at all," he added, now that he'd thought about it.

Carmichael grunted, which surprised him. He would have expected a "thank heavens" or some other kind of reassuring remark. Instead, she sounded almost displeased.

"Did you know her well?" he asked.

"No one knew her well," Carmichael said. "No one wanted to."

"Oh." He would have suspected as much. "What about the other people who died? Were they unpopular too?"

"What's it to you?" she asked.

He flushed. He usually wasn't that nosy.

"I'm sorry," he said. "I didn't mean to pry. I was just wondering."

"Murder really shouldn't be the subject of casual conversation, now should it?" Carmichael asked.

"I guess not," he said, refraining from pointing out that right now, the conversation wasn't as casual as she seemed to think. After all, three people had died on the ship, there was a fire, and now another person had died. Not that casual a conversation. Maybe even relevant.

They stopped at Carmichael's new room. He unlocked it for her and went in first, feeling a slight surge of adrenaline as he took his first breath. Would he always feel that now in his guest rooms? Would he always be afraid that a single breath could kill him?

"Well," Carmichael said following him in, "it's not quite as pretty as the other room, but it does look newer."

He hadn't thought of the other room as pretty, although it had personality which this one lacked. This one was like all the other rooms in this wing, big enough for a large bed, a table and two chairs, as well as an entire wall dedicated to in-room entertainment, if someone wanted to pay a premium price.

He didn't ask Carmichael what she wanted. He figured she could charge it to her bill if she decided she needed entertaining. He didn't want to be near her any longer.

He set her shoes and blanket on the floor, then backed out of the room. She didn't seem to notice. She was putting her clothing on top of the table as he left, as oblivious to his presence as a rich woman was to a robotic cleaner.

He hurried down the steps and back to the front desk, feeling unsettled. This group of people was beginning to frighten him. He had no idea when he'd

be rid of them either. The ship had to be repaired or some other ship had to come here and get them out of his hotel.

For the first time in a very long time, he missed having some kind of security on the station. Someone other than the burliest member of his staff threatening the guests with increased fees—which was usually enough to calm them down, since Hunsaker already had control of their accounts.

But he didn't want to threaten anyone here, because who knew how they would react?

He didn't want to think about it—any of it. Instead, he focused on a cleaning schedule for the vacated rooms. A cleaning schedule and a repair schedule. Time to make sure all the locks worked properly and all the equipment was tamper-proof.

Time he started doing his job.

Again.

Hideous man. Odious, actually. Who did he think he was to discuss other people's deaths as if they were entertainments?

Susan Carmichael sat on the bed in her new room, wide awake now, wondering if she would ever sleep again.

Agatha dead, here and not on the ship. That had shaken Susan as much as figuring out that Remy's death hadn't been suicide. Not that the thought of a suicide in the room next to her hadn't disturbed her too. Any death would have bothered her.

But the murders, the fire—somehow she had gotten it into her head as they fled onto Vaadum that they would be safe here, that their long nightmare was over.

She propped her pillows against the headboard and leaned her head back. She could feel the muscles in her back, so tight that any movement hurt.

She didn't like this room. The other one had the illusion of safety. She had gotten that room when she still believed that the outpost would be much better than the ship.

Now she knew it was no different. A limited group of people trapped in a limited amount of space.

There was nowhere to run, no way to escape. The ship was incapacitated, and—so far as she could tell—the *Presidio* was the only ship on the station.

Did the locals (what should she call them? Station rats?)—did they have a way to leave? She wasn't sure about that either, but she should probably find out.

She had been under the impression that Vaadum was one of the only safe stops between here and Commons Space Station.

But she didn't even know how far Commons Space Station was from here. Maybe she could convince someone to take her there. Or to hire a ship and have it arrive, getting her out of here.

Of course, some of the others would want to come, and that wouldn't work, because one of those others might be the killer.

She needed a way to defend herself. She didn't have one, at least not yet. And now she wouldn't be able to sleep again. She needed to stay awake, stay vigilant, should anyone try anything.

Susan pulled her knees to her chest. She needed a plan.

She just wasn't sure where to begin.

☼

The captain had found a spot in the bar, toward the back under the dim lights. Richard had to cross most of the room—which smelled of beer and sweat and spilled whiskey—to realize that the captain had five empty glasses in front of him.

Richard sighed.

The captain was a small man, former military—but with which army in what war, Richard had never asked (it was none of his business—and he'd learned, through his mother, politics was the most deadly business in the entire sector). The captain had run his ship on a tight schedule. He and the other two pilots had separate eight-hour shifts in the cockpit.

Richard had been hired on to do the menial work that had nothing to with flying the ship—keeping the passengers happy, making sure that the lower decks were spotless, maintaining the robotic cleaners and cooks. The food on the ship wasn't spectacular, but it hadn't been advertised that way. There were ships that made this run that were all about food, food every few hours, food from every culture in the sector, food as rich and varied as the passengers themselves.

But this ship hadn't been a cruise so much as a passenger vehicle. It took people from here to there in a modicum of comfort, with as little fuss as necessary.

Until the first death, Richard had mostly dealt with trivial complaints—broken entertainment sectors, malfunctioning avatars in the gaming area, the occasional sudden (and he thought humorous) switch to zero-g in a toilet. Agatha Kantswinkle had tried his patience—her bed was too soft, the equipment near her room too loud, the cooking smell from the galley too strong—but he'd had the leeway to move her twice, and her final cabin seemed to suit her more than the others, which had cut the complaints to about half of what they had been.

He'd settled in for a flight filled with irritations and hard work, but he knew once he got to Ansary, he'd be done with real work and he'd have money for the first time in months.

He had vowed not to get that low on funds ever again.

Now, here he was, unpaid and trapped on a space station that had at least one killer on board.

He peered at the captain. The man was staring blearily into his glass, as if he could read information written on the bottom of it. The captain was the one man Richard knew wasn't behind any of this, for two reasons.

The first was circumstantial—the captain had been with Richard during the first two killings. If the captain had been involved he would have had to have a collaborator, and the captain never consulted with anyone.

The second reason was more practical—the captain owned his ship. It was part of a franchise operation, and he got paid per passenger for the entire trip. If the ship was full, he made a hefty profit. Half full, he made some money. Empty, and he'd go bankrupt or have to get out of the business.

Richard could understand someone who wanted out so badly that he would destroy his own ship. But he couldn't understand doing it while paying customers were on board, nor could he imagine doing it with fire. There were so many other, much simpler ways.

Richard sat down across from the captain, jiggling the tabletop. The glasses clanked together, but it still took a moment for the captain to notice him.

Or at least to acknowledge him.

"Care to toast the end of my career?" the captain asked, lifting a glass.

"It's not as bad as all that," Richard lied.

"Ship's not reparable," the captain said.

"Yes, it is," Richard said. "I talked to them."

The captain shook his head. "Not flying that thing anywhere. Half the lower deck'd be unusable, it'd smell, and the environmental systems are whacked. Not safe. Least not by our standards."

By that, he meant the standards of the company he worked for.

"So are they sending a replacement ship?"

"Two weeks," the captain said. "Maybe. Or we can hire onto someone else's ship. Have to ask the passengers. What's left of them."

"Two weeks?" Richard asked.

"Coming from Ansary. We'd go back to the Dyo System. We'd be back where we started. Not that it matters. I get to have a hearing. Like it's my fault they let some murderous nutcase onto my ship."

"You didn't check the manifest?" Richard asked.

The captain glared at him. Or tried to. It wasn't that effective a look, considering how wobbly his head was and how bloodshot his eyes were.

"What'm I supposed to? Turn away paying customers with spotless records? Of course, I checked. Not an idiot. Or didn't think I was."

The captain sighed.

"Someone's trying to destroy me," he muttered.

Which was a distinct possibility, one Richard hadn't thought of.

"Does someone hate you that much?" Richard asked.

"You mean besides me?" the captain asked. "Oh, hell, I don't know."

"You didn't do anything wrong," Richard said.

"Sent that first body into space," the captain said. "Didn't turn around then and there. Shoulda brought everyone back."

"We thought it was a suicide," Richard said. "And when the other two deaths happened, we were closer to Commons Space Station than to the Dyo System. It would've taken a week to go back to Ynchyn."

This nightmare trip started in Ynchyn.

"Seems logical, doesn't it? They don't train you for this kinda thing, you know. Maybe I shoulda confined everyone to quarters."

Richard nodded. After all, that had been his initial suggestion—or at least, his suggestion after the second murder. Ignatius Grove, a professor, heading to a new job at some prestigious university in the largest city on Ansary. The man taught mathematics of all things, and he had died when the skin in his throat had a growth spurt, shutting off both sides.

Everyone would've thought that a freak death as well, particularly since Ignatius Grove and Agatha Kantswinkle spent each meal complaining about their various food allergies, if Richard hadn't seen that particular form of murder before. He knew that there were little nanosomethings that could activate the growth mechanism in the skin. If swallowed, the nanosomethings invaded the throat. No one had ever done studies to see if any of them made it to the stomach or if that would've made a difference if the throat hadn't closed first.

Ignatius Grove had died a particularly hideous death. So had Remy Demaupin, the first victim. In fact, all three victims had died terribly. The third, Trista Jordan, had died when someone had sealed her mouth and nose with some kind of bonding adhesive. Richard wasn't sure what was used—some kind of liquid glue. She should've been able to use her call button to ask for help—and she probably would have, if she hadn't also been glued to the chair in her room.

The killer hadn't tried to hide that death, not that it would've mattered. There was no time to investigate it, because shortly after they found Trista, the fire had started.

Or at least had been discovered.

"Confining people to quarters," Richard said, "probably wouldn't have helped. We had a pretty determined killer on board. Still do, actually. Have any ideas who it is?"

"I'd've shot the bastard if I knew." The captain picked up one of the other glasses and downed its contents. "Hell, maybe I should shoot everyone now. That'd take care of the problem. What do you think?"

"It's one solution," Richard said.

"It's as good as any," the captain said, and picked up the remaining full glass. "If I could just get my butt outta this chair. Which I'm not going to do. If someone wants to kill me, so be it. They might be doing me a favor. You want to kill me, Richard?"

The captain's gaze met Richard's. For the first time, the captain seemed sober. His expression was very serious. Richard had the sense that the captain knew more about him than Richard thought.

Richard had waited too long to pretend shock at the question. And he couldn't just wave it off, not considering the look the captain just gave him.

"If I kill you, what do I get out of it?" Richard asked.

The captain grinned and his head bobbled, that moment of clarity seemingly gone. "My eternal gratitude, my friend," he said, just before he finished the third drink. "My eternal gratitude."

☼

Hunsaker sat behind the desk and dug through the files. He had his back to the wall and, out of the corner of his eye, he watched the entrances and the stairway. He didn't want anyone to surprise him for any reason.

He had a pad propped up on his thighs. His personal screen, not the one tied into the resort proper. He had upgraded the pad dozens of times, sometimes illegally. More than once, he'd stolen programs from his guests, and from one—a well-connected gambler who liked the odds (and the breasts) in the casino—he had stolen an entire database of shady characters throughout the sector.

He didn't expect to see any familiar names in that database, but he found one.

Richard Ilykova, aka Yuri Flynn Doyle, Edward Michael Adams, and Misha Yurivich Orlinskaya, Mercenary and Assassin for Hire, believed to be responsible for more than two dozen deaths system wide.

Hunsaker shivered. He had known that Richard Ilykova hadn't been a common worker on a passenger ship. The man was too competent for that—not too mechanically competent, but too competent in the ways of death. He hadn't flinched when he had seen Kantswinkle's body, nor had he seemed too upset by his whole ordeal.

Yet all those deaths—the three on the ship and the fourth here—seemed awfully sloppy for a man who made his living killing people.

Hunsaker sighed softly and exited the illegal database. He felt dirty just thinking about Ilykova's job. About the man himself, actually. Ilykova hadn't seemed harmless—Hunsaker wasn't that naïve—but he had seemed…more efficient than deadly.

A movement caught his eye. Ilykova approached the desk. Hunsaker hadn't even seen him enter the room.

Hunsaker let out a little squeak. Ilykova raised an eyebrow in amusement. He'd clearly caught Hunsaker's moment of fear. Ilykova smiled—one of those knowing smiles—and then proceeded as if he had seen nothing out of the ordinary.

"Looking up the guests, are we?" he asked.

"So?" Hunsaker asked, then realized that probably wasn't the smartest response. Neither, he supposed, would be *What's it to you?* Or *Get the hell away from me.*

"So, does anyone have a history with lack of oxygen?"

"What?" Hunsaker asked, mostly because he hadn't been expecting that question.

"I realized when I was talking with the captain that all of our victims suffocated in one way or another. The fire would have caused the rest of us to suffocate as well. I was just wondering if we have some sort of revenge scenario going on here." Ilykova put his elbows on the desk.

"You tell me," Hunsaker said, his voice wobbling a little.

Ilykova frowned. "I don't have access to a deep database. You do."

Then his eyes widened just a little.

"Oh," he said. "You decided to research me first."

Hunsaker's heart was pounding. He had nothing to lose here—if Ilykova was going to kill him, it would happen here, now. So he called up the earlier screen, with Ilykova's history and pushed it across the desk at him.

"These things are so poorly done," Ilykova said. "It doesn't tell you much, does it?"

He looked up, his pale blue eyes twinkling. How could a man laugh about murder?

It made Hunsaker think of Carmichael: *Murder really shouldn't be the subject of casual conversation, now should it?*

Nor should it be something to smile about.

Apparently, Hunsaker's silence caught Ilykova's attention.

"We all have a past, Grissan," Ilykova said. "Yours involves embezzlement from every single resort you worked for. Quite creative embezzlement, I might add, the kind that would've made you very, very rich if you had kept to your original plan."

Hunsaker felt a warmth rise in his cheeks. No one knew about this. No one. How did Ilykova find it?

"The problem was, in your profession, that the younger, less experienced members moved from resort to resort, while the older ones got a well-deserved sinecure. That's the word, right? Sinecure?"

"Sinecure implies a job with little work. That's not true. To rise to the top of my profession, you must be willing to work at all times." Hunsaker's words were curt, showing his annoyance. He felt his face grow even warmer. He had let Ilykova irritate him.

Ilykova smiled slightly. "My mistake. I simply meant that you hit the top of your profession and remained in one place, a resort that became 'yours,' even if you didn't own it. You became the eyes and ears of the place, the face that everyone recognized. The person they associated with the resort. Which was why they bought you this place instead of prosecuting you. Did you know what a dive they got for you? It was the perfect revenge on their part, wasn't it? An effective banishment away from the populated areas of the sector. Did it embarrass you?"

Embarrassed, humiliated, *angered.* Hunsaker didn't say anything, though, although he expected all of the emotions ran across his face.

"Still," Ilykova said, "you got to keep the money you stole from the other resorts. You could've vanished. You just chose not to."

Too ashamed to leave. Hunsaker simply couldn't face any of his old colleagues ever again. Ever, ever, ever again.

"We all have a bit of history," Ilykova said. "I'm sure you had a reason for your sticky fingers. I have a reason for my history as well. My mother was Halina Layla Orlinskaya. Look her up in your little database."

Hunsaker took the pad back, his fingers shaking, dammit all to hell. He wasn't as practiced at controlling his physical reactions to his emotions, not like he used to be.

He looked up Halina Layla Orlinskaya. She had half a dozen aliases as well. A high-level spy, who defected with some devastating knowledge that changed the course of one of the border wars, she survived her last few years by hiring herself out as a mercenary to various governments.

"What it doesn't say there, I'm sure," Ilykova said, "is that she hired me out as well, as an assassin. She thought I had the personality for it."

"Did you?" Hunsaker wished he could take the words back.

But Ilykova didn't seem to notice. "Not really. I think one should feel passionate about his work. An assassin's job requires no passion at all. Don't you think that one should put his heart and soul into his job?"

"I used to," Hunsaker said.

"And I'll bet you miss that emotion," Ilykova said. "I did. I wanted to *do* something with my life. Ah, to *do* something. Of course, now I'm broke and hiring onto ships as a lower level employee just to get across the sector."

He leaned across the desk. Hunsaker couldn't lean away. His back was already pressed against the wall.

"So you see, I had no reason to kill those people," Ilykova said. "I didn't know them. And I'm certainly smart enough not to set a fire on a spaceship far from the nearest port."

"But," Hunsaker said, his voice smaller than he wanted it to be, "you knew Agatha Kantswinkle."

Ilykova smiled, a real smile, genuinely amused. "Didn't like her either, huh? No one did, so far as I can tell. But I didn't have to kill her. She would've gotten off the ship at Ansary. And here, on Vaadum, she was your problem, not mine."

Hunsaker swallowed. "So you're saying you didn't do it."

"That's right," Ilykova said. "Why would I?"

"Someone paid you?" Hunsaker asked.

Ilykova shook his head. "If someone paid me, I would've been a passenger. I wouldn't have signed on for *work.*"

It sounded logical. It all sounded very logical. Hunsaker just didn't know if he should believe it.

"So what's this about suffocation?" he asked.

"Oh, just a theory," Ilykova said. "Everyone suffocated in one way or another. So if you think of these crimes as related, then maybe the manner of death came as a form of revenge for a death by suffocation…?"

"I wouldn't even know how to look for that," Hunsaker said.

"I would," Ilykova said, and took the pad away from Hunsaker.

☼

Richard was finding a whole lot of nothing as he dug through Hunsaker's database. The database wasn't that good. It was old, for one thing, and the updates hadn't been meshed into the system all that well. They had been grafted on and not efficiently, certainly not efficiently enough for a proper search.

He would have to get onto the *Presidio*. It had a good database and he might be able to find what he was looking for there.

Because, in this cursory exploration, he couldn't find anyone with any links to any suffocation deaths, murdered, accidental, or even natural.

He was about to hand the pad back to Hunsaker, when someone screamed.

"Oh, not again," Hunsaker muttered.

Richard tossed him the pad and ran up the steps, half expecting to hear a thump. He didn't though. But he did hear another scream and, he realized, these screams were male.

They weren't frightened screams or startled screams (except maybe the first one), more likely horrified screams, end-of-the-world screams, the kind you emit when everything was hopeless and all was lost.

Another scream, and then another. Doors slammed as people left their rooms. He was joining quite a crowd as he ran up the stairs.

The screams came from the top floor.

He arrived, along with three other passengers from the ship (Janet Powell, Lysa Lamphere, and William Bunting) to find a man he'd never seen before on his knees, hands over his face, screaming like a stuck alarm.

Another body lay on the floor, this one a woman, also someone he'd never seen before either. Her eyes were open and glassy, her tongue protruding slightly.

She was clearly dead.

Someone sighed behind him.

Richard turned slightly. Hunsaker stood near his shoulder, and stared at the woman on the floor.

"Now what the hell am I going to do?" Hunsaker said with great annoyance. "I mean, really."

☼

Judging from the look on Ilykova's face, Hunsaker had spoken out loud. He felt that warmth returning to his cheeks. He kept his head down, so that he didn't have to look Ilykova in the eyes, and moved into the room.

He put his hand on Fergus's shoulders. Fergus had worked for Hunsaker since Hunsaker came to the resort. Fergus and his wife, Dillith, who now doubled as a corpse. Not that she was ever much livelier than a corpse. But for what Dillith lacked in energy, she made up for in precision.

She could find a speck of dust the robotic cleaners left behind. She could turn bed sheet corners perfectly. She was slow, but she was anal.

And in Hunsaker's "resort," precision mattered more than speed.

Fergus stopped screaming when Hunsaker touched him. Fergus looked up, eyes sunken into his face, and said, "What am I going to do?"

His use of the sentence was plaintive. Hunsaker's had been self-involved. He had jumped from corpse/murder/crisis to *who the hell was going to work for me in this godforsaken place?* in less than a minute. He wasn't proud of that, but he really wasn't a man who developed much affection for his employees.

In fact, he believed affection got in the way of work. He didn't know much about Dillith and Fergus besides their names, their work methods, and the fact that they both preferred late hours rather than getting up early.

"Stand up," Hunsaker said with as much sympathy as he could muster, which probably wasn't enough. "We'll figure something out."

Fergus stood. He was a slight man, and he fell into Hunsaker's arms, much to Hunsaker's chagrin. He hadn't invited the man to hug him. He certainly didn't want the man to touch him. But Fergus was beyond noticing subtleties. He was sobbing. Hunsaker could already feel his shirt getting wet.

He patted Fergus on the back and maneuvered him out of the room. Then he looked at Ilykova who was watching him with that look of amusement again.

"Do me a favor," Hunsaker said to Ilykova. "Get Anne Marie Devlin, would you?"

"Who?" Ilykova said.

"The base doctor," Hunsaker said.

"I think this woman is beyond a doctor—"

"Just do it," Hunsaker said, resisting the urge to move Fergus toward Ilykova. That would show him passion, all right.

Ilykova nodded, then hurried down the stairs. Three passengers from the ship stood around as if this were a theatrical event.

"Go back to your rooms," Hunsaker said. "There's nothing to see."

As if a woman wasn't already dead on the floor. There was plenty to see. He just didn't want them gawking at it.

They, of course, didn't move. He glared at them and tried to look tough, which was hard to do when you had a member of the staff sobbing in your arms.

"Go," he said, and that seemed to work. Maybe it was his tone, his clear disgust at everyone around him.

The three left slowly. He watched them go down the stairs, patting Fergus on the back the entire time as if he were a baby who needed to be burped.

Then Hunsaker peered at the room. It didn't look that much different than it had two hours ago.

When he'd helped Susan Carmichael move out of it.

☼

She heard the screaming, of course. How could she have missed it? And she resisted her first instinct, which was to burrow deep under the covers of this new room, and pretend like she couldn't hear anything.

But Susan Carmichael wasn't a hider. She wasn't the kind of person who ran to the scene of a crime either, although she couldn't be entirely certain what she heard was a crime.

But someone didn't scream with that level of grief—and that was grief, wasn't it?—without a precipitating event, and considering Agatha's murder, the best assumption—the only assumption, really—was that a crime had occurred.

Again.

Which meant she had to get the hell off this station. Somehow.

She changed clothes, slowly and deliberately, putting on the ivory blouse over the black pants. She slipped on her shoes, smoothed her hair, grabbed her personal information, and left this room as well.

The screaming had stopped, but she could hear faint voices in the distance. She glanced at the stairs to ensure that no one was on them, and then she quietly made her way down.

It was time she stopped all of this. She gave up. She had been fleeing her family, but really, life out here was much, much worse than life with them could ever be.

Besides, her father had the capability of getting a ship here within twenty-four hours. He had ships all over the sector. One of them had to be nearby.

She just had to contact him.

She made her way down the stairs toward the main desk. Surely, there was some kind of interstellar communications node. Or maybe just a sector-wide node.

Or worse case—which was a case she'd put up with, after all—she would simply contact the nearest ship and have them contact her father.

And then she would wait.

Although she probably needed some kind of guard.

There wasn't a lot of choice. Everyone from the ship was a possible murderer, and there weren't a lot of people on the station.

But all of the murders she knew of took place while the victim was alone.

So the next key was to be with someone at all times. Except right now.

Right now, she needed to contact Daddy.

After that, she'd find a companion—and find a way to stay awake until help arrived.

☼

Anne Marie Devlin was no longer drunk. She wasn't even under-the-surface drugged-sober drunk. She was so far past drunk that she felt giddy.

Actually, the excitement made her feel giddy. She felt useful for the first time in months.

If she didn't know herself better—and she knew herself quite well, thank you—she would say she had become a drunk because she was bored.

But she had been a drunk long before life ceased to be a challenge. She knew that excitement was just a temporary high, while alcohol numbed the senses, which was usually what she preferred.

Right now, however, she needed all the senses that she had. She was inside yet another room—this one a favorite of hers—standing over yet another corpse that had been murdered by yet another tampered environmental system.

The question was, how had it been tampered with? And why?

She was peering at the system itself, noting something off, when she realized one of the ship's passengers was also in the room. A tallish white-blond man with pale blue eyes.

The man who had fetched her. Richard Something-or-Other.

"I prefer to work alone," she said.

"So do I," he said.

They stared at each other for a moment. Hunsaker, who also preferred to work alone (she knew that because he had told her half a dozen times) stood near the doorway, his shirt soaked with Fergus's tears. She'd managed to get Fergus out of the room and down to the kitchen where the chef could watch him. Fergus was quite pliable most of the time. Right now, he was damn near catatonic.

Perhaps anyone would be after crying that much.

She turned toward Hunsaker. "What the hell were you thinking? Sending those two to work in these rooms with a murderer on the loose?"

"Who knew that the killer would come after one of us?" he said.

"I don't think the killer did," Richard Something-Or-Other said. "If you'll allow me."

He shoved—*shoved!*—Anne Marie out of the way, and peered at the control panel himself.

"You do realize if this man is the killer, he now has access to the evidence," she said to Hunsaker.

"You do realize if this man is the killer," Hunsaker said, mimicking her tone, "then you just gave him a reason to kill us."

They glared at each other again.

"I'm not the killer," Richard Something-Or-Other said, "but whoever is has some serious engineering skills."

She couldn't resist: she peered into the controls as well. These older models had digital readouts and mechanisms attached to mechanisms. She had just looked at the one in the room where Agatha Kantswinkle died—and that control did not have a secondary digital readout. This one did.

She looked at Richard Something-Or-Other. He raised his eyebrows at her, as if he were surprised as

well. Then he touched the whole thing with a single fingernail. The second readout was loose, but had been attached into the control's mechanism. She peered at the mix. When Dillith had been in here, the atmosphere's mix had been the same as it had been when Agatha Kantswinkle died.

Anne Marie frowned. She glanced over her shoulder at the door. Hunsaker was still leaning on the jam, glaring at her. He seemed to disapprove of what she was doing.

Or maybe he disapproved of Richard Something-Or-Other.

Or maybe he always disapproved of everything.

She sighed and walked to the door.

"Move," she said.

Hunsaker didn't.

"I mean it. Move. I need to see something."

"What?" he asked.

"It's easier to look than it is to explain," she said pushing him aside. Then she peered inside the locking mechanism. Another small digital readout had been attached.

"This door was closed when Fergus got here, wasn't it?" she asked.

"I don't know," Hunsaker said. "I didn't ask."

"You didn't bother to tell them to keep the doors open?"

Hunsaker's glare changed to something filled with a kind of fury. "Of course I did. It's part of the general instructions, anyway. The door should always be open with the staff is inside, even if no one else is."

"Hmm," she said.

"What?" Richard Something-Or-Other asked from his position near the environmental controls.

"This is a timer," she said. "It closes the door."

"And this timer," he said, "changes the environmental mix."

"It couldn't have been put in here when Dillith was here," Anne Marie said.

"Someone set it up earlier than that," Richard Something-Or-Other said.

"Which means that the killer wasn't after Dillith," Anne Marie said.

"He was after Susan Carmichael." Hunsaker said that last, breathed it in fact. Anne Marie could hear the shock in his voice. "If I'd gotten her just a little too late, then—"

"You would've died too," Anne Marie said. "We have to brace this door open."

"I doubt the room will kill again," Richard Something-Or-Other said.

"But the other rooms might," Anne Marie said.

"I moved everyone out of the older rooms," Hunsaker said.

"Let's hope that's enough," Anne Marie said. She actually felt a little chill. She liked the chill. Excitement—she had missed it so much. "Maybe he'll start coming after the rest of us too."

"Oh, don't get your hopes up," Hunsaker snapped and left the room.

Richard Something-Or-Other raised his eyebrows again. "What was that all about?"

Anne Marie shrugged. "I guess he's upset by all of this."

Richard nodded. "I think it would be surprising if he were not."

Hunsaker stomped down the stairs. Now he didn't know what to do. Did he warn Carmichael? Did he put all the guests in the same room and let them duke it out until a ship arrived and got them out of his resort?

He stopped halfway down the stairs and leaned his head against the wall. All of his training, all of his long and fancy education, all of his experience good and bad did not train him for any of this. He could just imagine the lecture titled *How to Handle a Murderer Loose in Your Resort*.

Simple: Call the local authorities.

And if there were none?

He banged his head against the metal just once. If he rounded them up, where would he take them? The restaurant? The casino?

The casino at least covered a big area. It would be hard to tamper with the environmental system.

Maybe he should just force them all back to their ship, and if they killed each other, so be it. Hell, if they died from smoke inhalation, so be it. It wasn't his concern.

While they were here, they bothered him.

While they were on their ship, they had nothing to do with him.

That's what he'd do. He'd get the maintenance guys and make them act as security guards. Even the chef and the blackjack dealer could work security (so long as she put her shirt on). They'd round up these horrible people and put them back on their own ship and if they died, they died.

His stomach turned.

Maybe if they all died, he could just jettison the ship into deepest darkest space. He'd set it on autopilot and get it the hell out of here.

For a moment, his spirits rose.

Then he remembered he'd already charged their accounts. There was a record he couldn't tamper with of them being on his station.

Dammit.

He had no idea what to do.

Richard helped Anne Marie get the corpse down to the medical wing. He'd had enough of carrying bodies. By his count, this was the fifth this trip, and the only one he hadn't met while she was still alive.

The medical wing was in the farthest part of the station, and certainly didn't deserve the appellation "wing." It was a medical suite at best, a smallish group of rooms set up as an afterthought.

Agatha Kantswinkle lay on one table, naked—which was an image he'd never get out of his mind again—and, to his surprise, the other two bodies from the ship in clear refrigeration units, looking no worse for being dead the last few days.

He set Dillith on the closest table, and stretched his muscles with relief.

"Thank you," the doctor said in that tone all professionals used which actually meant *you're done, now get the hell out*.

Which he did.

And as he stepped into the corridor, he realized he'd been going about this investigation all wrong. He'd been looking for common ties, for suffocation deaths, for *motive*, and he, of all people, should know that motive mattered a lot less than the entertainments said it did.

His motive for most of his early killings had been because his mother had hired him out to do the job. The later killings had been because he could make money at it. Only the first killing had had a real motive: the man had murdered his father and ruined Richard's life.

Richard didn't need to look at motive.

He needed to look for experience. Technical experience.

With environmental systems.

He scurried back to the hotel's main entrance, and hoped that Hunsaker's horrible aging database had at least enough information to solve all of this.

☼

She wasn't hysterical. Hunsaker could've dealt with her if she had been hysterical. He had training in hysterical. High-end hotel guests often got hysterical about nothing. And here, which was decidedly *not* high-end, people got hysterical because… well, because they were here.

Susan G. Carmichael had every reason to be hysterical. She could've died in her room had he not taken her out of it. But she had already figured out that she might die and she was calmer than he was.

She had even found a way to contact her father, who was such a famous Vice Admiral that Hunsaker had even heard of him, and he was sending a ship that would be here in 18 hours sharp, along with some kind of back-up that would take care of the problem.

Whatever that meant.

But she wasn't returning to her room.

To any room, really.

She wanted to remain with Hunsaker, thinking that somehow, Hunsaker would be safe.

He sat on his chair with his back against the wall, no longer sure what safe was. She was sitting on the edge of his desk, surveying the area as if she ran it instead of him.

He was still debating whether to get everyone else out of their rooms when Ilykova burst through the doors.

"I need your database," he said.

"Whatever happened to please and thank you?" Hunsaker muttered, knowing he was being a complete ass, as he handed over the pad.

Ilykova ignored that, although he did glance at Carmichael. He didn't seem that surprised to see her. Then he leaned against the desk and started trolling the database, his fingers moving faster than Hunsaker's ever could.

The three of them didn't say a word as Ilykova worked. Carmichael watched him. Hunsaker kept an eye on the doors and the stairs, not that it had made any difference in the past.

Then Ilykova looked over at Carmichael. "Were you and Agatha Kantswinkle ever alone?"

"Here?" she asked.

"On the ship," he said.

She looked down. "I talked to her once. After that incident—you know. I felt so sorry for her that—"

"What incident?" Hunsaker interrupted. It wouldn't have been his business had everything happened on the ship, but the ship's problems had spilled into his little resort, and he felt he had a right to know.

She looked at him. "We had a dinner hour on the ship. We all got fed at the same time, and the room wasn't that big. We got to know each other better than you usually got to know people on passenger ships, which wasn't necessarily a good thing."

Ilykova nodded, although he kept his head down, still searching the database as he listened.

"Anyway, just after Professor Grove died, we were all on edge, and Agatha started into how we needed someone to take charge, to make sure things wouldn't get worse, and Mr. Bunting had enough. He told her she was a nosy snobbish old woman who wouldn't know how to treat other human beings even if she had special training, and she certainly couldn't be in charge of anything, and he didn't believe anything she said about herself and—" Carmichael shook her head. "I was agreeing with him at first, she was an unpleasant woman, and I would've given anything to avoid her as much as possible, but he didn't stop, and by the end, she looked just devastated."

Ilykova was looking up now. Hunsaker was surprised as well. He couldn't quite imagine Kantswinkle looking devastated.

"I waited until everyone left," Carmichael said, "and told her that we were all on edge and that he had no right to lay into her like that, and she started to cry, which made me very uncomfortable. I walked her to her room, and told her to get some rest, that it would all seem better in the morning, and then I left."

"Then what?" Hunsaker asked, expecting more to the story.

"Then we found Trista's body and the fire and we barely made it here," Carmichael said.

"I got the distinct impression you wanted nothing to do with Ms. Kantswinkle," Hunsaker said.

Carmichael looked at him in surprise. "I thought I hid that."

"You avoided her in the lobby, checking in," Hunsaker said.

Carmichael looked down, sighed. "She was clingy. Halfway through our discussion, I realized she was bombastic because she was lonely and needy and I'd made a huge mistake trying to comfort her. If this had been some kind of normal flight, I wouldn't have been able to shake her for the rest of the trip."

"If it had been a normal flight," Ilykova said, "you wouldn't have spoken to her in the first place."

"True enough," Carmichael said. Then she frowned at him. "Why did you ask about us?"

"I have a theory," he said.

But he didn't say any more. And he continued to tap on the pad, which annoyed Hunsaker.

"Are you going to share the theory?" Hunsaker asked.

"I think someone thinks you saw something," Ilykova said. "Did you?"

Carmichael shrugged and shook her head.

"It would've been when you two were alone together."

She shook her head again. "Nothing."

He grunted as if he didn't believe her. He continued to work.

After a long moment, he said softly, "Well, I think I found something."

✿

"What did you find?" Hunsaker asked. Carmichael crowded close. Richard didn't answer right away. First he made certain no one else could hear. He checked the doors, and looked up the stairwell.

When he came back to the desk, he spoke as softly as he could. He explained his idea—that he searched for expertise, not motive. He didn't discuss how he feared the database would be limited (it was, but it didn't matter, he'd found enough).

"When I searched for expertise in environmental systems, I got two names. I expected at least one from the crew, but that was wrong."

"Which names?" Carmichael sounded panicked for the first time since he saw her down here.

"William Bunting and Lysa Lamphere."

"Bunting," Hunsaker said. "He was the one who yelled at Agatha Kantswinkle, you said."

Carmichael nodded.

"But," Richard said, "whoever killed Agatha and went after you, Susan, had a short window to do so. You had your room assignments already. Did you let anyone in your room?"

"Janet Powell," Carmichael said. "But I never left her alone and she never went near the controls."

"Anyone else?"

She shook her head.

"Where were you after we found Agatha's body?"

"I didn't leave the room," Carmichael said.

"Except to buy clothing," Hunsaker said.

"Yes," Carmichael said. "I bought clothing. But Bunting couldn't've done it then. He was in the boutique with me."

She used the word boutique with a touch of sarcasm. Richard frowned for a moment. Bunting had yelled at Agatha Kantswinkle, and made her cry. She wouldn't have let him near her. But another woman…?

"Did she have any troubles with Lysa?" Richard asked.

Carmichael shrugged. "I have no idea. I'm not even sure they spoke."

He didn't want to push her too hard. "Did you see either William Bunting or Lysa Lamphere that night you were alone with Agatha?"

"Lysa," Carmichael said. "But it was no big deal. She had forgotten something in the dining area. She went past us, looking a bit concerned. It wasn't important."

"Past you from where?" he asked.

"I assume she came from her room," Carmichael said.

"But you were walking Agatha to her room."

"Yes," Carmichael said.

"From the dining area."

"Yes."

"Which was nowhere near Lysa's room."

Carmichael looked at him.

"Her room was in a whole different area of the ship."

"And the fire started not too far from Agatha's room," Carmichael said.

Richard nodded. He felt certain they knew who the killer was now. Lysa Lamphere had killed Agatha and gone after Carmichael because they could tie her to the entire event.

"It all sounds so nice and pretty," Hunsaker said, "until you remember that Lysa nearly died from inhaling the same toxic air that Agatha died from."

"Did she?" Richard asked. "She went into the room, made the switch with the environmental controls, maybe even watched Agatha die, and then switched them back. She waited until everything cleared a bit, and then went through her charade. I have a hunch if we search her room, we'll find some small breathing equipment, something she hid before going back to 'discover' Agatha."

"Why would she do that?" Carmichael asked.

They were all so naïve. Or maybe he wasn't naïve enough. It seemed obvious to him. Once he had Lysa's name, he understood how everything happened. And a little bit of why.

"So that no one would ever suspect her. You ruled her out even after I discovered her expertise because she had suffered as well."

He almost added, any good professional would've done that. But he didn't. Still, he saw the way Hunsaker looked at him. Hunsaker knew that.

"May I have the pad?" Hunsaker asked.

Richard handed him the pad, bracing for the next question, which came with predictable swiftness.

"I don't suppose you have expertise in environmental systems?" Hunsaker asked.

Richard resisted the urge to smile. "No, I don't."

"I will check," Hunsaker said.

"Do," Richard said. "But remember what I told you before. I wouldn't have started the fire. If you want to scuttle a ship, there are better and quicker ways to do it. She didn't want us all to die. She knew we were close."

"But why kill five people?" Carmichael asked.

"That's what I mean to find out," Richard said.

✿

It took a bit of work. Buried deep in all the information was one single tie. To the mathematician. His new job was a promotion, one she didn't feel he deserved. She had studied under him, and he had refused to grant her a degree, saying she was sloppy. She moved to engineering, and graduated, although not with honors, and not in a way that gave her any currency in any job. She would've needed more education for that.

She had boarded that ship with a plan to follow him to Ansary, maybe destroy his career there. Or maybe kill him. But she didn't.

Trista died because she had seen the murder, and she planned to do something about it. Lysa had never planned for Trista's body to be discovered. She probably thought the fire would've been found sooner. By the time someone had found it, the entire ship went into a panic. Which, if Richard thought about it, meant that her calculations had been off.

Professor Grove, the mathematician, had been right about her after all. Her math skills hadn't been up to the task.

Then Agatha Kantswinkle and Susan Carmichael had seen Lysa in that area, and if there were an investigation, they might've mentioned her. She didn't want to risk it. So she planned the last two murders, and might've gotten away with all of it, if Hunsaker hadn't moved Carmichael out of her room.

What Richard couldn't figure out was why she killed Remy Demaupin.

"I didn't," Lysa snarled. They had tied her up and moved her to the bar, along with all the other passengers. No one wanted to be alone any longer. They all worried that Richard and Hunsaker and Carmichael had caught the wrong person, even though Lysa had made it pretty clear from the moment she got tied up that they hadn't.

"What do you mean you didn't kill Remy," Carmichael said. "We know you did."

Lysa shook her head. "He killed himself," she said. "In fact, he inspired me. I figured everyone would look for a connection between him and Professor Grove. Then we would have the emergency and everyone would forget and…"

She lowered her head. Richard watched her, realized he'd met her type before. The type that imagined what they'd do, then did it, and wondered why nothing quite worked the way they'd planned.

"You should've just shoved him out of an airlock," Richard said.

Everyone looked at him. He realized he'd said too much.

He shrugged, pretending a nonchalance he didn't entirely feel.

"What I mean is that had you done something simple, no one would've thought twice about it. All this elaborate stuff was your downfall."

That still sounded bad. He sounded like one killer giving advice to another. Which, in fact, he was.

Hunsaker crossed his arms, watching Richard, a slight frown on his face. Anne Marie stood in the back of the room, listening. The captain was still at his table, drowning himself in drink. Carmichael kept checking the time, hoping that her father's ship would get here soon.

Everyone else sat very far away from Lysa, as if her particular brand of insanity was catching.

Richard didn't stay that far away though. For all her brand of insanity, her elaborate kills, and her mistakes, she was what a murderer should be.

Someone who had a reason to do what she did— not a bloodless reason. A personal reason. An important reason. Something that was, to her, life and death. So she acted, in a life-or-death manner.

And he found that both inspirational and appropriate.

He didn't ask her any more. Carmichael's father could take them all in his various ships. Somewhere Lysa would get prosecuted for what she had done. Not that this was a happy ending for anyone.

The captain would probably lose his job. Carmichael was going back to a situation that she clearly didn't want to be in.

And Richard would have no way to get to Ansary.

Not to mention all the people who had died. Their families would never be the same.

He walked back to Anne Marie Devlin. Pretty woman. Or she would've been if she weren't a depressive and a drunk. She was sober right now, but he could see the tendencies. She was the kind who didn't want to change because she saw no point in it.

Besides, change was hard. That was becoming clearer to him, each and every day.

✣

The ships arrived in fifteen hours, not eighteen, and they took everyone away. Once Hunsaker realized who Carmichael's father was—he truly was a mucky-muck of high muck who had a lot of mucking money—he made noises about the damage to his resort and how embarrassing it would be if it ever came out that his daughter had been a target.

When that hadn't moved her father, Hunsaker added that it would also be embarrassing for people to know that his daughter had been fleeing from him when all of this occurred.

Hunsaker got a tidy payout, enough to renovate the entire resort if he felt like it. And he felt like it. He wanted this place as tamper proof as possible. He didn't ever want to be in this situation again.

Ilykova hadn't left with the rest. He wasn't going to testify either, no matter how much everyone pleaded with him. He sat in the bar these days and watched Anne Marie drink, which was a sight to behold. He didn't seem miserable, but he didn't seem happy either.

He was waiting for the next ship, for a way out. Although he clearly didn't know where he was going.

And Hunsaker had been thinking about it. The station was a world unto itself. Technically, anything that happened here was prosecuted in the Commons System, but no prosecution had ever happened.

Hunsaker wasn't sure what he would've done if Ilykova hadn't been here. Ilykova wasn't big or burly and he didn't seem tough. But he had experience.

And he had no qualms about doing what it took to keep the peace.

You should've just shoved him out of an airlock.

Hunsaker couldn't've done that to anyone. Ever. But he could pay someone to do it while he looked the other way.

That wouldn't've worked in this circumstance, of course. But it might in future circumstances.

And if Hunsaker had learned anything from this experience, he had learned it was better to be prepared.

If he had been prepared, none of this would've happened.

The doors would've locked properly, the environmental controls would've been up-to-date, and all the rooms would've been cleaned.

Woulda coulda shoulda.

He wasn't going to have any regrets. He was going to move forward.

He squared his shoulders and walked to the bar. He paused for a brief jealous moment when he saw how close Ilykova was sitting to Anne Marie. Then he saw the look of disgust on Ilykova's face, and realized that the man would never be interested in her.

So Hunsaker sat down at their table, and offered Ilykova a job.

No one was surprised when Ilykova said yes.

Jean Marie Ward writes fiction, nonfiction and everything in between. Her credits include a multi-award nominated novel, numerous short stories and two popular art books. The former editor of CrescentBlues.com, she is a frequent contributor to Galaxy's Edge *and ConTinual, the convention that never ends. Learn more at JeanMarieWard.com*

FROM ROCK STARS TO REDSHIRTS AND KAIJU: *GALAXY'S EDGE* INTERVIEWS JOHN SCALZI

PART TWO

by Jean Marie Ward

Galaxy's Edge *continues its conversation with John Scalzi, the award-winning author of such science fiction bestsellers as* Old Man's War, Redshirts, *The Interdependency series, and his latest novel,* Kaiju Preservation Society. *This segment focuses on his writing process; what it's like to sell to and work in movies, TV, and streaming services; and why* kaiju *are on this year's publication menu. (For more about Scalzi's origins as a writer and the importance of pop culture to his work, check out* Galaxy's Edge *No. 54.)*

Galaxy's Edge: Could you give our readers that general idea of your writing process? Do you start with a character or a scene? Do you write linearly, or do you do what they do in the James Bond movies, write five big scenes then tie them together?

John Scalzi: A lot of it depends on the particular story. In terms of the ideas, where they come from, most of the time what I basically do is *Hunger Games* in my brain, where I have all these ideas and I let them fight. Whichever one survives is the one that I end up writing. In many cases, the story that eventually gets published has been rolling around in my head for years, literally. The ideas pop in, and I don't write them down. I go, "Okay, that sounds like an interesting idea." Then I go to sleep and if I don't remember it the next morning, I guess it wasn't that interesting. I keep doing that, and the ones that I end up writing are usually the ones that stick around for a really long time.

Sometimes a whole idea just downloads into my brain and I'm like: "Oh, my gosh, I need to write this right now!" Which is what happened with *Kaiju*, and we can get into that a little bit later. But generally speaking, I just let [the ideas] roll around until one of them gains enough mass in my brain in terms of setting and characters and everything else that it finally drops, and I'm ready to write it. That's how that happens.

I mostly write linearly. I don't outline, I just sit down, and I write and see what comes out. Then I also edit as I go along so that when I type the end, ten minutes later it's off to my editor. I don't write second drafts or third drafts or anything like that, primarily because I edit as I go along, but also because drafting in many ways is an artifact of people having to type out on paper and then having to go back and rekey and retype.

On a computer, which is where I started writing—I started writing short stories the same year the Apple Macintosh came out—you don't have to do that. You can go back and fix things as you go along. My editing process has been informed by that. So, I have to write linearly. Every morning I wake up, I read what I wrote the day before, make tiny adjustments, all that sort of stuff. Then I start the day's writing. Usually, I can hit between 1,000 and 3,000 words. I try to do about 2,000 words. If I don't hit 2,000 words, I don't panic. but I do write from eight to twelve, because I haven't looked at the news, I haven't gotten angry, so I can focus on what I'm doing. After about twelve, I stop and I take care of email and everything else, and I let my brain think about what's going on for the next day. If I'm writing along, and I realize in chapter 15, I should have put something in chapter 3 so that it looks like I was foreshadowing what's happening in chapter 15, I'll go back to chapter 3 and I'll put that in, so that when the readers read it, they're like: "Oh, that was so clever. He'd foreshadowed that in chapter 3 and here it is in chapter 15. He must have really had that super organized in his head."

The answer is no. I just wrote, and I edited as I went along. I think that that's the important thing, I think

that writers do get really obsessed with their process. I don't think there's anything wrong with that, because this is what we do. Our process is our job. But at the same time, the readers don't read process, they read result.

So, however your process gets you to the point where you have a full book is your process, and it's a good process. If you outline and that works for you, that's great. If you make it up as you go along like I do and that works for you, that's great. The important thing is, is that you're doing something that works for you, and at the end, we all get to the same spot, which is a book with 100,000—or 250,000 words if you're an epic fantasy writer. Oh, my God, how can they write that much? But they do what they do, and we all put it out on the market. The process is interesting for us. The result is interesting for the reader.

GE: But a lot of readers are writers or aspiring writers, and sometimes—and I recognize this is an aside—it helps very new writers to know that they are not alone in their process and that it's all good as long as it gets the work on the page.

JS: Right. I don't know if that's an aside at all. I think that's actually really interesting. The point that I always want to make to writers is there is no one process. It's always very interesting to hear how other writers do it, and if there's something that clicks with you about how another writer does that, then you can try it. But I think one of the fallacies that writers have, particularly newer writers, is the idea of the one path. There's one way to do the writing. There's one way to publish it. There's one way to find an audience. There's one way to do all this stuff. If we could only divine what that one path is, we would all be successful, and we would all have Hugos, and we would all have movie deals, right?

The answer to that is no, there is no one path. There are many paths that people take to finishing that book, to winning that award, to getting that movie deal. Part of the thing is just assuring younger writers and newer writers—because they're not always the same thing—that, in fact, the path that is the best path for them is the path that gets them to finish the work, because once the work is finished, then everything else has potential to happen. You have the potential to sell it. You have the potential for it to be successful. You have the potential for it to win the awards. You have the potential for the movie deals. You have the potential to own a church, if that's your thing; or in the case of George Martin, a movie theater; or in the case of Neil Gaiman, an island. All of these things. But none of that happens unless the work gets done. So whatever path sets you to that first destination of getting that work done is the important path.

GE: And your path is linear once the idea has downloaded. Does that ever create complications when you've got a lengthy series, like *Old Man's War* or The Interdependency series, which are as close as you've ever gotten to doorstoppers?

JS: Absolutely. When I wrote *Old Man's War*, I had John Perry leave Planet Earth. Earth was only in the book for a chapter and a half. So, I was lazy, and I made twenty-eighth or twenty-fifth or whatever century it is Earth look like early twenty-first century Ohio, because I don't care. We're only here for a chapter and a half, right? I didn't expect to make any more Old Man's War books. I didn't expect anything. Then the book took off, and my editor was like: "Well, now you have to write sequels." And Charlie Stross of all people is like: "You know you have to explain why twenty-fifth century Earth looks like twenty-first century Ohio, right? Because that was some bullshit right there." And I was like: "Curse you Charlie Stross!" because he was 100 percent correct. Now I had to explain it.

As it turns out, I did explain it, and that became a narrative thread that went through the entire series. Basically the Earth was having its progress intentionally halted by the Colonial Union, so they could continue to farm it for colonists and for fighters. So, yeah, absolutely, writing the way that I do can get me in trouble, especially if I don't know that there's a series. The Interdependency was the first time that I wrote a series that was intended from the start to be two or three books. So, I could do that long-term, knowing that I wasn't going to answer all the questions in one book, and that there are things I could carry over. But everything else was that artifact of

dealing with the nonsense you try to slide by everybody before.

The other thing is the Old Man's War series is currently at six books. There'll be at least a seventh book. [The series was] written over the course of 15 years. There's lots that I've forgotten, and either I have to reread the books—which I can do obviously, or sometimes I have a question about my books, and I just go on the internet and be like: "Hey, somebody who's read *Zoe's Tale*, can you remind me the name of this particular character?" And the internet is helpful or wants to be helpful, and they're like: "Why, of course. That name was Metwalli. That was the last name." And I'm like: "Thank you." Once they say it, then it pops into my brain. *Oh yeah, I haven't heard that name in a long time. You know, you used that for that book. What was that name of the book? Zoe's Tale.* It's nice to have fans because they will do things like create wikis and answer your questions on Twitter. And mostly they don't lie to you, so that's good.

GE: Your stories form the basis of several episodes of the Netflix series, *Love, Death, & Robots*. In addition, several of your series have been optioned for film, TV, and streaming services. Can you tell us anything about the status of these projects?

JS: *Old Man's War* is at Netflix. It's been at Netflix for a couple of years. It was at Syfy before that, and it was at Paramount before that. It's been in development long enough to pay for my daughter's college education, so well done, Hollywood. Thank you very much for my daughter's education. Things at Netflix are going pretty well. The thing is, if they happen, they happen, and if they don't, they don't. That's kind of where that is. *The Interdependency* is also in development. It's been optioned by Working Title. We have a showrunner attached to that. I can't say who it is at the moment, but they are a terrific showrunner. I've seen the pilot script, and the pilot script is wonderful. Now it's just a matter of somebody saying yes or no, and we'll see what happens with that.

There are a couple of other things that are in development that I can't talk about, simply because they've asked us not to talk about it yet. But that's always the process. Things get optioned, everybody's excited, and then the real world happens. There are so many places where things can fall down.

One of the nice things about working on *Love, Death, & Robots* is that [the shows] actually happened. There are four episodes, three in Season One, one in Season Two, and there'll be a fifth in Season Three, which will hopefully be in 2022. They're all either made or in the process of being made. So, I can be like: "Look, there it is. 'Three Robots,' that's mine. 'Yogurt', that was mine." It's kind of fun because I have a *Love, Death & Robots* T-shirt, which Netflix sent to me. It was like: "Thanks for all your hard work. Here's a T-shirt."

GE: As long as they sent the money, the T-shirt's great.

JS: Netflix absolutely sent the money, and we're very thankful for that. Then also a T-shirt. [When I wear the T-shirt], I swear everywhere I go, there's somebody who's like: "*Love, Death & Robots*. I love that." Then I get to go: "Oh, good. Which shows did you like?" We'll like talk about a whole bunch of them, and inevitably, because I had three in the first season, out of 18, sooner or later one shows up, and I'll be like: "Oh, yeah, that one, I wrote that." And they go: "What? What are you doing out in the wild? I thought they kept you in a cage in Hollywood." Because you never expect to see a writer in the wild or anything like that. That's always kind of fun, unless they really hate it in which case I'm like: "Yeah. That one sucked. Who thought that yogurt would want Ohio? What complete jackass thought that was a good story?"

GE: Did you have any input into the actual episodes or did you just say, "Oh, great. Here's the story. Thank you."

JS: I was very, very fortunate. The people who are actually producing [the series] for Netflix—Blur Studio and Tim Miller, who is the head of Blur—were very good about keeping me in the loop. Also, as things went on, they were like: "Hey, what do you think? Do you have notes? Are these the things that you want us to do?" For the second and third seasons, I actually wrote the scripts for the episodes that were attached to [my stories], which was kind of fun as well. So, they have allowed me to be very

involved. Now, because I'm a writer in Hollywood, I don't have final say. Nor should I necessarily, because again, once you start working in Hollywood, you have a lot of people who are involved.

I'm perfectly willing to admit that as a novelist, my competence level is very high. As someone who is putting together a TV series, my competence level is not nearly as high. So, you learn to not only rely on the fact that other people are more competent than you, but you also get the chance to learn from them. I am better at doing TV series now than I was ten years ago when I started doing stuff with *Stargate Universe* and, later on, when I started doing other stuff. You get to learn, then you get to grow, and you build from there.

But no matter what, novelists do their thing by themselves. It's individual achievement. With TV and film, it's a team effort. If you can't accept that now you are part of a team and you don't necessarily have the final word—unless you are J.K. Rowling with the Harry Potter films, where she did get final say. Everybody else just has to accept that they're part of the team. If you can't accept that, then you don't play. And that's perfectly fine. There's lots of people who don't want to do that. I think it's reasonable if you don't want that, but if you do want to play, and you do want to see where things go, then you have to accept that it's just part of the price of playing the game in Hollywood.

GE: *Kaiju Preservation Society* was not the Scalzi novel that people expected in 2022, but it's the one I'm glad we got. Could you tell us a little bit about how the book came to be?

JS: What happened was I was trying to write a novel in 2020 that was a dark, moody, gritty, political thriller in space. It turned out that 2020 was a really bad year to try to write a dark, gritty, political thriller, whether or not it was in space, because 2020 was a nightmare year, not only for politics, but obviously because of COVID and the pandemic and everything else. Usually, no matter what's going on in the world, I have the luxury and privilege of getting into my head and disappearing in a different world where things aren't necessarily better, but they're more interesting. Unfortunately for me, the world that I had developed for this novel was really not any better or kinder to my mental state than the world that I was living in. So, it became difficult for me to write. Not difficult to write individual sentences or paragraphs or even chapters, because those were fine. But they weren't holding together, and I couldn't focus enough to get things done, partly because the world was pulling focus with everything that was happening, one after the other.

Then, at the end of the year, I got sick. All the nasal swabs and blood tests swear to me that it wasn't COVID, but whatever it was, for the last two months of 2020, I couldn't brain. My brain was pudding. Then finally the new year came and I was like: "New year, new me, new attitude. I'm gonna start writing on January 4th, get through the weekend." And January 4th I wrote 250 words. I was like: "Two hundred and fifty words. That's 250 words. It's the start." The next day I wrote five hundred words. I'm like: "I am geometrically progressing. Things are going great." Then January 6th happened, and I was like: "Fuck me. I'm not doing anything until at least the twentieth of January, and I know that we've had a transfer of power, because, Oh. My. God." Then January 20th rolled around, and I waited another week just to make sure that it took. Then I waited another week because, why not?

I started writing again in February. I wrote 3,400 words and it was great. Then that chapter just disappeared, and I was like—and pardon my language—I was just like: "Fuck this book! *FUCK IT*!" I just couldn't do it anymore.

I sent an email to Patrick, and I was like: "I loathe this book. I loathe everything about it. And I loathe what it is doing to my brain. I just can't write it anymore. I know it's supposed to come out real soon. I know that I'm supposed to be reliable, and I just can't."

Patrick totally got it. He can't have been happy, but he was empathetic, and he understood. He was just like: "We'll make it work. Don't worry about it. Go take a nap."

I didn't take a nap. I went and took a shower, and when I took the shower, my brain was like: "Oh yeah,

kaiju. Kaiju Preservation Society. Ka-kathunk." And I wanna spell this out so that you have it: KA-K-A-T-H-U-N-K *Ka-kathunk.* Right into my brain, literally, that whole story. And I was like: "Oh, my God! Oh, my God!" Because my brain was still working in 2020. Some part of my brain was rebelling against the other part of my brain going: "I don't know about the rest of you, but I'm gonna have fun in this secret corner." Then when I finally gave up on that book I couldn't write, the dark and moody thing, the part of my brain that was working in the secret corner was like: "I made you this gift. I made you this thing made out of twine." And it was perfect.

I got out of the shower, went to the computer, and emailed Patrick: "Hey, remember how I was freaking out, and I wasn't gonna have a book, and we didn't know what was gonna happen, and pain, and death, and angst? You'll have a book in six weeks."

And that's what happened. I just sat down, and I was like: "Here we go, bump, bump, bump, bump, bump, bump." Because, like I said, my brain seemed to have it all there. And it was such a relief to write a book that was fun and silly. It has serious moments and stuff in it, but there was a lot of joy in the writing, and I think that it comes through in the text as well. What I've been saying to people about it is: I was trying to write this dark symphony, and what I really needed to be doing and was writing a pop song. And I wrote a pop song, and it's what I needed as a human. Forget as a writer, it's what I needed as a human after everything that we've gone through. For now, for two years, I just needed something that was like: "It's okay to be light. It's okay to have a laugh. It's okay to do big monsters."

So, it was not the book I was expecting to write. It was not the book that people were expecting to get. It was not the book my publisher expected to get. But I think in every case, it was absolutely the book that needed to be done. I think everybody who's read it so far has had the same sort of response. It's like: "Thank you for writing something where I can forget the world for as long it takes to read." And I'm like: "You're welcome. But honestly, I didn't do it for you guys. I really did it for me, and I'm glad it works for you too."

GE: It really does. The opening both engages with what was happening in 2020, and at the same time, there's a strong sense of wonder, which serves as a true anodyne right now. Thank you for that.

All right, we've reached the end of the interview. Is there anything you'd like to add? Any closing thoughts for the readers of *Galaxy's Edge*?

JS: Look around. Obviously, look around in the pages of *Galaxy's Edge*, but look around beyond there. We are really in a new golden age of science fiction. The writing now is as good and as vital as it has ever been in science fiction. We are getting so many new writers and new perspectives and new stories and new worlds that is really an embarrassment of riches. I'm happy as a writer to be writing in this period, not only because I get to know all these cool writers, but what their writing inspires me both as a reader and as someone who is like: "Oh wow, they're doing such a good job, I've got to…not so much like a competition of step up the game, but this is the landscape. How do we do this?"

It feels the same way that I think musicians feel when someone drops an amazing album, and you're like: "What? This is where we get to be right now? Holy crap!" Then you'd be like, "Yes, I see what you did, but watch this." Having that happen, at such a high level right now in science fiction and fantasy, and in speculative fiction in general, is such a privilege as a reader and is such a privilege as a writer that every day I look around at what my friends and peers are doing, and I'm just like: "How did I luck out to be doing what I do right now?" So, readers of *Galaxy's Edge*, be cognizant of the fact that this is some of the best of times that we've ever had in the genre.

Copyright © 2022 by Jean Marie Ward.

Richard Chwedyk sold his first story in 1990, won a Nebula in 2002, and has been active in the field for the past thirty-two years.

RECOMMENDED BOOKS

by Richard Chwedyk

IT AIN'T WHAT YOU KNOW

"Science fiction isn't what it used to be."

I keep hearing this, usually but not exclusively, from older members of the community. I can at times understand it, even sympathize with it. Things just ain't what they used to be. Time was, so say some, when you knew who the big writers were, and they were doing what you wanted them to do. You knew the history and you knew all the quirks and corners. Not so anymore. Time was, you knew where you stood. You knew your stuff.

I for one welcome our not-like-it-used-to-be authors, not because the new work dishonors the past (did I mention the grumblers feel disrespected too?). It cannot help but build upon that past. What it tries not to do is to repeat it. A "literature of change" *has* to change by its very nature. If it feels too comfortable or familiar, it's not doing its job. We'd no longer be following a vital form of literature, but preserving an artifact.

There are times in reading when I feel thoroughly confounded. And that's good. In all the imaginative literatures, but especially science fiction, it's not what you know—it's what you *don't* know that makes all the difference. As a favorite writer of mine from outside the field, Nelson Algren, used to say, "Any writer who knows what he's doing isn't doing very much."

The authors of the works noted below may know what they're doing, or not, but they're doing a lot.

◆ ◆ ◆

Sweep of Stars
by Maurice Broaddus
Tor
March 2022
ISBN: 978-1-250-26493-0

I've been waiting for this book for a while. I'm familiar with some of Broaddus's other writings and was excited to see what he would do with a now-familiar form like a science fiction epic trilogy. I am not disappointed.

The beginning has the now-common lists of characters and time line that you're going to skip back to later but you have no time for now. You want to see how the novel opens and if it will compel you to keep reading until you reach the final page:

> Your name is Leah Adisa. For now.

> Choosing a name for yourself is not something to be entered into lightly. It is a promise you make to the universe. Or it to you. A name is the story of yourself you present to the world, a label to define you. That is the entire point of the Naming Ceremony: you are finally of age to interpret yourself and into the Muungano community as a full free member.

The paragraphs that follow continue to orient you to a world you've not encountered in a novel before: the African-based hegemony (of sorts) of the Muungano people, which extends from Earth to Titan, and a little further to a mining colony named Oyigiyigi. We may be familiar with spacefaring empires extending to the outer planets, but we've usually seen them from a Western perspective, a sort of continuation of "American" middle-class culture, or

how Octavia Butler once put it, "The same as now, only more so." In this novel, we're not just discovering new worlds but old worlds seen in new ways, from a new perspective. We're discovering what, for we readers, is a whole new culture.

It's not as if this hasn't been attempted before, but Broaddus seems to have found the right angle or point of view from which to address we readers that neither frustrates us with opaque "strangeness" or presumes we are simpletons who need every little detail explained. The result is a clarity of narrative that is truly splendid.

And that narrative is…complex. To say the least. You expect that in a trilogy. But that same angle or point of view, or better still, that *voice*, never leaves you confused as it shifts from setting to setting and person to person.

And I was intensely impressed with Broaddus's focus upon his people. He has great insight into human concerns, their desires and needs, how they express them and how they attempt to conceal them. Some authors of this sort of work become so overwhelmed by their own world building, they can only manage to "populate" their novels. With *Sweep of Stars*, one gets the feeling this story began with the people. The world came later, or simultaneously, so the human scale is never lost.

Sweep of Stars exercises the best traditions of science fiction while providing new perspectives and redefining the expectations we place upon such works. Some readers may find it rough going, but I encourage them to stay with it. On rare occasions, even for science fiction readers, one encounters a book that truly changes the way one sees the world, yesterday, today and most certainly tomorrow. I believe this is one of them.

Star Eater

by Kerstin Hall
Tordotcom
June 2021
ISBN: 978-1-250-62531-1

Fantasy readers, I can guarantee you have never read a novel like this. I can extend that guarantee to everyone else who may be curious. The borders between fantasy, science fiction, and horror are here either discarded or ignored. And to you aspiring writers out there: remember all those things your esteemed writing teachers said you can never get away with? Well, Kerstin Hall gets away with most of them. Honestly, I don't know how. I suspect she does it through a modicum of chutzpah and a great deal of skill.

Something about this novel reminded me of one of those profound pronouncements Marlow makes in Conrad's "Heart of Darkness": about "The fascination of the abomination." But not in a bad way. I will add, though, that some other reviewers have added trigger warnings to their comments, and they can be justified. There are some really rough scenes in here. Be warned.

But…what can be expected from a novel where, if someone were to ask you what it was about, you'd say something like, "Well, it takes place in a city that's elevated over the world, because on the surface all the men have become zombies. In the city, there's a sisterhood that acquires magic through cannibalism, and once they have it the magic is manifested in lace. Literally, lace. And that's just the background for some really Machiavellian intrigue."

And if this someone asks you further, "Well, who are the good guys?" you will most likely answer, "Well, I'm still trying to figure that out."

The thing is, you're still fascinated by these people, either because they have real human facets that accompany these atrocious activities, or because you keep turning pages, muttering to yourself, "They can't *possibly* get away with that! Can they?"

They can, with Kerstin Hall telling the tale, and doing so with masterful precision.

❖❖❖

Destroyer of Light

by Jennifer Marie Brissett
Tor
October 2021
ISBN: 978-1-250-26865-5

As with Kerstin Hall's novel, readers should take note that there's some strong stuff here.

Aspects of this story will strike you as familiar, and I'm not referring to its reimagining of the Persephone myth. Aliens boot us off our planet, genetically modify us and relocate us to a world called Eleusis, where things go "not as planned" from the get-go. There are three habitable areas of the planet, named Day, Dusk and Night. Resources, material and intellectual, and some things more, are not equally distributed. And often, this situation, rather than encouraging cooperation, spawns greed and violence.

We may have read versions of this kind of thing before (suddenly, I'm remembering a Bradbury story called "Frost and Fire"), but not in this way. The central character, Cora, is sympathetic enough, as you might expect, but also enigmatic, but not in any bad way. She is, after all, Persephone, and everything we encounter on Eleusis is a little bent, a little twisted, like what we might encounter through Lewis Carroll's looking glass if it were being held by James Tiptree Jr. I'm not saying Brissett writes like Tiptree, but her vision shares that same uncompromising intensity.

When you're dealing with myths, it's difficult to be otherwise. To paraphrase R. A. Lafferty, the myths aren't inside us; we are inside them, struggling to get out.

You won't "get" this book on a first read. It will haunt you, though. And that's likely one of the things in *Destroyer of Light* that goes exactly as planned, by Brissett.

The Reinvented Heart
edited by Cat Rambo and Jennifer Brozek
Caezik
March 2022
ISBN: 978-1-64710-042-1

Last November, when I went to Windycon, my first "in person" convention in what seemed like ages, I very often heard a word that I really hadn't encountered much at conventions heretofore: "Romance."

And that word being used in the denotation of a literary category: those books in the store with the label "Romance" on the spine. Many of us in fandom made fun of those books. We believed them all to have been built on a steadfast, indestructible narrative skeleton: young woman of modest means falls in love with a handsome young man of higher social status, or some other condition which seems to doom their relationship, though the young man reciprocates her feelings. Whatever, their hardships are overcome by the last page and the beautiful couple prepare for a lifetime of happiness. Thousands of novels were built on that skeleton, and billions of copies of those novels were sold. They were reliable. And predictable. And we made fun of them. Their fungible structure seemed a polar opposite of what science fiction was all about. They were allegedly more predictable than Nancy Drew, the Hardy Boys, or Tom Swift.

But the picture was never quite that simple. At least a couple of new generations of readers have grown up since we callow old fogies sniffed at the romance market. Many new science fiction readers began by reading romance novels, then switched over to several of the many "cross-genre" variations, like romances set in fantasy worlds or science-fictional universes. Not to mention the explosion of romances catering to a number of diverse, non-traditional audiences. And many of the newer writers in our field not only got their start in the romance market, but they maintain a presence in that genre while doing other work in ours.

All of that is to say that we should no longer be surprised at having romance fiction discussed at SF cons. It's here. Get used to it.

And frankly, I'm not really sure if the preceding tangent of mine has any relevance to the brilliant anthology edited by Cat Rambo and Jennifer Brozek, *The Reinvented Heart*, but I started there, so be it.

The marvelous thing about this anthology is that it left me far removed from the simple definitions of what we're talking about when we talk about "relationships," romantic or otherwise.

In her foreword, Rambo quotes the call to authors she made for this book:

> Science fiction often thinks about the technology without considering the ways social structures will change as tech changes—or not. What will relationships look like in the future when we have complications like clones, uploaded intelligences, artificial brains, or body augmentation? What happens when emotions like love and friendship span vast distances—in space, in time, and in the heart? And as we acknowledge differences in gender in a way we never have before, what stories are finally given the space in which to emerge?

Any sort of devoted reader of science fiction will no doubt immediately recall any number of stories—by Octavia Butler, or Sturgeon, or Delany, or Sheckley, or Le Guin, or Tiptree, to name just a few—that already address what Rambo and Brozek were looking for, but you'll have to admit that those gems are rare—exquisite, but rare.

The marvelous thing about this anthology is how successful the editors were in their search to increase this number. This is all fine work, written with great skill, great intelligence, great wit and, perhaps most of all, a discerning and sympathetic eye for the way change can seem at once surprising and inevitable in this world (and any other world you choose to imagine). My favorites, not necessarily the best, works are by Rosemary Claire Smith, Lyda Morehouse, Naomi Kritzer, Fran Wilde, Lauren Ring, Sam Fleming, Xander Odell and Devin Miller. The three sections: "Hearts," "Hands" and "Minds" are prefaced with poems by Jane Yolen. One need say no more.

Full disclosure: yes, it's published by Caezik, but I would have grabbed up this anthology no matter who published it. Dozens of themed anthologies come out every year. This one is significantly a keeper.

◆ ◆ ◆

Drunkard's Walk
by Frederik Pohl
Ballantine Books (first book publication; previously serialized in *Galaxy* magazine)
1960

You may be puzzled at my choice for a not-so-recent novel worthy of attention this time. After all, for an author like Frederik Pohl, the works that would first come to mind might be *Gateway*, or *The Space Merchants* (co-authored with C.M. Kornbluth), or any of a dozen other novels for which Pohl is already well known. In this respect, to choose one of them would be a cheat, for if you are an enthusiastic reader of science fiction (as I know you are), you are already familiar with these works (or should be).

I have a suspicion that this novel may not be familiar to even some of Mr. Pohl's most ardent fans.

Also, it happens to be a work about which I was corresponding with Pohl's widow, Dr. Betty Anne Hull, shortly before her health took a turn for the worse last year, when we lost her. I was telling her about how pleased I was at finally acquiring a copy after the college where I teach, in its infinite wisdom, decided to pitch this volume with about half of its entire fiction collection, not knowing (I guess their wisdom is finite after all) that their edition was a rare Gnome Press hardcover published after the first Ballantine paperback came out. My college's loss was, perhaps, Goodwill's gain. Book collectors out there: be on the lookout.

I stumbled upon the novel when my teacherly duties were getting the better of me and I wandered the aisles, as I often do, when my frustrations compel me to look at almost anything other than the assignments I'm supposed to be reading. Frederik Pohl was obviously a familiar name, but I'd never heard of *Drunkard's Walk*. Well, I pulled it off the shelf and started reading it. And after I read it once I kept going back to it, whenever I needed a break from the endless deluge of first-person present tense student narratives that narrate scarce little.

Is *Drunkard's Walk* a lost masterpiece? Unlikely. But it is a prime example of one of Pohl's greatest strengths as a writer, though it is a strength that is rarely noticed even by his biggest fans: his voice.

And by voice I mean that quality that renders even a "third person" into a character, a storyteller. And the storyteller was communicating directly to *you*, the reader, whoever you may be. He may have best demonstrated this "sense of address," as we used to call it in my undergraduate fiction workshops (thank you, John Schultz), in his famous short story, "Day Million," but it is present in almost everything he wrote. In some works, like *Drunkard's Walk*, brilliance with voice shines on nearly every page.

Suppose you are a picture on his wall—perhaps the portrait of Leibniz, taken from Fiquet's old engraving. Out of the eyes under your great curled wig you see this young man stand up and walk slowly toward his window.

His room is eighteen stories up.

If a picture on the wall can remember, you remember that this is not the first time. If a picture on the wall can know things, you know that he has tried to leap out of that window before, and he is about to try again.

He is trying to kill himself. He has tried nine times in the past fifty days.

If a picture on the wall can regret, you regret this. It is a terrible waste for this man to keep trying to kill himself, since he does not at all want to die.

There is something incredibly effective about ascribing the witnessing of a presumed suicide attempt to a portrait on the wall—the sense of isolation, of aloneness. And it's done in present tense. The funny thing is that even though the young man, a math professor named Cornut, is apparently alone, he isn't. There is another witness in the room, as we find out a little later. But without giving too much away let me say that for Pohl to take this narrative approach is perfectly logical and perfectly appropriate. The prose is an echo to the paranoiac tone of the story.

The story? Yes, it's about subtle, intrusive suggestion of the sort we've all become accustomed to since the middle of the previous century: how to alter thinking without our being aware of it—but suggestion used to much more nefarious ends.

Does the tale creak with anachronisms, predicting a future from six decades before our time? Yes, you can find them, but not as many as you might suspect, since Pohl has constructed a future quite unlike the futures his colleagues at the time (and in truth, Pohl himself) would have imagined. It's a subtly authoritarian world, hierarchical, and the further up you go in the hierarchy, the more it feels like paradise. And such elevated status affords you medical treatment that promises the next best thing to immortality. This disparity is played strongly by understatement. And of course, there are consequences. All good stories are about consequences.

Two aspects of this world should resonate with contemporary readers to a surprising degree of familiarity, conceived as this story was over sixty years ago: the use of TV/video in college teaching (think not only of those recent, often disastrous, Zoom sessions, but the many video courses offered by big-name celebrity authors and artists, selling the "secrets" of instant best sellerdom or whatever) and pandemic plagues spreading like wildfire across the world taking millions upon millions of lives.

Even old mirrors can reflect the present moment.

And now, reading *Drunkard's Walk*, I can't help thinking as well of Professor Hull—Betty Anne—and the brilliance of her husband.

The memories of those two are great blessings.

L. Penelope is the award-winning author of the Earthsinger Chronicles. The first book in the series, Song of Blood & Stone, was chosen as one of TIME *Magazine's 100 Best Fantasy Books of All Time. Equally left and right-brained, she studied filmmaking and computer science in college and sometimes dreams in HTML. She hosts the My Imaginary Friends podcast and lives in Maryland with her husband and furry dependents. Visit her at: http://www.lpenelope.com.*

LONGHAND

by L. Penelope

FROM INSPIRATION TO MANUSCRIPT: DEVELOPING STORY IDEAS

The most frequently asked question I receive as a writer is, "Where do you get your ideas?" While the answer is different for each author, it's also universal—ideas come from everywhere. Life is an idea factory and all you need to do is pay attention.

A few months ago, while in Vermont for my anniversary trip, my husband and I were driving across a bridge. I peered out over Lake Champlain, not thinking about anything in particular, and *boom!*, an idea popped into my head. Who's to say where it actually came from—would crossing any body of water have given me the same inspiration or was it that water, that bridge, that day? The idea was small, just a tiny seed, no plot, no characters, no theme—nothing but the hint of what it could be.

At the time, I was finishing another manuscript and beginning the process of idea generation for the next stand-alone novel in my contract with my publisher. This brand-new shiny idea seemed like the perfect one to follow up the book I had just completed.

There are many ways an idea can present itself. I almost never have fully formed characters appear in my mind ready to tell me their story. Usually I get a phrase or question or situation. I can often trace the moment of inspiration back to an event—a movie I watched that kept playing in my head after the credits rolled, or a dream I had, or a song that moved me. Author Elizabeth Gilbert says in her book, *Big Magic*, "The universe buries strange jewels deep within us all, and then stands back to see if we can find them."

So once you unearth your own strange jewel, how do you go about honing it and turning it into something beautiful? Now keep in mind, I am a plotter, or a story architect, as opposed to someone who writes by the seat of their pants, or "gardens," and allows their story to grow without an outline. So all of my experiences are through that lens. But even if the thought of outlining gives you hives, pantsers still need to go from idea spark to flame.

My first step is to identify what is exciting about the idea. That spark or jewel resonates with you in some way, which is why it's burning so brightly in your mind. One such idea for me several years ago was a "what if" question: "What if a girl fell in love with an invisible boy?" That idea was so bright that I wrote two different manuscripts addressing that question in different ways with totally different worlds and characters.

My current process is to brainstorm why the idea made me light up. I'll use a notebook or a mind mapping application to capture everything I want to explore about a given idea. If I'm not sure of the genre, that usually becomes clear quickly and working this way can also suggest characters or story situations.

Brainstorming often leads to research, which is a backbone of my idea honing process. I found the characters and plot of my upcoming novel, *The Monsters We Defy*, during the research. The spark for that book was, "Harlem Renaissance era fantasy heist." That's all I knew. It was easy to identify what excited me about the idea—basically everything that phrase suggests.

The genre was ingrained in the idea spark, but I still had to do a fair amount of research there because I hadn't written a heist story before. I needed to ensure I knew the structure and audience expectations. I "filled the well" by watching movies and reading other heist novels to get inspiration and develop a sense of building blocks I would need to use.

Scenes and potential situations came to mind, but it wasn't until I dug deep into researching the time period and the societal issues that I discovered who and what I was going to be writing about. This is certainly true with a historical novel, but even in second world fantasy, or any of the other subgenres I've dabbled in, research is a large part of architecting a story.

Worldbuilding requires research to design everything from magic systems, technology, culture, mythology, folklore, and countless other aspects. Part of finding those jewels buried inside of us requires falling down rabbit holes and exploring everything that catches your fancy. This process can be chaotic; finding a balance between letting your mind run free and keeping your goal in mind is key. Especially when time is a factor. Idea generation is difficult to do on a schedule. The process can take several months to several years depending on the writer and the idea. Publishing contracts can compress the process (especially when you've sold a book you haven't even conceived of yet) so as much as you need mental freedom, you also need boundaries.

Creating a system to record all the ideas, notes, and research is key. I brainstorm in multiple places: a physical notebook, a text file, spreadsheets, plotting software, voice memos, etc. I want to be sure I can catch every idea because the process of capturing them is almost more important than being able to find that specific note later, which, in my case, can be difficult. With research notes, I try to be more organized and note the source in case I need to return to it later.

After brainstorming and research, it's time to wrangle the story into submission and apply a structure to it. You can plan and daydream and design forever, but the point of this is to create a finished product in your lifetime. At this point, the story could go in nearly infinite directions, so finding some fixed points is very helpful. For me, this means going back to the spark and why it lit me up in the first place and holding that in the forefront of my mind. That way, I can weigh every potential story path and character arc against the initial inspiration.

The next step is to identify the main turning points of the story. I like to run it through at least one, often many, story structure systems or beat sheets. For this, I turn to one, often many, of my craft books and start to build the scaffold that will hold up the narrative. Story beats and character arcs need to work

together and be woven along with theme. I often bounce back and forth between developing the plot and the character to make sure they're intertwined.

The last step is just to tell myself the story. Once I know the major turning points, I can then visualize the narrative, allowing it to play in my mind like a movie. I write everything I see in a very messy synopsis that encapsulates the entire thing. You can't edit a blank page, so I don't worry about how muddled or disorganized this synopsis draft is. I just need to get it all out of my head. I'm constantly testing the character development against the plot development and ensuring that they all lead back to the theme, or if I haven't identified the theme, at least all of these elements lead back to that original spark.

Once the synopsis is complete, I'm ready to write. I use the same process for short stories or full-length fantasy novels, though condensed or elongated as the situation requires. Building a story from spark to flame, from rough jewel to honed gem is hard work. Don't we all wish that the Muse poured the completed tale from our fingers directly onto the keyboard without months or years of struggle? But developing the idea is the journey, and the final product is the destination. Of course, this is just the way things work for me. There are as many ways to accomplish this as there are writers with stories to tell.

Copyright © 2022 by L. Penelope.

HARRY TURTLEDOVE

ORIGINALLY WRITING AS H. N. TURTELTAUB

*Harry Turtledove writes alternate history, science fic-
tion, fantasy and historical fiction and has won a Hugo
Award, two Sidewise Awards for alternate history, and
the Hal Clement Award for YA science fiction. With more
than a hundred books, a couple of hundred pieces of short
fiction, as well as a translation of a Byzantine chronicle
and four academic articles published throughout his career,
Turtledove also ended up with a doctorate in Byzantine
history from UCLA. He wrote his dissertation alongside
the first novel he sold. Along with teaching at UCLA, Cal
State Fullerton, and Cal State Los Angeles, he worked as a
technical writer for the Los Angeles County Office of Education before resigning from that job to freelance in 1991.
He is married to Laura Frankos, herself a writer. They
have three daughters (one also a published author) and
two granddaughters. Two cats, Boris and Hotspur, run
the household with iron, clawed fists.*

OVER THE WINE-DARK SEA

by Harry Turtledove

X

Menedemos was like a child with a new toy. "We'll make the family rich with this run!" he said. "We'll throw grain into the *Aphrodite* till we're down to about a digit's worth of freeboard, and we'll get paid for it as if we were that full of fine wine. What could be better?"

His cousin, predictably, was like a mother watching her son play with a sword he thought was a toy. "What could be better?" Sostratos said. "Not getting sunk could be better. So could not getting caught. Not getting killed. Not getting sold into slavery. Not getting gelded. If you give me a little while, I can probably think of some more things."

"Oh, nonsense." It wasn't altogether nonsense, as Menedemos knew. But he didn't want to dwell on that. Had he dwelt on it, he would have been just like Sostratos. He had trouble imagining a fate less appealing—or, for that matter, a fate less interesting.

As a brisk, hot breeze from out of the north pushed the *Aphrodite* ahead of it towards Rhegion, Sostratos scowled. Sostratos, in fact, did everything but stamp his foot on the timbers of the poop deck. "It isn't nonsense. What you want to do is senseless. We already have a profit. This is a needless risk."

"We'll be fine." Menedemos did his best to sound soothing. "From what Xenodokos said, there'll be a whole fleet down at Rhegion. The polluted Carthaginians can't nab everybody."

"Why not?" Sostratos retorted. "And you didn't see Xenodokos setting out for Syracuse, did you? Not likely! He went the other way. I wish we would, too."

"You worry too much," Menedemos said. "You were jumping up and down about putting in at Cape Tainaron, too, and that worked out fine. Why shouldn't this?"

"We weren't sailing into the middle of a war when we put in at Cape Tainaron," his cousin answered. "You're just asking for trouble."

"The wind should be with us and against the Carthaginians," Menedemos said. "We'll just slide right into the harbor at Syracuse along with all the round ships—and if the barbarians do get after this fleet, they'll have an easier time catching round ships than they will with us."

Sostratos exhaled angrily. "All right. All right, by the gods. You're going to act like an idiot—I can see that. You lust for this the same way you lusted for that Tarentine's wife. But promise me one thing, at least."

"What is it?" Menedemos asked.

"This: if Xenodokos is wrong, if there is no fleet of merchantmen gathering at Rhegion, you won't load the *Aphrodite* up with grain and try to sneak into Syracuse all by your lonesome."

"We might have a better chance that way," Menedemos said. Then he saw just how furious Sostratos looked. He threw his hands in the air. "Oh, very well. If there is no grain fleet, we'll head for home. There! Are you satisfied now?"

"Satisfied? No," Sostratos said. "I won't be satisfied till we do sail for home. But that is a little better—a very little better—than nothing."

Menedemos didn't think it was anything of the sort. The more he thought of tiptoeing into Syracuse past the Carthaginian fleet, the better he liked it. A man could dine out on such stories for the rest of his life. But he'd gone and given his word, and he felt obliged to keep it.

I hope there's a fleet at Rhegion, he thought. *There'd better be a fleet at Rhegion, because I want to do this.* Sostratos was right, and Menedemos was honest enough with himself to admit it: he did lust after going to Syracuse the same way he lusted after some frisky young wife he'd chanced to see.

"Remember," Sostratos said, "whatever else you do, you're not supposed to risk the ship."

"I don't intend to risk the ship," Menedemos snapped, wishing Sostratos hadn't put it quite that way, "and I'm the one who judges when the ship's being risked and when it isn't. You aren't. Have you got that, O cousin of mine?"

"Yes, I have it." Sostratos looked as if he liked it about as much as a big mouthful of bad fish. He stormed down off the poop deck and up toward the bow. *Daft*, Menedemos thought. *Daft as Aias after he didn't get Akhilleus' armor. Anybody who'd rather deal with peafowl chicks than stand around and talk has to be daft.*

The peafowl chicks! Menedemos brightened. "*Oë*, Sostratos!" he called.

Reluctantly, Sostratos turned back toward him. "What is it?"

"How much do you think young peafowl will bring in Syracuse?"

"I don't know," Sostratos answered. "How much do you think they would bring in Carthage?" Having got the last word, he went on up to the little foredeck.

When Menedemos steered the *Aphrodite* into the harbor at Rhegion, he anxiously scanned the quays. If things looked no busier than usual, he would have to sail on toward Rhodes. He let out a whoop on seeing a couple of dozen large round ships all tied up together. If that wasn't a fleet in the making, he didn't know what was.

His cousin saw the ships, too, and also knew them for what they were. The look he gave Menedemos was baleful. Menedemos grinned back, which, by Sostratos' expression, only annoyed him more.

With a handful of men at the oars to put the merchant galley exactly where he wanted her, Menedemos guided her toward the quays alongside which the round ships floated. "Go somewhere else!" a man called from the stern of the nearest big, tubby merchantman. "We're all together here, loading up on grain for Agathokles."

"That's what I'm here for, too," Menedemos said as Diokles eased the *Aphrodite* up against the pier.

"You?" The fellow on the round ship laughed loud and long, displaying a couple of teeth gone black in the front of his mouth. "We can carry eight or ten times as much in the *Leuke* here as you can in that miserable little boat. Take your toy home and sail it in your hip-bath." He laughed again.

"Toy? Hip-bath?" Menedemos was tempted to yell, *Back oars!* and then spurt forward to ram the round ship. How much grain would that sneering fellow carry then? But, unfortunately, no. It wouldn't do. Menedemos said, "However much or little we haul, Syracuse'll still get more with us than without us—and Agathokles'll pay us for it, too, same as he'll pay you."

"Well, all right. When you put it like that, I suppose you've got something," the other Hellene said. "And when the Carthaginians come after us, you can be the one who fights 'em off." He laughed again, louder than ever.

But he wasn't laughing by the time the *Aphrodite*'s crew finished screaming abuse and the details of their battle with the Roman trireme at him. He was white with fury, his fists clenched, his lips skinned back from his teeth. He had to stand there and take it, as did the other sailors on his ship. Had they chosen to answer back, the men from the akatos would have made them regret it—for, while the round ship held more cargo, the merchant galley held more crewmen.

A fellow wearing an unusually fine, unusually white wool chiton bustled up the pier toward the *Aphrodite*. "Are you here to carry grain to Syracuse?" he asked.

"We certainly are," Menedemos answered—this chap, unlike the man aboard the round ship, looked to have some clout. "Who are you, sir?"

"My name is Onasimos," replied the fellow with the fancy tunic. He also, Menedemos saw, had buckles on his sandals that looked like real gold. With a bow, he continued, "I have the honor to be the Syracusan proxenos here in Rhegion, and I'm doing what I can to help the polis I represent."

In normal times, a proxenos looked out for the interests of citizens of the polis he represented in the polis in which he dwelt. He was, necessarily, a man of some wealth and importance in his home town. He might aid in lawsuits. He might, at need, lend money. He got no pay for his services, only prestige and business connections. When the polis he represented was in danger, he might do extraordinary things, as Onasimos looked to be doing now.

"How do we get the grain?" Menedemos asked him.

"It's in the warehouses," Onasimos said. "Gods be praised, Great Hellas had a good harvest this past spring. I have plenty of slaves and free men ready to bring it aboard for you."

"Good." Menedemos dipped his head. "Now—about arrangements for payment."

"You've probably heard Agathokles is offering four times the going rate for grain delivered to Syracuse," Onasimos said.

Menedemos tossed his head. "I hadn't heard exactly how much he offered, as a matter of fact. But I have heard a lot of Agathokles himself—including the way he got rid of the Syracusans who weren't of his faction earlier this year. Anyone who could come up with that little scheme wouldn't think twice about going back on a promise to pay a merchant skipper."

The Syracusan proxenos looked pained. "I assure you, my dear fellow—"

But Menedemos tossed his head again. "Don't assure me, O best one. Let me ask some of the other captains and see what I find out."

Had Onasimos called his bluff and told him to go ahead, he might have believed the proxenos' protests. As things were, Onasimos sighed and said, "Oh, very well. I'll pay you the going rate now, and you can collect the rest on delivery."

"I'm sorry." Menedemos tossed his head for a third time. "The going rate isn't enough to make me want to risk the Carthaginian fleet. I know the Carthaginians are supposed to be splendid torturers, but I don't want to find out how they do what they do for myself."

He waited to see what Onasimos would say to that. The proxenos glared at him. He smiled his sweetest smile in return. Onasimos sighed again. "You're one of the canny ones, I see. All right, then—one and a half times the going rate in advance, but not an obolos more. If I give you everything promised ahead of time, you might just sail off with the grain and never go near Syracuse."

Menedemos thought about squeezing the proxenos some more. He glanced toward Sostratos. His cousin ignored him—Sostratos wanted no part of the Syracusan venture. Menedemos sent him a covert dirty look. He wanted to know what Sostratos thought, for his cousin was often better at haggling with these fancy types then he was himself. But Sostratos seemed determined to sulk.

That left it up to Menedemos. Onasimos had a point. Some men, with silver in their hands, *would* sail away from Syracuse. *Not me, of course*, Menedemos thought. But Onasimos didn't, couldn't, know that. "All right," Menedemos said. "One and a half times the going rate it is. Sostratos!"

His cousin jumped. "What?"

"You'll keep count of how many sacks of grain Onasimos' men bring aboard the *Aphrodite* here," Menedemos said. "As soon as we get paid our first installment for hauling them, we're off with the rest of the fleet."

"I'll have a man of my own doing the counting," Onasimos said.

"Good." Menedemos smiled that sweet smile at him. "I'm sure his count and Sostratos' will match very closely, then." The Syracusan proxenos' answering smile looked distinctly forced. *He was going to try to cheat me*, Menedemos thought. *Why am I not surprised?*

Muttering under his breath, Onasimos tramped back down the pier. About half an hour later, a line of men carrying leather sacks, each with a talent of grain, came out from the interior of Rhegion. "Where do you want these?" asked the man heading up the line. He carried no sack himself; he was obviously the fellow who would do the counting for Onasimos.

"Sostratos!" Menedemos called, and Sostratos, still seeming just this side of mutinous, went up onto the pier and stood beside Onasimos' man. For that worthy's benefit, Menedemos continued, "Now—I'll want you to start at the stern, just forward of the poop deck, and work toward the bow, one row of sacks at a time, till she holds as much grain as she can."

"Right," Onasimos' man said, and shouted orders at the men he was in charge of. They came down the gangplank and started loading the grain.

By the time they finished, the *Aphrodite* rode a great deal lower in the water. That worried Menedemos. Not only the extra weight but also the extra amount of hull now in the sea would slow the merchant galley. She didn't need to be slow, not when she might have to flee from Carthaginian warships. But he couldn't blame Onasimos for wanting to put as much grain into her as he could: the proxenos was doing his best to feed the people of the city he served.

"How many sacks of grain did we take on?" Menedemos asked once the last sweating hauler left the akatos.

"By my count, 797 sacks," Sostratos answered.

Onasimos' man sneered. "I reckoned it as 785." Sostratos bristled. Anyone who accused him of inaccuracy was asking for trouble.

Menedemos had no time for that kind of trouble. He said, "We'll split the difference. What does that come to?"

Sostratos counted on his fingers, his lips moving. "It would be 791," he said. "But I still think this fellow—"

"Never mind," Menedemos broke in. He nodded to Onasimos' man. "Tell your master we've got 791 sacks of grain aboard. As soon as we get paid, we're ready to go. Agreed?"

"Agreed," the other said. "Some of these round ships hold more than ten times as many sacks as that, you know."

"Every bit helps," Menedemos replied. Onasimos' man dipped his head and went back into Rhegion as his master had before him: to get money, Menedemos hoped.

Diokles said, "I hope the wind stays with us. The men'll break their backs and their hearts rowing with us laden like this, and she'll handle like a raft—if we're lucky, that is."

"If the wind fails, we're not going anywhere, not with all these round ships," Menedemos said. "They have to sail."

"Mm, that's so," the oarmaster agreed. He flashed Menedemos a sassy grin. "In that case, skipper, maybe we ought to hope for south winds for the next three months, so Syracuse falls, we don't have to come close to all those Carthaginian war galleys, and we pick up a nice pile of silver anyway."

"You sounds like Sostratos," Menedemos said, and Diokles' grin got wider and even more provocative. Menedemos mimed throwing something at him and went on, "I wouldn't mind getting paid for doing nothing, either—who would? But if we don't get to deliver the grain, they'll just take it off and make us cough up the money again."

"If we were proper pirates, we'd sneak out of the harbor if that looked like happening," the keleustes said. "We're a galley, after all. We could do it."

"We *could*, sure enough." Menedemos wished Diokles hadn't put the idea in his mind. It was tempting. But he had no trouble finding reasons it wouldn't work: "You said it yourself—we'll be slow as a cart-ox with all this grain aboard. And my bet is, Rhegion would send her navy after us if we made off with the grain *and* the money. This Onasimos fellow looks to pull a lot of weight here."

"Well, so he does," Diokles said. "All right, then. I'd sooner pray for fair winds than foul, anyway."

"So would I," Menedemos said.

✧

Sostratos thought of himself as a modern, rational man. He'd been embarrassed to spend the past couple of days praying for contrary winds. And he'd been embarrassed all over again to have his prayer fail so ignominiously, for a fine breeze blew from the north this morning. *So much for the gods*, he thought, *and a solid point for rationalism.*

Menedemos was up before dawn, too, smiling at the sky. *He'd* probably been praying for fair winds, so his belief in the gods was bound to be vindicated, too. That thought made Sostratos grumpier than ever. But, instead of gloating, Menedemos just pointed to the thin crescent moon rising a little ahead of the sun. "Another month almost done," he said.

"Sure enough." Sostratos peered into the brightening twilight between that little cheese-paring of a moon and the horizon. "And there's Aphrodite's wandering star."

"Why, so it is," Menedemos said. "Sure enough, your eyes aren't so bad if you can pick it out against the bright sky. The sun's almost up."

"I knew where to look," Sostratos answered with a shrug. "It's been sliding down the morning sky toward the sun for weeks now. Before too long, we'll see it in the evening instead. People used to think the evening appearance was a different star from the morning one—the same with Hermes' wandering star."

"What do you mean, used to?" Menedemos said. "Half our sailors probably still believe that."

"I meant educated people," Sostratos said. "The sailors are fine men, but…" Most of them thought of little save women (or, with a few, boys), wine, and tavern brawls. *How does one talk with such people?* he wondered.

"I like 'em fine," Menedemos said.

"I know." Sostratos did his best not to make that sound like a judgment. Still and all, what did it say about his cousin's taste?

Menedemos didn't seem to notice Sostratos' tone, which was just as well. He said, "We'll sail today."

"I know." Sostratos knew how unhappy he sounded, too, but he couldn't help it. "Do you think we'll make Syracuse by nightfall?"

"*We* would, if we weren't so overloaded," his cousin answered. "These fat scows we'll be keeping company with? Not a chance. We'll put in at one of the Sicilian towns tonight, or spend the night at sea, then go on in the morning."

"All right." Sostratos sighed. "One more night to spend worrying."

"Nothing to worry about," Menedemos said. "What could possibly go wrong?"

Sostratos started to answer. Then he started to splutter. And then he started to laugh. "Oh, no, you don't. You're not going to get me to turn purple and pitch a fit. I'm wise to you, Menedemos."

"A likely story," Menedemos said. They grinned at each other. For a moment, Sostratos forgot how much he wished the *Aphrodite* weren't sailing for Syracuse.

But he couldn't forget for long. All around the harbor, captains were waking up, tasting the breeze, and realizing it would be a good day to sail. They called orders to their crews and to the longshoremen who came down the wharves to cast off their mooring lines and bring them aboard once more. The sailors grunted and heaved at the sweeps even round ships carried, and slowly, a digit at a time, eased the ships away from their berths so they could make sail and head for Sicily.

Seeing their struggles to get started, Sostratos laughed again. "Our rowers may have to work hard, but not that hard."

"You're right." Menedemos waved to a couple of longshoremen. "Over here, too!"

"You're going to take this little thing to Syracuse?" one of the men said as he tossed a line down onto the sacks of grain in the *Aphrodite*'s waist. "Good idea—you can be a boat for all the real ships." He laughed at his own wit.

That sort of remark was as calculated to make Menedemos furious as Menedemos' crack had been to infuriate Sostratos. But Sostratos' cousin only shrugged, saying, "Onasimos likes us well enough to pay us to haul grain." The longshoreman turned away, disappointment on his face. Menedemos raised his voice: "Come on, boys, let's show these round-ship sailors how to row."

Diokles set the stroke. The men—all of them at the oars—pulled as hard as they had in the fight with the Roman trireme. And the *Aphrodite*…moved as if she were traveling through mud, not seawater. Diokles said, "I think this is about as much as we'll get from her, captain."

"Yes, I think you're right," Menedemos agreed. "I'd hoped for a little more, but...." He shrugged.

"She feels different in the water," Sostratos said. "More solid, more as if we were on dry land. She doesn't shift so much underfoot."

"I should hope she doesn't," Menedemos said. "She's carrying twice as much as usual, so the waves don't seem to hit her so hard."

"That's true. We've never really felt what she's like fully laden before, have we?" Sostratos said, and Menedemos tossed his head. The merchant galley didn't have to travel full up to hope for profit, as a round ship did. She carried luxury goods, valuable for their rarity, instead of being a bulk hauler. Now Sostratos got a glimpse of what the usual sailor did on a usual voyage, and found he didn't much care for it.

One by one, the round ships lowered their great sails from their yards. One by one, the sails bellied out and filled with wind. The tubby ships began their southward journey, but not at a pace above a walk. The *Aphrodite*'s sail came down, too, and Menedemos called the rowers off the oars. Before very long, he had to order the men to brail up half the sail; otherwise, the akatos would have shot ahead of the other ships in the fleet despite her load.

When Sostratos let some peafowl chicks out of their cages to exercise, they ran around over the leather sacks of grain as happily as they had over the planking. They picked at spilled wheat as happily as they had at the cockroaches and other bugs that normally infested the *Aphrodite*—not that loading hundreds of sacks of grain onto the vermin had got rid of them.

Once the crew helped chivvy the chicks back into the cages, Sostratos could take a long look at the scenery. Indeed, he had little choice, unless he wanted to find a place to stand and brood. Considering where the *Aphrodite* was going and what she was liable to face when she got there, that didn't strike him as the worst idea in the world, but he refused to give in to it.

Because the merchant galley couldn't make anything close to her usual speed if she wanted to stay with the fleet of round ships, Sostratos had plenty of time to admire each bit of scenery as it passed. There was a great deal of Mount Aitne to admire. Now that Sostratos had seen both Aitne and Mount Ouesouion from fairly close range, he realized how much more massive the Sicilian volcano was than the one on the mainland of Italy. The soil on its slopes and around its base, though, had the same grayish, ashy look he'd seen near Pompaia. The Sicilian vineyards looked very rich, too, though the fields lay fallow under the hot summer sun.

Slowly, slowly, the fleet sailed past Taruomenion and Naxos and Akion. Sostratos looked longingly at each inviting little harbor, and sighed as the *Aphrodite* and the round ships crawled past each one. That summer sun seemed to speed across the sky. Before the fleet reached Katane—the largest polis on the east coast of Sicily except for Syracuse—it set behind the island. Anchors splashed into the water as the captains got ready to spend a night at sea.

"Unless I'm wrong, those merchant skippers wish they were tied up at a quay," Sostratos remarked to Menedemos.

"Well, when you get right down to it, so do I," his cousin answered. "If a storm were to blow up all of a sudden, we'd be in trouble, especially when we're heavy with grain."

"A storm, right now, is the least of our worries." To show what he meant, Sostratos pointed south.

Menedemos tossed his head. "A storm is never the *least* of your worries, not when you're at sea. If you want to worry about the Carthaginians more, I don't suppose I can stop you."

"I wonder how you say, 'Sail ho!' in the Phoenician language," Sostratos said. "Himilkon would know. I wish I were back in the harbor of Rhodes so I could ask him."

"After we deliver the grain and get paid, we'll be going home," Menedemos answered. "You can find out, if you still want to know by then."

He kept his tone light. If he didn't believe everything would go well when the fleet got to Syracuse, he didn't let on. Some of that, no doubt, was to keep the crew from fretting. The rest, Sostratos was convinced, sprang from his cousin's natural self-confidence—or was it arrogance? Menedemos had never yet found himself in a spot from which he couldn't wiggle out, and so seemed convinced he never would.

Sostratos hoped his cousin was right without believing it. That wasn't how things worked. Hoping Menedemos would prove right this particular time seemed a better bet…though not a very good one. *We'll know tomorrow*, Sostratos thought. He wrapped himself in his himation and lay down on the sacks of grain. They were a little more yielding than the planks of the poop deck, if lumpier.

He thought he would worry too much to find sleep, but exhaustion proved stronger. Next thing he knew, Menedemos announced the new day like a rooster. Several sailors let out groans and sleepy curses. Sostratos said, "If I were wearing shoes, I'd throw one at you."

"It's a day worth celebrating," Menedemos said, his voice full of the false heartiness some traders used to sell things that weren't worth buying. "Tonight we'll feast in Syracuse, a polis famed for its feasts wherever Hellenes live."

That made some of the sailors cheer up. It did nothing to raise Sostratos' spirits. For one thing, Syracuse was a city under siege. What kind of feast would the Syracusans be able to make? For another, weren't the *Aphrodite*'s crew and those of the rest of the fleet likelier to make opson for the eels and crabs than to feast off seafood themselves?

But all around the fleet captains were shouting their crews awake, even if none of the others chose to crow. There was Aphrodite's wandering star glowing through the twilight in the east, with the very thinnest sliver of moon not far from it. Were it not for the blazing beacon of the wandering star, Sostratos doubted he would have noticed the moon at all.

Menedemos wasn't worrying about either the moon or Aphrodite's wandering star. Like any captain worthy of the name, he was tasting the wind. "Out of the north, sure enough," he said. "As long as it holds, we can slide right into the northern harbor—the Little Harbor, they call it—at Syracuse."

Well, we could, if it weren't for the Carthaginian war galleys, Sostratos thought. *They're between us and where we want to go, and with oars driving them they don't care which way the wind blows. Those are the things Menedemos conveniently forgets to mention.*

His cousin went right on not mentioning them, too. The crew raised the dripping anchors. They lowered the sail from the yard. The round ships' big sails

were coming down, too, and filling with the fine breeze that would waft them in exactly the direction they were mad enough to choose to go.

Again, the *Aphrodite* felt much more solid, much more stable, in the water than usual. And again, she moved through the water much more slowly than usual. Sostratos went up onto the poop deck. "If we had to," he asked Menedemos, "could we have the men who aren't rowing throw sacks of grain overboard?"

"You mean, to lighten ship if the Carthaginians were chasing us?" Menedemos asked, and Sostratos dipped his head. His cousin shrugged. "We could have them do it. I doubt it would help much."

The answer struck Sostratos as honest if uninspiring. He watched Katane come into view and then disappear behind him. It *was* a good-sized town, bigger than Messene. He clicked his tongue between his teeth. He still thought it would be a good place to pause for, say, twenty or thirty years. But Menedemos didn't care what he thought, and Menedemos was in command. Sostratos wondered why more soldiers led by a bad general didn't simply run away.

He couldn't run away, not in a ship. Katane was too off away to swim to, and a lot of sailors couldn't swim at all. And Sostratos didn't *know* Menedemos was a bad captain. He did, however, have a strong opinion about that.

His cousin was doing all the little things he needed to do to succeed. He had sharp-eyed Aristeidas in the bow as lookout. And, some time past noon, Aristeidas called, "Ship ho! Ship ho dead ahead!" He pointed south, toward Syracuse. There was the city on the mainland. There was the small island of Ortygia, a few plethra offshore and also heavily built up. And there, worse luck, was the Carthaginian fleet blockading the Little Harbor north of Ortygia and the Great Harbor south of the island.

Aristeidas had spoken with the precision a good lookout needed: he'd called, *Ship ho!* and not, *Sail ho!* The Carthaginian war galleys had their masts down; as warships on active duty did, they moved with oars alone, ready to fight at any moment. Only specks in the distance now, they would look bigger all too soon. Sostratos knew that better than he wanted to.

"What do we do now?" he called to Menedemos.

"Hold our course," his cousin answered. "What else can we do?" *Run* sprang to Sostratos' mind again. But Menedemos went on, "I still think we've got a pretty good chance of sneaking into the Little Harbor. The Carthaginians will go after the round ships before they bother us."

"And how do you know that, O sage of the age?" Sostratos demanded.

"For one thing, all the round ships carry a lot more grain than we do," Menedemos answered with surprising patience. "That's what the Carthaginians want to keep from getting into Syracuse. And, for another, we can fight a little bit, and the round ships can't. Why should the Carthaginians make things harder on themselves than they have to?"

All that made a certain amount of sense to Sostratos, but only a certain amount. He pointed toward the oncoming war galleys, which were closing with the fleet of grain carriers at a frightening clip—it certainly frightened him. "Do you really think we can fight *those* even a little bit?" Some of the galleys had two banks of oars—those would be fours. Others had three banks—those would be fives. All of them dwarfed the Roman trireme the *Aphrodite* had crippled. And Sostratos could see how smoothly the rowers handled the oars. These weren't half-trained crews, like the one in that trireme.

"Of course we can," Menedemos said, so heartily that Sostratos knew he was lying in his teeth.

Sostratos couldn't even call his cousin on it, not without disheartening the crew. The Carthaginian galleys scurried toward the round ships like so many scorpions. The sternposts that curved up and forward over their poops like upraised stings added to the resemblance. But the galleys carried their stings at the bow, in their rams. White water foamed from the three horizontal flukes of those rams. Sostratos could see it much more clearly than he would have liked.

But then Aristeidas proved he was indeed a first-rate lookout. "Ships ho!" he sang out. "Ships so off the port bow!" He'd kept looking around while everyone else thought of nothing but the Carthaginian war galleys, and pointed southeast, where another fleet of warships was rounding Ortygia, heading north as fast as their rowers could take them.

"Are those the Carthaginians who'd been patrolling outside the Great Harbor?" Sostratos asked. "If they are, why aren't they coming after us?"

"How should I know?" Menedemos, for the first time, sounded harassed. He'd seemed ready to deal with one fleet. Two…

Sostratos hadn't been ready to deal with even one fleet. He didn't think his cousin had, either, no matter what Menedemos said. But, when he saw something strange, he wanted to find out about it.

And find out about it he did. The Carthaginians had come within three or four stadia before they noticed the compact formation of ships to the east. Then Sostratos heard cries in the harsh Phoenician language. The Carthaginian war galleys forgot all about the fleet of grain ships. They turned their prows to the east, ready to ward off the onslaught they expected from the other ships.

Menedemos whooped for joy. "Those aren't more Carthaginian galleys!" he exclaimed. "Those are Agathokles' ships, sailing out of Syracuse to save us!"

The sailors aboard the *Aphrodite* cheered. They couldn't have been any happier than Sostratos at the thought of those Carthaginian fours and fives bearing down on the akatos, and could know nothing but relief when the enemy fleet's rams turned in a new direction. But then Sostratos said, "If Agathokles aims to rescue us, why aren't his ships turning in on the Carthaginians?"

He'd expected Menedemos to have an answer ready for him. He wasn't ignorant of the sea himself—few Rhodians were—but his cousin knew as much as a man twice his age. All Menedemos said, though, was, "I don't know."

Diokles undoubtedly knew more about the sea than Menedemos. He too sounded baffled: "They're rowing north right on past us, fast as they can go. What *are* they doing?"

"I haven't the faintest notion," Sostratos said. Menedemos dipped his head to show he didn't know, either.

Agathokles' fleet kept on heading north, at the best speed the rowers could make. Again, Sostratos heard shouts from the closest couple of Carthaginian war galleys. He wished he understood the Phoenician language. Before long, though, the Carthaginians' actions showed what was in their minds: they began to row after the ships from Syracuse, forgetting about the round ships they'd been on the point of capturing or sinking.

"They're more worried about Agathokles than they are about us." Menedemos sounded affronted.

But Sostratos said, "Wouldn't you be? Those ships can fight back. This fleet can't."

He waited for Menedemos to tell him the *Aphrodite* certainly could fight back. His cousin only sighed, dipped his head again, and said, "But what's Agathokles *doing*? He's sailing out of the harbor where he's safe, he's sailing away from Carthage, not toward it...." His voice trailed off.

What had to be the same thought struck Sostratos at the same time. "If they go along the north coast of Sicily..." His voiced faded away, too.

Menedemos took up the idea for him: "They can make for Carthage that way. If that's what Agathokles is doing, he's got balls and to spare." He let out an admiring whistle.

"Look at the way the Carthaginians are chasing him," Sostratos said. "They have to think that's what he's after."

"I do believe you young gentlemen are right," Diokles said. "At least, I can't think of anything else Agathokles'd be up to. And he's a son of a whore who's always up to something, if half the stories you hear about him are true."

"That's the truth," Sostratos said. "Look at how he let his enemies leave the polis and then got rid of them."

"He's ready for anything, sure enough," Menedemos said. "Now we've got to get ready to get into Syracuse ourselves."

"We've got to get ready for more than that," Sostratos said.

"How do you mean?" his cousin asked.

"We've got to get ready to see if we get paid."

"Yes, I suppose that does matter," Menedemos agreed.

"Matter?" Sostratos said. "Matter? Now that we've come all this way without getting killed or captured, making what we were promised would almost make up for the fear we went through getting here. Almost—though I can't think of anything else that would even come close."

Menedemos grinned at him and said, "You worry too much." He pulled back on one steering oar and

forward on the other, guiding the *Aphrodite* toward the waiting, welcoming harbor ahead.

☼

"Yes, of course you'll be paid," the Syracusan official said—officiously—as slaves carried sacks of grain off the *Aphrodite* and down the quay into hungry Syracuse. "Come to the palace on Ortygia tomorrow, and you shall have every obolos owed you. So Agathokles promised, and so shall it be."

He spoke as if the sun wouldn't rise if Agathokles broke a promise. Menedemos wondered how the Syracusan tyrant's political enemies felt about that. A moment later, he stopped wondering: being dead, they doubtless felt nothing at all.

No matter how bold a front he'd put up for Sostratos and the akatos' crew, he knew he'd stuck his head in the lion's mouth by sailing down to Syracuse. Now he was going to have to put his head there again. If Agathokles—or rather, Agathokles' brother Antandros, who was in charge of the city while the tyrant led the fleet to Africa—didn't feel like living up to the bargain Onasimos the proxenos had made in Rhegion, what could anyone do about it? Not much, as Menedemos knew too mournfully well.

Some of the sweating slaves taking grain off the *Aphrodite* and the round ships were big, pale, fairhaired Kelts. Some were stocky Italians of one sort or another (Menedemos hoped there were plenty of Romans among them, but couldn't tell by looking). Most, though, had the swarthy, hook-nosed look of Carthaginians.

"Plenty of Hellenes enslaved in Carthage, too," Sostratos said when Menedemos remarked on that. "If you get captured instead of doing the capturing, that's what happens to you. We were lucky, you know."

"Maybe we were." Menedemos could admit it now that they were tied up in the Little Harbor. "But Tykhe is a strong goddess."

"Fortune is a fickle goddess, too," Sostratos said. "Remember what happened to the Athenians who came here a hundred years ago. Most of them would have been lucky with anything so light as lugging sacks of grain."

"I think I've heard you tell that story before," Menedemos said. "Me, I'm more worried about what will happen tomorrow than what happened a hundred years ago."

He'd hoped that would annoy his cousin. It did, but not quite enough to suit him. Instead of going off in a huff, Sostratos answered seriously: "What happens tomorrow will happen in part because of what happened a hundred years ago. How can you understand the present if you don't understand the past?"

"I don't know, and I don't much care," Menedemos said. That *did* affront Sostratos. He stalked toward the bow, dodging men with sacks of grain on their shoulders. Menedemos smiled behind his back.

The slaves weren't the only people on the pier. A tavern tout called, "First two cups of wine free for all the sailors who brought us grain when we needed it so bad. Come to Leosthenes' place, right off the harbor."

A cheer went up on the *Aphrodite*. The cheers that rose from the round ships were smaller—they carried fewer sailors. Menedemos said, "Diokles, I'm going to want half a dozen men on board through the night. Two days' bonus pay for anybody who's willing not to drink and screw himself blind tonight."

He hadn't tried to keep his voice down—on the contrary. He wanted the sailors to hear, and to volunteer to pick up an extra three drakhmai. Along with the sailors, Sostratos also heard. He whirled in alarm: he hated spending extra silver. Menedemos thought he would protest out loud, which wouldn't have been good. But Sostratos proved to have sense enough not to do that. Menedemos beckoned him back to the stern as Diokles found volunteers.

"Don't worry," Menedemos told his cousin. "Once Antandros pays us, a few drakhmai won't matter one way or the other."

"They always matter," Sostratos said primly, "and I always worry. One of the things I'm worrying about now is, suppose Antandros doesn't pay us?"

"His man said he would," Menedemos said, that being the strongest reply he could make. He was worried, too, and doing his best not to show it. "And even if he doesn't, we still got half again the going rate up in Rhegion—and we're in *Syracuse*, by the dog of Egypt! We've got a fresh chance for top prices on peafowl chicks and silk and Ariousian—and a fresh chance to unload what's left of our papyrus

and ink. If we can't sell 'em here, we can't sell 'em anywhere this side of Athens. And everybody takes them there, so nobody gets a good price for them."

He waited to see if his cousin would stay mulish. Most men would have. But Sostratos was uncommonly reasonable—sometimes, as far as Menedemos was concerned, too reasonable for his own good. Instead of growling, he stopped and thought. At last, grudgingly, he dipped his head. "Fair enough, I suppose. You were right about coming here, as things worked out. Maybe you'll be right again. I hope so."

"Me, too," Menedemos said. And then, because Sostratos had gone halfway toward healing the quarrel, he tried to do the same himself: "I'd have had more faith myself coming down here if I'd known ahead of time that Agathokles would pick that moment to sally forth. Good luck, like we said before."

Sostratos snapped his fingers in annoyance. "By the gods, I'm an idiot! Why didn't I see that before?"

"If you'd asked me, I could have told you you were an idiot," Menedemos said cheerfully. Sostratos glowered. Menedemos went on, "But what didn't you see?"

"It probably wasn't just good luck," Sostratos answered.

"What wasn't?" Menedemos hated it when his cousin got ahead of him. Sostratos thought too well of his thinking as things were.

"Agathokles' sally, of course," he said now. "It all fits together, don't you see? Agathokles had to use something to break the Carthaginians' blockade if he was going to get his own fleet loose. What would be more likely to make the Carthaginians move than a gaggle of nice, fat grain ships?"

Menedemos stared. It *did* fit together, provided.... "That Agathokles must be one sneaky rogue." He held up a hand; this time, he was running even with Sostratos. "We already know he is, from the way he treated his enemies."

"We can't prove any of this, you know," Sostratos said. "I wonder if Antandros would tell us."

"If you ask him, I'll hit you over the head with the biggest pot I can pick up," Menedemos said. "How can you be clever enough to see plots and schemes and foolish enough to want to get in trouble sticking your nose in where it doesn't belong, both at the same time?"

"Hmm." Sostratos pondered again. "Well, maybe you're right."

"I should hope so!" Menedemos said. "Are you going to stay aboard the *Aphrodite* tonight?"

"I think so," Sostratos replied. "Why?"

Menedemos grinned. That was the answer he'd wanted to hear. "Why? Because, O best one, I intend to go into Syracuse and celebrate getting here without getting sunk the way such things ought to be celebrated."

"You're going to have a couple of girls and you're going to get so drunk you won't remember having them," Sostratos said with distaste.

"Right!" Menedemos said. His cousin rolled his eyes. Menedemos couldn't have cared less about his cousin's opinion.

As the oarsmen rowed the *Aphrodite*'s boat across the narrow channel separating the Sicilian mainland from the island of Ortygia, Sostratos took a certain somber satisfaction in Menedemos' condition. His cousin's eyes were red, his face sallow. He shaded his eyes from the sun with the palm of his hand. Even though the sea in the Little Harbor was calm as could be, he kept gulping as if he were about to lean over the gunwale and feed the fish.

"I hope you had a good time last night," Sostratos said sweetly.

"I certainly did," Menedemos answered—not too loud. "This one girl—by the gods, she could suck the pit right out of an olive. But…" He grimaced. "Now I'm paying the price. If my head fell off, it'd do me a favor."

Sostratos hadn't had the pleasure, but he didn't have the pain, either. As he usually did, he thought that a good bargain. The boat slid up to one of the quays on Ortygia. The fellow standing on the quay looked more like a majordomo than the usual harborside roustabout, but he made the boat fast. As he did so, he asked, "And you are…?"

"I'm Menedemos son of Philodemos, captain of the merchant galley *Aphrodite*," Menedemos told him, still speaking softly. He pointed to Sostratos. "This is my toikharkhos, Sostratos son of Lysistratos."

"You will be here for payment, I expect?" the Syracusan servitor said.

Menedemos dipped his head, then winced. Carefully not smiling, Sostratos said, "That's right."

"Come with me, then," the servitor said, and walked off toward a small, metal-faced gate in the frowning wall of gray stone that warded the rulers of Syracuse from their enemies. Over the past hundred years, those rulers had had a good many foes from whom they needed protection. Not only had the Athenians and Carthaginians besieged the city, but it had also gone through endless rounds of civil strife. *I don't always remember how lucky I am to live in a place like Rhodes*, Sostratos thought. *Coming to a polis that's seen the worst of what its own people can do to one another ought to remind me.*

Inside the grim wall, Ortygia proved surprisingly lush. Fruit trees grew on grassy swards that sheep cropped close. The shade was welcome. So were the perfumes of oleander and arbutus and lavender. Sostratos breathed deeply and sighed with pleasure.

So did Menedemos. "I'm glad to be here," he said. "The light doesn't hurt my eyes nearly so much as it did before."

"That's because you're in the shade now," Sostratos said: only tiny patches of sunlight dappled the path along which they were walking.

"No, I don't think so, Menedemos replied. "I guess my hangover is going away faster than I thought it would."

Sostratos scarcely heard him. He was staring at those little sun-dapples, the places where light slid through gaps in the leaves above. They should have been round. They should have been, but they weren't. They were so many narrow crescents, as if the early moon had broken into hundreds or thousands or myriads of pieces, each shaped like the original.

He looked into the morning sky. It did seem dimmer than it should have, and more so by the moment. Alarm and something greater than alarm, something he belatedly recognized as awe, prickled through him. "I don't think it's your hangover," he said in a voice hardly above a whisper. "I think it's an eclipse."

The sky kept getting darker, as if dusk were falling. The chatter of wagtails and chaffinches died away. The breeze caressing Sostratos' cheek felt cooler than it had. But his shiver when he peered up toward the sun had nothing to do with that. Like the shadows, it too had been pared to a skinny crescent.

"By the gods!" Menedemos was whispering, too. "You can see some of the brighter stars."

So Sostratos could. And seeing them, oddly, touched a chord of memory in him. Speaking a little louder than he had before, he said, "'In the same summer, at the time of the new moon—since, indeed, it seems to be possible only then—the sun was eclipsed after noon and was restored to its former size once more: it became crescent-shaped, and certain stars appeared.'"

"It's not after noon," the Syracusan servitor said, his voice raucous in the sudden, uncanny gloom. "It's only about the third hour of the morning."

Menedemos knew his cousin far better than the stranger did. He asked, "What are you quoting from?"

"Thoukydides' history, the second book," Sostratos answered. "That eclipse happened the year the Peloponnesian War broke out, more than a hundred and twenty years ago. The world didn't end then, so I don't suppose it will now." He shivered, hoping he was right. In the face of something like this, rationality came hard, hard.

Screams—from women and men both—showed that a lot of people weren't making the least effort to stay rational. "A horrible monster is eating the sun!" someone howled in accented Greek.

"Is he right?" the servitor with Sostratos and Menedemos asked anxiously. "You fellows sound like you know something about it."

Sostratos tossed his head. "No, he's mistaken. It's a natural phenomenon. And look—it's one that doesn't last long. See? It's already getting lighter."

"Gods be praised!" the servitor said.

"I can't make out the stars any more." Menedemos sounded sad.

Birds started singing again. The clamor that had echoed through Ortygia—and, no doubt, through all of Syracuse—ebbed. The small speckles of sunlight on the ground and walls remained crescent-shaped rather than round, but the crescents seemed wider to Sostratos than they had when the eclipse was at its height.

"Well, *that's* something I can tell my grandchildren about, if I live to have any." Agathokles' man—Antandros now—recovered his aplomb quickly.

So did Menedemos. "Lead on, if you would," he told the fellow.

Following them both, Sostratos thought, *I should be making notes, or at least standing still and remembering all I can. When will I see another eclipse? Never, probably.* But he kept on after his cousin and the servitor. With a sigh, he strode into the palace from which Agathokles had ruled Syracuse and in which his brother now held sway for him.

Before they came into Antandros' presence, more servitors patted them most thoroughly to make sure they carried to weapons. Sostratos thought himself more likely to want to kill someone after that sort of indignity than before it, but kept quiet.

Antandros sat on what wasn't quite a throne. He was older than Sostratos had expected; he'd lost much of his hair, and gray streaked what remained. When a steward murmured to him who Sostratos and Menedemos were, he leaned toward the man with a hand cupped behind his ear. "What was that?" he asked. The steward repeated himself, louder this time. "Oh," Antandros said. "The chaps from the akatos." He turned his gaze on the two Rhodians. "Well, young men, between the Carthaginians and the eclipse, I'd bet you've had more excitement the past couple of days than you really wanted."

We certainly have! Sostratos thought. But before he could speak, Menedemos said, "I always thought a quiet life was a boring life, sir."

Antandros held his hand behind his ear again. "What was that?" As the steward had, Menedemos repeated himself. Antandros said, "My little brother would agree with you. Me, I don't mind sleeping soft in my own bed with a full belly every now and again, and that's the truth."

I'm with you, Sostratos thought. But Antandros' homely desires went a long way toward explaining why Agathokles ruled Syracuse and his older brother served him.

"How many sacks of grain did you bring into the polis?" Antandros asked.

Menedemos looked to Sostratos, trusting him to have the number at his fingertips. And he did: "It was 791, sir," he replied, loud enough to let the man in charge of Syracuse hear him the first time.

Antandros' smile showed a missing front tooth. "Paying you won't even hurt. A merchant galley doesn't hold much next to a round ship, does she?"

"She wasn't built to haul grain, sir," Sostratos agreed, "but we were glad to help your polis as best we could." *Menedemos was, anyhow.*

Amusement sparked in Antandros' eyes. Sostratos got the feeling Agathokles' brother knew he was lying. But all Antandros said was, "You'll be glad to get paid, too, won't you?"

"Yes, sir." Sostratos wouldn't deny the obvious.

"You will be," Antandros said. "No, you aren't made for hauling grain, sure enough. What other cargo have you got aboard?"

"Rhodian perfume, Koan silk, Ariousian from Khios, papyrus and ink—and peafowl chicks," Sostratos answered.

"What was that last?" Hearing something unfamiliar, Antandros hadn't got it.

"Peafowl chicks," Sostratos said again. "We sold the grown peacock and peahens earlier, mostly in Taras."

"Can't let the polluted Tarentines get ahead of Syracuse," Antandros exclaimed. "Now we have plenty of grain to feed birds, too—plenty of grain to feed everyone. We went from hungry to fat in one fell swoop when the fleet got in. What do you want for these chicks? And how many have you got?"

"We have seven left, sir." Sostratos flicked a glance toward Menedemos. His cousin's lips silently shaped a word. Sostratos fought back the urge to whistle in astonishment. Menedemos didn't do things by halves. But Sostratos had, in a way, asked, and the gamble struck him as good, too. In a calm voice, he went on, "We want three minai apiece."

The steward looked horrified. Privately, Sostratos didn't blame him a bit. "I'll take all of them," Antandros said. "To the crows—no, to the peafowl—with the Tarentines. As soon as I get the chance, I'll send one on to my little brother in Africa."

"Ahh!" With the pleasure of curiosity satisfied and a guess confirmed, Sostratos forgot about the dismayed steward. "So that's what Agathokles was up to! He *is* sailing around the north side of Sicily, then?"

"That's right." Antandros dipped his head. "Up till now, all the fighting in this war has been here in Sicily. But my brother decided it was time for the Carthaginians to see how they like war among their wheatfields and olive trees. No one has ever invaded their homeland—till now."

"May he give them a good kick in the ballocks, then," Menedemos said. Sostratos thought the same thing. The Macedonian marshals littering the landscape in the east of the Hellenic world were bad enough. Having barbarians overrunning poleis in Great Hellas struck him as even worse.

A moment later, he wondered why. What could the Carthaginians have visited on Syracuse that Hellenes hadn't already inflicted on other Hellenes? The question struck him as no great compliment to Carthage, but rather a judgment on what Hellenes had visited on one another.

Antandros spoke to the steward: "Take them to the treasury. Pay them for the grain and for these birds."

"Yes, sir," the steward replied, though he looked as if he would have said something else had he dared. He turned to Sostratos and Menedemos. "Come with me, O best ones." He didn't sound as if he meant that, either.

Can it be this simple? Sostratos wondered as he followed the steward out of what would have been the throne room had Agathokles called himself a king. *Will Antandros really just pay us for the grain and the peafowl and send us on our way? Nothing this whole voyage has been that simple.*

Seeing the treasury did nothing to reassure him. Ortygia was a fortress. The rulers of Syracuse stored their silver and gold in a fortress within a fortress, behind massive stone walls, gates whose valves seemed to Sostratos as thick as his own body, and a veritable phalanx of soldiers: some Hellenes, others Italians and Kelts. Sostratos tried to imagine what those soldiers would have done had he and Menedemos approached them without the steward's protective company. He wasn't sorry to find himself failing.

But the steward, whatever he thought, did not dare disobey Antandros. The clerk to whom he spoke looked surprised, but asked no questions. How long would a man who asked questions last in Syracuse? Sostratos couldn't have gauged it by the water clock, but thought he knew the answer nonetheless: *not long.*

Instead of asking those dangerous questions, the clerk started bringing out leather sacks. When Sostratos hefted one, he asked the fellow, "A mina?" The clerk dipped his head and went back for more silver.

By the time he was done, what seemed like a small mountain of sacks stood on the broad stone counter that separated him from the two Rhodians.

Solemnly, Menedemos said, "We have just made a profit."

"So we have," Sostratos said. "I ought to count the drakhmai in a few of these sacks." Cheating by one part in twenty, maybe even one part in ten, would be easy if the treasury clerk didn't offer the use of a set of scales to weigh the silver, something he showed no sign of doing.

The silence that came crashing down was so very frigid, it put Sostratos in mind of snow: only a word to most Rhodians, since none had fallen on his island in all the days of his life, or, for that matter, his father's, but he'd seen the stuff in a hard winter in Athens. Now Menedemos spoke quickly: "I think we're all right."

"But—" Sostratos was the sort of man who liked to see everything pegged down tight, so there could be no possible doubt about where it lay.

"I said, I think we're all right." As if trying to get something across to Antandros, Menedemos spoke louder than he had to. He spoke so loud, in fact, that his voice echoed from the stone walls and ceiling of the treasury.

Hearing those echoes reminded Sostratos of exactly where he was. It also reminded him of his earlier thought about what happened to Syracusans who asked questions. That thought led to another: what would happen to a stranger who asked questions in Syracuse? Sostratos decided he didn't really want to find out the answer to that one.

"Well, I suppose we are, too," he said, with what he hoped wasn't too sheepish a smile. Menedemos' sigh of relief was loud enough to raise echoes, too. The steward and the treasury clerk relaxed.

Menedemos said, "Could we have two large leather sacks and a couple of guards to take us back to the *Aphrodite*'s boat? This is a *lot* of silver, and all of Ortygia knows by now that we're getting it."

When the steward hesitated, Sostratos said,"If you like, they could come across to the akatos with us, and bring the peafowl chicks and their cages back for Antandros."

"All right." The steward dipped his head. "That does make sense."

Sostratos felt like cheering. The peafowl had been a weight on his back like the world on Atlas' ever since he first heard the peacock screech in the Great Harbor at Rhodes. Now, at last, after spring and most of summer, he would be free of it. He hadn't known just how heavy it was till he faced the prospect of having it lifted from him.

And he gave a sigh of relief of his own when the guards the steward summoned proved to be Hellenes. Had he had a couple of tall, beefy Kelts for an escort, he would have worried that they might set on Menedemos and him. Of course, Hellenes could be light-fingered and murderous, too, but he chose not to dwell on that.

"How much money have you got there?" one of these fellows asked in interested tones.

"As much as Antandros wanted us to have," Menedemos answered before Sostratos could come up with a reply to a question with so many implications. He admired the one his cousin had found.

From somewhere or other, the rowers in the *Aphrodite*'s boat had got hold of a jar of wine. When they took the Syracusan soldiers across the narrow channel to the merchant galley's berth in the Little Harbor, their stroke suggested that this was the first time they'd ever handled oars in their lives. Sostratos was embarrassed. Menedemos, plainly, was mortified. He couldn't even yell at the men without making themselves look even worse to the Syracusans than they did already.

Menedemos cursed in a low voice as he boarded the *Aphrodite*. But Sostratos' exasperation melted away as sailors loaded the peafowl chicks and their cages into the boat. He even tossed the two Syracusans a drakhma each, more in sympathy with them for having to deal with the birds than as a tip for getting him and Menedemos back to the akatos unrobbed.

"Thank you kindly, O best one," one soldier said. The other waved and grinned. The boat's crew took them back to Ortygia. The channel between mainland and island was narrow enough to let them escape misfortune.

As the crew returned—still rowing most erratically—Sostratos said, "It's a good thing they didn't have to do anything difficult."

"What's so good about it?" Menedemos growled. He screamed at the men in the boat: "You idiots!

If you're on your own polluted time, I don't care what you do, you whipworthy rogues. I'll do it right alongside you, as a matter of fact. But you've got no business—none, not a dust speck's worthy—getting drunk when you know you're going to have to do something important in a little while. Suppose Sostratos and I had been running for our lives. Could you have got us away safe? Not likely!"

The rowers wore wide, wine-filled, placating smiles, like so many dogs that had somehow angered the leader of their pack. One of them said, "Sorry, skipper. That eclipse knocked us for a loop, it did. And everything worked out all right." His grin got wider and more foolish.

Sostratos thought that a fair excuse, but not his cousin: "No, it didn't, the gods curse you." Menedemos' voice rose in both volume and pitch. It got so shrill, in fact, that Sostratos dug a finger in his ear. "You wide-arsed simpleton, you made the ship look bad. Nobody makes my ship look bad—nobody, do you hear me?"

Half of Syracuse heard him. By the way he was shrieking, Sostratos wouldn't have been surprised if Agathokles, somewhere off the north coast of Sicily, heard him. He tried to remember the last time he'd seen Menedemos so furious, tried and failed. *It's been a long time since anyone embarrassed him in public*, he thought.

If the sodden rowers had had tails, they would have wagged them. "Yes, skipper," said the one who felt like talking. "We *are* sorry, skipper—aren't we, lads?" All of them solemnly dipped their heads.

But Menedemos, like a Fury, remained unappeased. "Sorry? You aren't sorry yet!" He spun toward Sostratos. "Dock every one of those bastards three days' pay!"

"Three days?" Sostratos said—quietly. "Isn't that a bit much?"

"By the gods, no!" Menedemos didn't bother lowering his voice. "One day because they've wasted a days' work with their antics. And two more to remind them not to be such drunken donkeys again."

Instead of getting angry themselves, as they might have done, the men in the *Aphrodite*'s boat looked contrite, as if they were sacrificing their silver in place of a goat in expiation for their sins. That too was the wine working in them, Sostratos judged.

"It'll never happen again, skipper," their spokesman said. "Never!" A tear rolled down his cheek.

Sostratos nudged Menedemos and spoke one word out of the side of his mouth: "Enough."

He wondered if his cousin would listen to him, or if Menedemos' anger, like that of Akhilleus in the *Iliad*, was so great and deep as to leave him beyond the reach of common sense. For a moment, he feared passion held complete sway over Menedemos. But at last, gruffly, Menedemos said, "Oh, very well. Come aboard, you clods."

The drunken sailors scurried away from him. Another Homeric comparison occurred to Sostratos. In a low voice, he asked, "How does it feel to be Zeus, father of both gods and men?"

Menedemos chuckled, the rage finally ebbing from him. "Not bad, now that you mention it. Not bad at all."

"I believe you," Sostratos said. "You don't often see anybody put men in fear like that."

"Every once in a while, a captain needs to be able to do that," Menedemos said seriously. "If the men don't *know* they have to obey, know it down deep, you won't get the most out of them. Sometimes you need to—when a trireme is coming after you, for instance."

"I suppose so," Sostratos said, "but wouldn't it be better if they obeyed you out of love? As the godlike Platon said, an army of lovers could conquer the world."

His cousin snorted. "Maybe it would be better, but it's not likely. Try to make your rowers love you, and they'll just think you're soft."

Sostratos sighed. Menedemos' words had the hard, clear ring of probability to them, like silver coins dropped on a stone counter. As for an army of lovers…The soldiers of Philip, Alexander the Great's father, had killed the Theban Sacred Band—made up of erastoi and their eromenoi—to the last man, after which Alexander went out and conquered the world without them. Platon hadn't lived to see any of that. Sostratos wondered what he would have had to say about it. Nothing good, he suspected.

Platon *had* come here to Syracuse, to try to make a philosopher out of the tyrant Dionysos' worthless son. That hadn't worked, either. Sostratos sighed again. People seemed harder to change than lovers of wisdom wished them to be.

Menedemos changed the subject like the captain of a round ship swinging the yard from one side of the mast to the other to go onto a new tack: "Now all we need to do is a little more business here, maybe, and then get our silver home. Even my father won't have much to complain about.

"It'll be a shorter trip, or it should," Sostratos said. "We won't have to stop at nearly so many places." He coughed delicately. "And we'd do better not to stop at Taras after all, wouldn't we?"

"What if we would?" Menedemos said. "We can visit Kroton again, and then sail across the gulf there to Kallipolis. Old what's-his-name in Taras won't hear about us till we're gone."

"You hope Gylippos won't," Sostratos said. "Was Phyllis worth it?"

"I thought so then," Menedemos answered, shrugging. "A little too late to worry about it now, wouldn't you say?"

"A lot too late." But Sostratos didn't sound amused or indulgent. "When *will* you grow up?"

Menedemos grinned at him. "Not soon, I hope."

continued in issue 56…

CAT RAMBO & JENNIFER BROZEK
EDITORS

JANE YOLEN
LISA MORTON
PREMEE MOHAMED
SEANAN McGUIRE
MERCEDES M. YARDLEY
NAOMI KRITZER
AND MORE

THE
REINVENTED
HEART
TALES OF FUTURISTIC RELATIONSHIPS

EBOOK MARCH 2022
HARDCOVER MAY 2022

www.ingramcontent.com/pod-product-compliance
Lightning Source LLC
Chambersburg PA
CBHW082227140626
46556CB00020B/3374